25/3   NOV 1 5 2001

W

SC

W9-CNB-127

WITHDRAWN

Your receipt

Items that you checked out

Title: Man without a past : frontier stories
ID: 0030302324485
Due: Monday, May 06, 2019

Total items: 1
Account balance: $0.00
4/8/2019 12:01 PM
Checked out: 1
Overdue: 0
Hold requests: 0
Ready for pickup: 0

Thank you for using the bibliotheca
SelfCheck System

Man Without a Past

Man Without a Past

FRONTIER STORIES

T. V. Olsen

Five Star • Waterville, Maine

Acknowledgments on pages 230–231

Five Star First Edition Western Series.

Published in 2001 in conjunction with Golden West Literary Agency.

Cover photograph by Johnny D. Boggs.

Set in 11 pt. Plantin.

Printed in the United States on permanent paper.

Library of Congress Cataloging-in-Publication Data

Olsen, Theodore V.
  Man without a past : frontier stories / by T. V. Olsen.
    p. cm.—(Five Star first edition western series)
  Contents: Man without a past—A time to fight—The ambush—Tenderfoot—End of the trail—Deadline day — Killer's law—Midnight showdown—Trouble from Texas—The reckoning—The broken spur—The man we called Jones.
  ISBN 0-7862-2732-X (hc : alk. paper)
  1. Western stories. I. Title. II. Series.
PS3565.L8 M34 2001
813′.54—dc21   2001040526

Table of Contents

Editor's Note

At the time of his death T. V. Olsen left behind six unpublished Western novels and nine unpublished Western short
stories. Of the nine short stories, one was an earlier version of
"Gold Madness," collected in LONE HAND: FRONTIER
STORIES. Two of these unpublished stories also appeared
in that collection for the first time. Of the remaining six stories, five appear here for the first time: "Deadline Day,"
"Midnight Showdown," "The Broken Spur," "The Ambush," and "Tenderfoot." In effect, virtually all of T. V.
Olsen's shorter Western fiction can now be found in the present collection, in LONE HAND: FRONTIER STORIES,
and in WESTWARD THEY RODE (1976), this last title
most recently reprinted in a paperback edition by Leisure
Books. It was due primarily to Bill Pronzini, who had pro-
posed preparing a new collection of T. V. Olsen's previously
published Western magazine fiction, that the author revised,
edited, and had newly typed all of his previously published
stories for possible inclusion. It is the enhanced versions of
those stories, benefiting from the author's greater maturity
and depth of understanding, that form the basis for the texts
used in this book. The only exceptions, of course, are the stories new to publication that previously existed only in holo-
graphic manuscript form. Based on common themes, but not
characters or events, some of these unpublished stories may
have been first drafts of short stories published later. Since
the majority of T. V. Olsen's short stories for magazines was

published in the years 1956 through 1959, it is probable that these unpublished stories were written by the author during that period. The one possible exception to this may be "The Broken Spur." It might possibly date from 1975, the period at which T. V. Olsen wrote "One for the Money" and "Point of Honor," both of which were published for the first time in WESTWARD THEY RODE.

Man Without a Past

I

First of all, as he opened his eyes, he saw the girl. She was standing by the narrow cot where he laid, her gaze cautious and holding only a trace of concern. That was strange to him, as strange as this broad adobe-walled room. He did not remember it, or the girl.

He pulled his forearm over his eyes, because they ached intolerably. That single twinge of movement told him that he was sore from head to foot, and his face and hands felt raw. He groaned.

"Rest," the girl said. "You've been through a bad time."

He closed his eyes tightly. He could remember only that he had staggered for what had seemed hours under a blazing sun. He could remember falling and getting up to stagger on under the prod of a nameless urgency, only to fall again. His mouth had become an oven; his tongue was still swollen with thirst.

"But where am I now? Then he had another, more terrifying, thought: *Who am I? What . . . what am I?"* He tried to recall, groaned again with the effort, and gave up.

He heard the girl say: "He's in here, Doctor."

He opened his eyes again to see a stout, gray-haired man in a baggy suit crouch by the cot and open his black bag. The

9

doctor was mournful-faced, but officious-looking. He began his examination, probing his fingers carefully along the patient's body.

The sick youth could see a second man standing behind the doctor. He was whiplash-lean; he looked to be in his early fifties and as brown and hard as mahogany. His drooping, steer-horn mustaches hid the expression of his mouth, but his gray eyes held a kindly concern. He wore the rough clothes of a ranchman.

This man said to the girl: "When did he wake up, Lottie? Give you any trouble?"

"He come to just now, Angus," she said. "Been quiet till now. He's in pain, though."

"No wonder," Angus grunted. "Arizona plains at high noon is no place to be taking a stroll. Face and hands are sunburned. Must have been pretty pale before. City fella, judging from his clothes."

"Uhn-huh."

The girl folded her strong tanned arms, bare where she'd rolled her flannel shirtsleeves to the elbow. The young man on the cot saw a glint of humor add itself to the mixed expressions in her green eyes.

She wasn't tall, but her body looked compact and firm in the flannel shirt and loose pants. Her chestnut hair was gathered toward the back of her head with a bit of ribbon. The young man looked away, feeling embarrassment even above the pain that overlay his hurts.

The doctor, finished, stood up with a grunt. "No broken bones. Beat black-and-blue, though. Did he get thrown by his horse?"

"Anyone's guess," Angus drawled. "He came staggering up to the house couple hours ago, on foot, babbling and out of his head. Brought him inside, then hitched up and came into town to fetch you."

"Nasty cut here," the doctor said, touching a raw line of fire over the patient's temple. The sick young man jerked his head away. "Easy, boy. Lottie, how about you boil some water? I'll soak away the dried blood and put on a dressing." He looked down speculatively at the young man's hard, wary eyes. "What's your name, boy?"

The young man said nothing.

"Well?"

"Trying to remember." His voice sounded parched and cracked to his own ears, and the movements of speech hurt his throat. He was suddenly aware of a burning thirst. "Can I have a drink? Water?"

"Don't see why not." The doctor nodded to Angus, who silently fetched a dipperful of water and handed it to the doctor. The medico tilted it to the youth's cracked lips who gulped eagerly and drained it. "Enough for a while," the doctor said. "How do you mean, you can't remember?"

"I can't, that's all."

The doctor said sharply: "Where are you from, son?"

The sick man shook his head helplessly, wincing with the motion.

An expression of wonder replaced the doctor's professionally impersonal briskness. He felt gingerly around the gash on the young man's head. Then he lifted his stubby-fingered hand and held it a yard from the young man's face.

"How many fingers am I holding up?"

"Two."

The doctor straightened up, shaking his head, and turned to Angus.

"Skull's intact, vision as clear as a bell. That knock on the head must have fouled up his memory."

"How's that, Doc?"

11

"Medical profession calls it amnesia."

Angus stroked his silky steer-horns and said thoughtfully: "Might be another crack on the head. . . ."

"On the theory," Doc snapped, "that loss of memory incurred by a head blow might be restored by a similar blow?"

"Had something of that sort in mind."

"Well, get rid of it. Could kill him or permanently impair the damaged cells. Lots of rest, good food, and proper care are his best chance for recovery. Who's going to give it to him?"

"Why, Doc, you never heard of Angus Horne turning out a man who needed help, did you?"

Doc snorted testily. "Hog-tie me hand and foot if I'd abandon any patient to your tender mercies! If Lottie will play nurse, though, I'd say he'd be as well off here as anywhere."

He glanced a question at the girl as she came in with a pan of boiling water, and she nodded an agreement.

The doctor dressed the cut, closed his black bag, and headed for the door, giving Lottie instructions for the patient's care. "His physical hurts don't amount to much," the young man heard the doctor say as he and the girl stepped into the yard. "As for his memory, it should come back under proper treatment. I'll be around in a couple days."

Angus Horne pulled a chair up to the cot and drew a blackened pipe from his shirt pocket. He lit it, puffing slowly. "Son," he said, "I'll lay it on the line. This is a one-loop spread I got. My brother . . . he was Lottie's father . . . owned it back ten years ago when the Mescaleros was still rampaging through the territory. They raided this place, burned it, and massacred my brother and his family. 'Cept Lottie. She was staying at the ranch of her older sister and her husband at the time. My brother Jim might have foreseen something of the sort. I dunno. But he willed me his property with the provision I'd care for any surviving members of his family. Me . . . I was a no-'count drifter, a mite too quick with a gun. Was old enough by then to know it, so I welcomed the change. Re-built the place and took Lottie in. She growed up here."

Angus paused, puffing fitfully at his pipe. "We hold the place down alone. Lottie can work, ride, and shoot like a man. But that ain't no way for a seventeen-year-old miss to grow up. You'll be well shortly. You want to stay here and work for your keep, be glad to have you. Then my niece can take over a woman's rightful duties in the house, where she belongs."

"I don't know anything about. . . ."

Angus waved his pipe. "Guessed that. City man, ain't you? Forgot, you can't remember. Well, you're young and husky-looking for a city lad. You can learn . . . that's if you don't mind some trouble along the way."

Uncertain, sick, and bewildered, the young man said he'd stay.

"Fine," Angus said meditatively. "Now, we should have some name to cuss you by."

He thought a moment, then absently knocked his pipe out against the chair, littering the clean-swept floor with ashes. The gesture was a quick, almost embarrassed one.

"You know, when I was younger, I had most of my wild times below the border. Had a Mexican wife. She died bearing my son, and the boy didn't live a year." Angus's hard-planed face softened a little. "I'd made a lot of plans for little Johnny. If he'd lived, he'd be about your age. Would as soon call you Johnny as anything else. That all right with you?"

The young man nodded his head.

"Good," Angus said. "And you're a green hand, so there's your second handle, Johnny Green."

II

In the next two days, Johnny Green's battered body recovered with the quick resilience of youth, while his past remained a staring blank in his mind. During that time, he heard no more about the "trouble" Angus had mentioned.

On the second day, Johnny Green limped outside and watched the sun die in a crown of gold fire on the distant mesa that closed off the western horizon, where the vast sweep of land was lost to sight. It was all strange to him, yet held a pleasant sense of homecoming. He could find no reason for the feeling, although he wracked his memory endlessly. He told Angus Horne as much.

At dawn of the third day, Angus roused him out, saying: "You feel well enough to ride to town? Thought we might buy you an outfit. And might be you'll see something familiar."

Johnny agreed eagerly. He still felt a little cramped, a little sore, and his sunburn had begun a painful peeling, but he was alert and restless, ready for anything. Lottie served their breakfast. He hesitantly returned her pleasant smile, then bent to his plate.

These were real folks, he thought. He was amazed at their open-handed acceptance of an injured stranger. He felt awkward and grateful in the face of this kindness, and made a silent promise they wouldn't be sorry.

After breakfast, Angus hitched the team to a buckboard and, with Johnny beside him, lifted the horses into a trot along the old wagon road.

They hit the town of Moreno an hour later. It was a hybrid Mexican-American hamlet, a patchwork of adobe buildings flanking a mud-rutted street. Johnny Green eyed it with a strained expression.

Angus pulled up the team at a tie rail and glanced at him. "Nothing familiar, eh?"

He shook his head.

They climbed down and went into the general store. Angus scooped up a handful of crackers from a barrel, munched them, and said to the clerk: "This fella needs some work clothes, Harvey, a complete outfit. Fix him up."

The clerk sized up the young man, then took shirt, trousers, hat, and boots from the shelves. "Try these on for size. You can change in the storeroom."

Johnny took off his dirty, wrinkled traveling suit, rolled it in a bundle, and left the storeroom in stiff new clothes, feeling almost like a new man. He found Angus leaning against the counter in conversation with a ruddy-faced, pot-bellied man.

Angus looked up, eyeing his new hand with an approving nod. "Looks more like it." He indicated the pot-bellied man. "This is Gus Withersteen, who owns the GW Corrals down the street. Gus, my new hand, Johnny Green."

"We've met," Gus boomed, extending a fleshy hand. "Well, young fella, you straddling any more tough ones these days?" He guffawed.

Angus eyed the corral owner narrowly. "You know him?"

"Not much. But this tenderfoot got off the train here four days ago. Come straight over to my place and wanted to buy a horse. Well, Bull Munson . . . you know, Cliff Sanders's foreman. . . ."

"Yeah," Angus said dryly. "Go on. What happened?"

"Bull and some of the other Long S crew men was loafing around my place, it being Saturday. When they seen this lad come in, with tenderfoot written all over him, you can guess what happened."

"Sure," Angus said. "But tell it anyways."

Johnny Green realized that the request was for his benefit.

"Well, hell." Gus sounded a little defensive. "You know how the boys like to josh a green hand. They picked out a half-broke broncho for the lad here, told him it was gentle as pie. Then slipped a burr under his saddle. Kept my mouth shut, 'cause the last time I tried to stop one of their jokes, they dunked me in the water trough. Soon as the boy hit the saddle, he got throwed. Sailed clean into a corral post and fetched his head a wallop you could hear halfway across town. Knocked him cold. Thought he was killed, so did Bull and the boys. They cleared out fast. I felt for his heart then, and it was still strong, so I took off to find Doc Lane. But he was out on a call. Time I come back, the kid was gone. Looked as if he come to, dusted himself off, and walked away. Lad, you must have a skull of iron."

"Try to remember, Gus," Angus said sharply. "Did he give you his name?"

"No. Say, is something wrong here?"

Angus explained Johnny Green's predicament.

"Hellfire!" Gus said admiringly. "He must have picked hisself up and walked clear to your ranch under an Arizona sun 'thout knowing it. That's some tenderfoot."

Johnny said: "I remember walking for a long time. I don't recall this town or the horse. Or you or those others."

Gus clucked sympathetically, said he was sorry he couldn't be of more help, and they left the store.

"Well, that's something," Angus said. "Now we know how it happened. Might as well step across the street and baptize you right. Less'n you're a teetotaler?"

Johnny smiled and shook his head. "I wouldn't know, yet."

In Rudabaugh's saloon, Angus told the bartender: "Rudy, we're here to break Johnny in on that bottled

16

lightning you call whisky."

The first shot brought tears to Johnny's eyes and scoured his throat with fire. But when the fumes began rising to his head, he found it was easy to identify himself with Johnny Green, ranch hand. Maybe it was for the best, having a new name for a new life.

They were pouring a second round when the swinging doors parted and three cowhands jostled in. The sight of Johnny brought them up short.

The man in the lead was built like a bull. His head sank like a bristling bullet, necklessly, into his shoulders, and black hair protruded in all directions from under his hat brim. His eyes were as small and savage as a wild peccary's.

"Boys," he said, "it's our friend from the corral. Looks like we didn't finish the job, hey?"

Angus whirled from the bar, dropping his hand to the holstered Colt at his hip. "Bull, you and your men done enough to this boy."

"Angus Horne, the old mother hen." Bull Munson smiled. "Well, no man in this country ever did claim to match you in gun play. Long as the tenderfoot's attached himself to your apron strings. . . ."

"Just a minute," Johnny Green said softly. He set his glass on the bar and faced Bull. "I fight my fights."

"Don't be a damned fool, boy," Angus snapped. "He'll break you in half."

"He can start anytime . . . if he's not afraid he'll get choked by one of those apron strings."

Bull Munson growled in his throat. "Dude, come ahead."

Without hesitation, Johnny moved to meet him. He slipped under Bull's first blow and came up slashing unreservedly at his face and body. Bull Munson stopped his offensive and retreated, backpedaling, throwing up his crossed

17

arms to protect his face from a flurry of jabs.

Johnny sank his fist deeply into Bull's yielding stomach. When Bull dropped his arms, Johnny hit him squarely on the point of the jaw with a straight-arm blow that buckled him to the floor.

Johnny stepped back, fists still doubled, breathing only a little faster. He settled a stare on the other two Long S 'punchers. "Well?"

Johnny Green wasn't a big man, but he was a wiry bundle of stockily built muscle. Although he'd moved almost too fast for the two 'punchers to follow, they'd somehow known from the moment Bull Munson had moved against this dude stranger he hadn't stood a shadow of a chance. That knowledge held them motionless.

Angus touched Johnny's arm, saying quietly: "All right, son, you proved your point. Now let's get the hell out of here."

Outside, as they moved across to the buckboard, Angus demanded: "Where'd you learn to fight like that?"

Johnny smiled and shook his head.

Angus growled: "I forgot again. Right now, though, I'd give a peck of gold double eagles to know your past."

As they rode back to Angus's Whippletree spread, Johnny said: "Does this Munson have anything to do with that trouble you mentioned the other day?"

Angus gave him a sidelong glance. "Sorry I brought it up. Didn't want no stranger involved with our problems."

Johnny smiled faintly. "Maybe I'm already neck-deep in 'em."

"Could be. Well . . . here's the story."

Angus explained that the huge Long S ranchlands bordered on his own Whippletree and a number of smaller ranches. The main water supply for all the ranches on this side of the big mesa was one water hole called Indigo Springs. It was on the boundary between Cliff Sanders's Long S and Angus's Whippletree, open by tacit agreement for the use of all. But the present dry season, the worst Angus had ever seen, had lowered the water level considerably. There wasn't enough to supply all the small ranches' stock and Long S's, too.

Lately Cliff Sanders had shown a tyrant's hand, saying that his father had used that water hole before any of the others had built here (true enough) and that, therefore, Long S had a prior claim. He wanted to fence the hole off from the little men. He'd have done it, too, for they were a docile lot, except, Angus modestly mentioned, for himself. Angus had never backed down in his life, and, having had a considerable reputation with a gun in his younger days, he was the mainstay of the small ranchers. The ranchers knew it, and so did Cliff Sanders. Cliff was still cautious enough not to make any effort to monopolize the water supply by force.

Angus fingered the reins for a while in silence after his explanation. Then he said: "Cliff's like his old man. Old Jard sent his kid East. Got him an education in some big university. Come back here two years ago to take over the Long S when old Jard died. Cliff's only twenty-six now, but damned if he don't handle the Long S as well as Jard ever did. Has gone into other interests, too. Reckon he's near doubled the fortune the old man left him. The East didn't soften Cliff none. He's tough as nails and smart as a whip. Got it into his head about a year back that he wanted to marry Lottie. Come up to my place courting her quite a bit for a while. She would have none of him, for all his Eastern sass. Cliff was too swell-headed to see it. Kept right on coming till this trouble over the water begun."

Johnny didn't say anything, although he thought that for

all her spunk (which Angus had mentioned as coming mighty close to mulishness at times), Lottie had too much depth to be happy with the man Angus had just described.

III

Angus took him on a tour of the ranch the next day. Lottie rode with them, close to Johnny's stirrup. She made quite a picture, with the sun shining on her hair.

They had been riding for an hour when she said: "What you think of the country, Johnny?"

"I like it fine," he replied. "I suppose you mean how do I think of it as cattle country? As to that, I couldn't say."

She gave him a faint smile. "You'll learn. That's if you stay long enough."

He felt a warmth rising to his face.

Angus grinned. "Don't let her get your goat, son. Long as she knows she can, she'll keep riding you. Indigo Springs is just ahead, over that rise. You'll get a chance to see what all the foofaraw is about."

They pulled up at the summit of the rise. They saw bawling cattle, milling around what appeared to be a shallow water hole about a hundred feet in diameter. The water looked brown and roiled. A few stunted willows grew near the seep.

"Don't look like much for men to fight over, does it?" Angus asked somberly. "Looks as if Long S stock is being watered down there."

"Long S stock," Lottie said, "with Long S men herding them. And isn't that Cliff standing by the seep?"

"Yeah, with Bull Munson," Angus said. "Well, this should be interesting."

He gigged his horse down the slope, followed by Johnny and Lottie. They pulled up by the seep.

Angus swung down from his horse, saying: "Howdy, Cliff."

Cliff Sanders grinned and lifted a lazy hand in greeting. Bull Munson's battered face bore a fixed scowl, but he said nothing. Sanders was taller than his foreman, not as thick-bodied, but cat-flanked and with a powerful sweep of shoulders. His face was good-natured, handsome, and open-looking, but with a latent shrewdness Johnny didn't miss. Whether it was fun or a fight in the offing, Cliff Sanders wasn't a man who would be caught napping.

Cliff pushed his Stetson back from his sweat-matted flaxen hair, gave Lottie an admiring nod, and looked at Johnny, and then at Angus. "New man, old-timer?"

Angus said coldly: "Yeah. His name's Johnny Green."

Cliff gave Johnny a tolerant once-over. "What's your specialty, friend? Rope, guns, fists?"

"You looked at your big bad foreman's face lately, sonny?" Angus asked gently.

A brief, wicked slanting of Cliff's eyes was the only sign of his irritation. He eyed Munson for a moment; the bull-like foreman flushed under his swarthy skin.

Cliff spoke, biting each word off. "You mean to say this undersized kid did that to you?"

"Well, boss. . . ." Munson managed a gray smile. "I was pretty who-hit-john at the time, you know."

"Yeah," Angus said with satisfaction. "Drunk with his own meanness. Don't let Johnny Green's size fool you, Cliff. So . . . you're still watering here."

Cliff's eyebrows lifted a quarter inch. "Why, yes. Didn't I

21

tell you I would? Mean to continue doing it."

Angus gave an impatient jerk of his head. "There's enough good water for your stock on the other side of your property. The rest of us can't reach it without driving across your land."

Cliff grinned. "And you'd better not try it, Horne."

"We don't intend to. But I'm asking you straight, why hog this water that we need, when the other is available to you? You only got to push your cattle a little farther to reach it."

Cliff rubbed a finger across the bridge of his long nose, nodding thoughtfully. "That's a straight question. Deserves a straight answer. So I'll tell you." His cheerful gaze turned diamond-hard. "I'm expanding. Will need all the water I can get. Want it understood now that I claim the right to this spring. Anyway, not you or any of these hard-scrabble hangers-on can tell a Sanders where he will or won't water. You think you can, just try it now."

That was the overriding arrogance of the old-time cattle baron speaking. Angus glanced at the Long S herders, about a half dozen men occupied with their work. They'd be no trouble. There were only Cliff and Bull facing Angus, and only they wore guns. Johnny could see the temper boiling high in Angus and knew that the older man was strongly tempted to have it out here and now.

Then Angus glanced back over his shoulder at Lottie and Johnny, remembering suddenly that they were in the line of fire. He sighed and shook his head regretfully.

Cliff had become aware that he was staring at the face of danger for the length of one hard-held breath. He let his breath out and relaxed. But Bull Munson, dully imperceptive, seemed not to notice the falling off of tension. His thick hand brushed his holster.

Angus might have been forced to a showdown then, if it

hadn't been for Lottie. Her hand snaked down to the saddle boot under her right leg and came up holding her carbine.

"We don't want trouble," she said quietly. "Don't you start it."

Bull rumbled a laugh. "She look like Dan'l Boone to you, Cliff?"

Angus said mildly: "Don't make a mistake. She can likely outshoot any man in your outfit."

Bull laughed again

Cliff didn't even smile. "Can you, Lottie?" he asked.

"Angus taught me," she said simply, not taking her cold gaze off Munson.

"Relax, Bull," Cliff said good-naturedly. "You, too, honey."

His gaze strayed insolently from her face, down to the fullness of her flannel shirt. Johnny's hands clenched on his reins. Cliff's gaze flicked suddenly to him.

"You do look sort of mean, kid," he observed. He seemed to mull that over, then said: "So you whipped Bull. You know, I did some boxing back East. Was champion at the university, as a matter of fact. I wonder how you'd fare outside of a barroom brawl. Bet you might get cut to pieces in a . . . shall we say . . . a scientific bout."

"I don't know," Johnny said softly. "But you can find out any time."

Cliff eyed him for a speculative moment, then laughed suddenly, and slapped his thigh. "Good! I've been afraid of getting rusty. The boys at the ranch are a total loss as sparring partners . . . except for Bull. But he's an easy mark when he has to fight clean. Step down, kid. Let's go a bout."

"Here?" Angus barked.

"Why not?" Cliff grinned. "Your boy's not scared, is he?"

For answer, Johnny Green swung to the ground.

"No, Johnny," Lottie said softly, but he didn't even glance at her. He pulled off his hat and handed it to Angus. Cliff unstrapped his gun and passed it and his own hat to Munson.

"We'll square away over here, back of the seep," Cliff said cheerfully. "I'll need room to lay you out. Marquis of Queensbury rules, eh? Or wouldn't you know about that?"

Strangely the words struck an answering chord of familiarity in Johnny's mind. *Queensbury.* He wanted to follow up that track of thought and then found there was no time to think, for Cliff was moving after him.

Cliff's left was up; he jabbed with his right. Johnny backed cautiously away, circling. There was something familiar, too, about Cliff's stance. Yet Johnny was bewildered. Rashly he tried the same rushing tactics which had brought Munson down the day before. He bored in at Cliff and flung a punch high to Cliff's face with the speed of a striking snake. To his surprise, Cliff blocked it easily. Then that poised right fist, waiting for just this, exploded fully on Johnny's unguarded chin.

Light and darkness burst as one in Johnny's brain. He felt the ground tilt and rise and slam him in the face. Doggedly, shaking his head, he raised himself on his hands. His head cleared, and he looked around, seeing Lottie's imploring face, as if she were asking him without words to quit now.

"No," he whispered to himself. He looked up at Cliff.

The rancher's smile held a hint of admiration. "That punch should have put you away for an hour," Cliff said. "But, hell, you can't box."

He began to turn away.

"Just a minute," Johnny said huskily.

Cliff paused, waiting.

Johnny came to his feet slowly, giving himself time to gather his faculties and assess his situation. *Keep away from him,* he thought. He began to circle again, moving always away from Cliff, not pressing an offensive, just getting the feel of his opponent, warding off Cliff's light jabs.

Now, more and more, there was a sense of something remembered, something familiar about this. It was beginning to become simple, this pushing away of Cliff's jabs. Annoyance flickered across Cliff's face. He was becoming impatient with this stalking of a moving figure that steadily eluded him. He moved in abruptly, landing another hard right slam. But this time, although awkwardly, Johnny guarded his chin, deflecting the punch. The blow hit him in the chest, knocking him off balance. He let himself fall, but rolled instantly on his side and spun cat-like to his feet, facing his antagonist again.

Cliff swore and went in after him. Johnny saw Cliff's breath coming harder, faster. Out of condition, he was already winded. His own breathing easy and controlled, Johnny sank into a crouch. It was an automatic reflex, purely without thought, and now, easily and naturally, he countered Cliff's offensive with a flurry of jabs, yet backing away in a circle. Cliff began to pant and flounder in his follow-ups; his blows lost timing. His foot slipped in the sand, and he went down on one knee. For a moment he stayed there, hauling in hard-drawn breaths.

"Want to take the count, Mister Sanders?" Johnny asked tonelessly.

Cliff's reply was choked with fury. "No, damn you!"

He lunged to his feet and forged in, wind-milling punches. His scientific training was a thin façade; now he was fighting with a primal fury. He drove a looping overhand right to the middle of Johnny's face. Johnny slipped easily under it, letting it graze his hair.

Cliff's own momentum carried Johnny inside his guard to

the chance Johnny was waiting for. He slammed lightning lefts and rights to Cliff's mid-section. When Cliff doubled up, Johnny straightened him with an uppercut.

He moved back one step as Cliff's knees began to bend. Then he drove in a straight right and felt the cartilage of Cliff's nose crunch under his fist. Cliff crashed down like a falling tree. He plowed on his face, then lay motionless with his arms out-flung.

Johnny had moved back to let him fall. Now, without a break in his fluid movement, he turned on his heel and walked straight for Munson, who backed off quickly. The Long S 'punchers had stopped working and were staring open-mouthed.

Johnny gently lifted Cliff's hat from Bull Munson's lax hand and bent to fill it with tepid water from the pool. He carried the full-sloshing hat back to Cliff and poured the water over him slowly, letting it spray off his head.

Cliff groaned, stirred, maneuvered to a sitting position. Blood and dirt caked his face.

"If you want to know," Johnny said pleasantly, "it was I who hit you. Any time you want to give me lesson number two, you let me know, Mister Sanders."

He tossed the hat into Cliff's lap and walked back to his horse.

Angus said nothing; his face was grim. But for just a moment he settled one big hand on Johnny's shoulder and squeezed it hard. "Let's mount up," Angus said then, and they swung up to their saddles.

"Wait a minute."

It was Cliff's hoarse croak. He had swayed to his feet and was stumbling drunkenly toward them. When he reached Johnny Green's horse, he reached up one big raw-knuckled hand.

26

"You licked me fair," he said. "Just to show there's no grudge."

The words belied the cold hatred in his eyes, but Johnny silently shook hands with him.

Cliff stepped back, looking up at Angus Horne. "You want to end this water hole feud without gun play?"

The question was blunt enough. But Cliff was full of subterfuge, and Angus studied him warily, wondering what was behind his words.

"Sure I would."

"I have a proposition. Your boy's quite a fighter. Would you give him odds against any man I could dig up?"

Angus showed a brief frosty smile. "Reckon I would. Why?"

"Well, I'd like to arrange a fight between him and a man I'll select. If he wins, I'll forfeit all rights to this water hole with a signed quitclaim. If my man wins, you forfeit."

"You got an axe to grind, Cliff?" Angus asked bluntly.

"Hell, no," Cliff said impatiently. "I'm making you a sporting proposition. Of course, if you're not sure of your boy. . . ."

"I'm sure of him," Angus said flatly. "It's you I got my doubts about. Never did like risking a whole pot on a single throw."

Cliff laughed. "Think I've got something up my sleeve, eh? Look . . . we'll arrange the bout on neutral ground, with an impartial outsider as referee. All aboveboard and to the satisfaction of both parties. How's it sound, kid?" He nodded at Johnny.

Johnny shrugged. "It's for Angus to say. If he wants, I'll meet your man."

Angus pursed his thin lips. "Who you have in mind for your fighter?"

"I'll let you know later." Cliff smiled crookedly. "There's a lot of details to iron out. Place, time, and so on. I'll be in touch with you."

"All right." Angus turned his horse abruptly and swung back toward Whippletree, with Johnny and Lottie falling in beside him.

"You don't sound too enthusiastic, Angus," Lottie said. Her tone was chiding, but it sounded worried, too.

Angus grunted sardonically. "Any proposition of Cliff's is likely to have more hidden teeth than a close-mouthed 'gater. Still, he's a born gambler and sportsman. If there's one thing he might take seriously, it'd be something on this order."

He reached out and slapped Johnny on the knee. "Thanks for the support, son. You ain't obliged to fight Cliff's man, you know."

"I think I can," Johnny said quietly.

Angus was generous; it was like him to discount a debt. But a man had to pay his due.

Angus was nodding to himself now, as though confirming something. "Had a hunch when I saw you lick Bull. After the way you just took Cliff apart, I'm sure of it. You're a trained fighter. Must've played a big part in your past. Maybe you ought to follow that up, 'stead of wasting time around here."

"Could be." Johnny shrugged. "Only I happen to like it here."

He felt strangely indifferent to this new knowledge of his forgotten past. Maybe it was part of what he'd been trying to leave behind when he'd gotten off the train in this arid, little-settled country. He felt strongly that there had to be something he was trying to leave behind. . . .

IV

The week rolled by. Johnny began to acquaint himself more and more with ranch work, liking it. He made up in interest and aptitude what he lacked in experience. Both Angus and Lottie complimented him on his progress.

Meanwhile, as the days passed, there was no word from Cliff. That worried Angus; he was now sure that Cliff was up to something.

On Saturday night, Johnny came in tired and dirty from a day of repairing fence. He washed up and wolfed down his supper, Angus watching him approvingly.

"You been working like a horse this last week, son," Angus said, his frosty eyes holding a latent twinkle. "You deserve to relax a little."

He glanced at Lottie, who was beginning to clear the table. "Lot, there's a dance in town tonight, ain't there?"

Lottie stacked the dishes with a clatter, pushed a strand of hair back from her forehead, and said carefully: "Now how would I know?"

Angus pulled out his pipe and began to fill it. He chuckled. "You know, all right. Bought some dress goods when we went to town the other day. And you been sewing every damn' night."

A faint flush rose in Lottie's face as she carried the cleared things to the dishpan. Johnny watched the movement of her trim back. Then he looked guiltily down at the red-and-white oilcloth. He knew his face was probably redder than even his deep sunburn warranted.

Angus chewed his pipe stem. "Fighters make good dancers, I've heard. Nimble on their feet." He winked at Johnny.

Johnny fidgeted for a while in his chair, then got up and walked over to stand by Lottie. "I'll dry the dishes for you," he offered roughly.

"Fine. Thanks." There was a high color in her cheeks, and she didn't look at him.

"Lottie," he got out in a rush, "do you want to go to that dance?"

Her voice was cool. "You don't need to do me any favors, Johnny."

"Well . . . you'd sort of be doing me the favor."

"And that's sort of gallant." She bit her lip, but couldn't hold back her smile now. "Oh, Johnny. Sure, of course, I'll go with you. Angus, don't you have a suit? And do you think it would fit Johnny?"

"I reckon," Angus said, nodding his gray-thatched head and puffing quickly on the pipe, the only sign of his pleasure. "Never wore it much and don't fill it out any more. Was about Johnny's size when I was younger. Yeah . . . should be a good fit."

The suit was well-tailored black broadcloth of a rather old-fashioned cut. Johnny stood stiffly in it, uncomfortably pacing the kitchen while Lottie dressed in her little curtained-off alcove.

"You look fine, son," Angus assured him. "Relax."

Lottie swept from her alcove, whirling for their inspection. The checked gingham clung to her rounded upper body, flaring from her hips into a full skirt. She was surprisingly slender and graceful in feminine attire. She'd fussed with her hair, and there was an excited sparkle in her eyes.

"Makes me kind of wish I was young again," Angus said. "You're a fine-looking couple. Now go along. I got the wagon hitched up outside."

"Aren't you coming?" Lottie demanded.

"Afraid such pleasure is past for me." Angus smiled. "And I'll be too strong reminded of it, sitting in the stag-line shooting the guff with aging cronies. You two have a good time."

The wagon rolled briskly through a sage-pungent night, neither the boy nor the girl saying much. There was a beginning wonder to this for them both, although possibly more for Johnny who was discovering life all over. The tacit confidence of Angus, entrusting a near stranger with Lottie for the evening, and having her here beside him, was the fulfillment of a promise he'd felt from his first recollections of this country.

The crowded community hall of Moreno was the nucleus for young and old tonight. Johnny discovered that he knew how to dance well, once he got the hang of the steps, as Angus had predicted, and Lottie showed her pleasure. Between sets she introduced him to many people, and he tried desperately to keep track of names and faces. Finally in the whirl of dance, noise, laughter, and the kaleidoscopic blur of faces, he gave up.

Everyone knew everyone else, everyone was out for a good time, and nobody stood on formality. Lottie was whirled away for a varsoviana with a grinning young cowboy, and Johnny lost track of her for most of the evening. He danced with two buxom settlers' daughters, and then a group of young men drew him aside with the slyly whispered remark that one of them had a jug cached outside.

They stood in the patio back of the hall, and the jug was brought out. Johnny took his pull when it was passed to him and, with the fiery corn liquor burning his gullet, knew finally and for good that he was accepted. There was the bragging talk, the drink-blurred young men's voices lifted in song, the slapping of calloused hands on brawny shoulders, and the telling each other what fine fellows they were. Then the jug was empty, and there was the almost stealthy straggling back into the noise and brightness of the hall to face, with sheepish grins, the teasing or scolding of sweethearts and wives.

Lottie was sitting on the sidelines, chatting with another girl. When Johnny came, shuffling his feet, his face red with drink and shame, she gave him a chiding look because that was what he expected. But then she couldn't help laughing.

A heavy hand fell on Johnny's shoulder.

Cliff Sanders stood there, tawny-haired, handsome, and affable-looking in a well-cut suit. He indicated the portly, white-mustached man at his side. "Kid, this is the J.P., Judge Hasker. He'll referee your fight."

Johnny shook hands with the judge, wondering if the man was to be trusted. His suspicion was swiftly dispelled when the judge nodded to Lottie, courteously greeting her by name, and Lottie's reply was warm. Judge Hasker must be solid and respectable, and, if Lottie accepted him as referee, so would Angus. If Angus was right and Cliff had an ace in the hole, Johnny decided it must be that Cliff was mighty certain of his fighter.

"Understand, young man," the judge said to Johnny, "I will name the time and place at which the bout will ensue . . . and my judgment will be final and unquestionable. If, for any reason, one side should renege on the agreement, or should choose to back out prior to the fight, that side will forfeit the stakes . . . that is, the right to water at Indigo Springs . . . to the other party. Also, Mister Sanders has already named his fighter, and I understand that you will represent Angus Horne. His choice of adversaries must be considered final. There will be no changes. Mister Sanders suggested these conditions, and I find them sound. Will you accept the terms?"

Johnny hesitated. "I can't speak for Angus, sir."

The judge smiled for the first time. "You're a young man of scruple. I meant, however, to receive only your own approval. I'll speak to Angus personally."

Lottie spoke up. "That won't be necessary, Judge Hasker," she said clearly. "I reckon Angus would agree, seeing you're handling things. I'm sure he'll let Johnny speak for him."

She looked at Johnny as she spoke, and he saw the full measure of her confidence in him.

"Very well, my dear," the judge said. "It will be as you say. And you, young man?"

Without hesitation now, Johnny agreed.

Cliff slapped him heartily on the arm. "Fine, kid. Now that's settled, maybe you'd like to meet the man you'll fight. He came in on the train a couple of hours ago."

Lottie's eyes sparked. "So. You imported a fighter, a professional prize-ring killer, I got no doubt. Suppose we might've expected something of the sort from you?"

"Temper, Lottie girl," Cliff said, bathing her in a bland smile. "Don't recall anything that stipulated against my bringing in a man from outside. Well, kid, you want to meet him?"

Johnny nodded. He and Cliff and the judge headed for the entrance. "That's him, leaning against the door jamb," Cliff said, as they threaded their way among the dancing couples.

The man indicated was a pale city fellow in a checked, flashy suit. He was a bull-chested man of Johnny's height, but older and a good deal heavier. His nose was flattened gristle, his ears twisted cauliflowers. He was surveying the festivities with bored and jaundiced eyes.

Johnny felt a sharp pang of recognition, brief and tantalizing. They reached the man, and Cliff performed the introductions.

"Buck, meet Johnny Green, the kid you'll slaughter. Kid, this is Buck Kendricks, from Frisco." Cliff grinned, not pleasantly. "They call Buck 'Killer' Kendricks. Saw him fight in Frisco last year. Tore some young punk to pieces. So I got in touch with him, paid his fare to Arizona."

Taking his time, maybe to show his contempt, Kendricks turned his battered face toward Johnny. His jaundiced gaze froze, then widened with surprise and something close to . . . fear?

The pug turned on Cliff with a yellow-toothed snarl. "You want me to fight *him?*"

Cliff's eyes narrowed in surprise, then hardened. "What did you expect, a babe in arms?"

"But you told me the kid I'd fight was named Green! That's why I took your offer. Never heard of a pug named Green! I figured this kid was a hick slugger, a pushover. But him! Don't you know who he is?" Without waiting for an answer, Kendricks added: "The hell with it! Deal's off, Sanders. You think I'll fight him, you're crazy."

"Now just hold on," Cliff said in a softly outraged tone. "If you think I paid out good money for a half dozen telegrams, more money for contacts to get hold of you, plus the expense to bring you here . . . and think you can back out now. . . ."

"Here's my traveling money." Kendricks dug out a thick wallet, stripped out some bills, and rammed them in Cliff's breast pocket. "As for the rest of the dough . . . that's your tough luck, pal. I'm taking the next train out."

He spun on his heel and stamped from the hall with Cliff at his heels, saying furiously: "Now, damn you, Kendricks, listen to me!"

The judge turned with puzzled impatience to Johnny. "What does this mean, sir?"

"Excuse me," Johnny said dazedly, and turned to

maneuver back through the whirling couples toward Lottie. The movements of the dancers, the noise, only added to the swimming confusion he felt. He'd nearly reached Lottie before the full impact of what had happened burst across his mind. *Why, that man knew me!*

He pushed backward roughly through the dancers, muttering: "Sorry . . . 'scuse me."

He ran past the startled judge and burst onto the boardwalk, flinging glances up and down the street. No sign of Cliff or Kendricks.

I've got to find him!

He spent the next half hour rushing in and out of a half dozen saloons and the hotel and railroad station before coming to a dismal acceptance that Kendricks, the link with his lost past, had disappeared, as if swallowed by the oppressive Arizona night.

Feeling drained and empty, he returned to the hall, reasoning that he was upset over nothing. Cliff had probably argued Kendricks into staying and going through with the fight, and had taken him out to Long S for his stay.

Judge Hasker met Johnny with red-faced anger. "What the devil are you and Sanders trying to bring off?" he demanded.

Johnny was trying to explain his personal problem to the judge when Lottie, understanding that something was wrong, came over and calmly told Hasker about Johnny's dilemma.

"I see," Hasker said, not so much angry now as puzzled. "So . . . this man Kendricks knew you before?"

"Seems that way," Johnny said tiredly. Then he started in surprise as Cliff Sanders reëntered the hall. He moved swiftly in front of Cliff, bringing him to a stop. "Where's Kendricks?"

"Gone," Cliff said sourly. "Judge, about the fight. . . ."

"Where?" Johnny cut in. "Gone where?"

"How the hell should I know! He's gone, that's all! Forget him."

"Well, Cliff," the judge said coldly, "what is there to say? If your man has run out, the terms of the agreement are broken . . . the terms you yourself offered, I might add."

"You mean I lose the stake? Is that it?"

"If you mean to abide by your given word," Judge Hasker retorted. "The entire agreement was verbal, of course, though Miss Horne and I witnessed it. Then," he added icily, "I detest a cheat, Cliff. If you should be inclined to renege, I might be inclined to prosecute you . . . and, believe me, boy, I'll snare you in every technicality I know."

"Nobody said anything about cheating," Cliff said sullenly. But his fists were closing and unclosing with repressed fury.

"Then," the judge said quietly, "you'll be in my office tomorrow morning. And Miss Horne, please tell Angus to be there. Mister Sanders has a paper to sign."

Cliff hesitated for a moment, his face dark with a flood of violence, but he held it in. He pivoted on his heel and left the hall. Hasker tipped his hat to Lottie, clamped it back on his sparse white hair, and followed Cliff.

Lottie turned to Johnny, letting go her held breath. "Well, doesn't this call for a celebration?"

"Yes, miss. May I have the next dance?"

Sometime after midnight, the festivities broke up and folks began straggling to buggies and horses, calling good byes. Johnny gave Lottie a hand up to the buckboard, took his seat beside her, and picked up the reins, driving the wagon down the street, then onto the moon-washed plain.

Lottie eased off the flimsy slippers she'd worn, wincing. "Ouch."

36

"Quite an evening," Johnny said.

"Not all ranch hands dance as well as you," she said rue-fully, massaging her sore feet.

Johnny grinned and lifted the horses into a brisk trot.

"Not so fast," Lottie protested. "It's a pleasant night. Let's enjoy it."

Soon, too soon, they reached the cottonwood-bordered lane that branched off the road into the ranch yard. "Pull up, Johnny," she said. "Here, under the trees. I want to talk."

He pulled up the horses and sat in silence, waiting.

"It better be said," Lottie murmured, pleating a fold of her skirt between her fingers, "and I got a feeling you'll never say it. So I will."

"What?"

"What about us, Johnny?"

He wondered how long he'd been wearing his feelings on his face. But he hadn't been sure of himself in anything as important as this—when he was so unsure of his own life. And he'd hoped she might respond, but without any real belief that she would.

"I guess I can say it now," he said slowly. "I love you, Lottie. Have from the first day."

Her skirt whispered as she shifted to face him directly. "Then what are you waiting for?"

Her voice was a tender sound, mingling with the hammering of blood against his temples and the rainy murmur of the cottonwood leaves. Her mouth joined his, warm and pliant, the slim young body arching up to him with the hard pull of his hands.

They moved apart breathlessly. There was hurt in Lottie's voice. "I'm not sure I liked that, Johnny."

"I'm sorry," he said stiffly.

"Oh Johnny! It wasn't you. It was your . . . your manner.

As though you were angry. As though you were trying to hurt something. Me?"

"Not you," he said miserably. "Just myself. It's no good, Lottie. Nothing I can give you. Not even a name."

"Nothing except yourself. I wouldn't ask for anything else. But that I insist on. Is it too much?"

"No. What I'm saying is that I can't give you myself. Not with this damned blank in my brain!"

She said softly: "But you haven't given yourself time. Doctor Lane said it would be slow. Wait, Johnny. You can wait. And I'm willing to."

He searched her dimly lit face. "And you're not afraid? Of who, or what, Johnny Green might have been?"

"I'd never be afraid of you." She reached over to kiss him lightly.

"Listen," Johnny said quietly.

She straightened, alert to the night sounds. Then turned a look of puzzled wonder to him. "I hear a rider," she said. "Seems to be coming toward the ranch from . . . from another direction."

"Yeah," Johnny said.

They listened for another straining moment. Suddenly there was a rifle shot, high and sharp, not from the house, but close by it. Then the sound of a hard-driven horse vanishing in the night.

"Let's get up there," Johnny said.

He shouted at the horses, careening the wagon sharply up the lane. In a minute the lights of the house shone among the trees.

Lottie jumped from the high seat, tearing her skirt in her haste, as the wagon hauled to a stop. She ran toward the house. Johnny quieted the horses before he vaulted down and followed her.

They found Angus face down on the floor, a toppled chair beside him. He'd been sitting at the table when the shot had spun him backward. Blood had pooled on his back and run down his side to stain the floor. Lottie fell on her knees by him.

"Oh Johnny, he's . . . !"

At that moment, Angus groaned. His lank body twitched.

"Not dead," Johnny said. "Yet."

He moved to the broken side window, his boots crunching on shards of glass littering the floor. The rifleman had stationed himself well beyond the house and picked an easy target through the lighted window. He turned to Lottie. "Can you take care of him till I get Doc Lane?"

"Yes." Her tear-stained face had gained a hard composure. "Cliff," she said bitterly.

V

Johnny made the churning buggy ride to town and back in record time. He and the stocky doctor tramped into the house and found that Lottie had made Angus as comfortable as she could without moving him. She'd stoked the stove, too, and had a kettle of water boiling briskly.

"Good girl," Doc said. He made a cursory examination, then said to Johnny: "Let's get him up on the bed. I can work better there."

Gently they lifted Angus to his cot, and then Doc set about his work in silence, except for an occasional snapped order. He had to probe for the bullet, which was dangerously near the right lung.

The quick gray hours of pre-dawn had laid spectral fingers over the land when Dr. Lane finished dressing and binding the wound and turned to tell them that Angus would live.

With a choked sob, Lottie buried her face in Johnny's shoulder. He held her for a moment, then told her: "Get some sleep." Then he added flatly: "I can go without sleep. I'll sit up. And wake you, Doc, if there's any need."

Doc exhaustedly agreed and sought Johnny's cot, while Lottie retired to her alcove.

Johnny sat by Angus's side through long, dragging hours. Angus was only slightly restless. He had revived, very briefly, but he was breathing steadily in normal sleep now, and that was good.

When Lottie got up, she came from her alcove in her rough, familiar work garb. She stood for a moment, silently watching Johnny, who had already changed his clothes and was now carefully folding Angus's suit and replacing it in the commode behind his cot.

She didn't miss the hard decision in Johnny's manner. "What are you thinking?"

"I'm riding out to Indigo Springs," Johnny said quietly. "I could be wrong, but I don't figure Sanders will waste any time now."

"I'm going with you," she said instantly. "They'll have guns, Johnny. And you never even held a gun as far as you know. You'll need me."

He let out his held breath. "Yeah," he said reluctantly.

Johnny woke the doctor, apologized for keeping him away from other business, but asked if he could watch Angus for a while. They'd be back as soon as possible. Doc Lane replied waspishly that he hadn't any intention of leaving until he was sure Angus was past the critical stage.

Johnny and Lottie saddled up and rode out with few

words. Their concern for Angus and the knowledge of the danger they might meet at the springs, along with the iron certainty that it must be faced, held them mute.

They topped the rise above the watering place and saw a stir of activity in the dawn light. Men were unloading cedar posts from a wagon. Bull Munson was supervising the work, while Cliff Sanders stood by, watching. Lottie said softly: "They're going to fence off the spring."

Johnny said tonelessly: "I don't think they are."

He nudged his horse down the slope, hearing Lottie keeping pace behind him. Bull Munson saw them first and grunted a warning to Cliff, who set his hands on his hips and waited with a hard grin. One by one, the men left off work and stood awkwardly by, as though ashamed of what they were doing.

Johnny swung his horse around near Cliff. "I see the vultures are gathering," he said thinly.

Without hurry, Cliff began shaping a cigarette. "When I heard about old Angus's mishap, and knew he wouldn't be needing this water, after all, didn't see any sense in letting it stand unused."

"How did you hear about Angus?"

Cliff shrugged. "Maybe Doc dropped by a while ago and mentioned it."

"Doc's still with Angus," Lottie breathed in a trembling voice. "You devil, Cliff Sanders! It wasn't enough to shoot him. Now you mean to cheat on an honorable debt."

"Hell," Cliff said imperturbably, cupping his hands to light his cigarette against a gust of wind, "I made the bet with Angus, not you, honey. Or the kid here. I owed Angus, not you. And it doesn't look much as if Angus will be collecting. . . ."

"I suppose that was your logic when you had him shot!"

"Prove it."

"We won't have to. It didn't work, Cliff. Angus is still alive!"

"Don't waste words, Lottie," Johnny cut her off in a steely voice. "Just get out your long gun and hold it on these others."

As he finished speaking, Johnny left the saddle in one lithe motion, lifting his feet from the stirrups and diving straight at Cliff from horseback. He hit the rancher with an impact that took Cliff by complete surprise and drove him backward, the wind gushing from his lungs as Johnny's weight smashed him to the ground.

Johnny rolled away from Cliff and came to his feet, his face flushed with a cold, killing savagery. The movement brought his back to Munson and the others, but he didn't even look their way. He gave Lottie one flicking glance, saw her rifle come out of its scabbard and train waveringly on the startled Long S men.

Johnny Green's mind held room for one thought only: to beat Cliff Sanders to within an inch of his life. Circumstantial evidence and the rancher's money might save him in the courts, but they wouldn't save him now from a hell of a beating.

Johnny watched Cliff gasp for breath, get up on one knee, and then labor to his feet. Seeing Cliff's face, Johnny knew there would be no holds barred in this fight, and that was how he wanted it. In his rage, Cliff forgot his science.

Johnny ducked under the rancher's first wild swing and pistoned both fists to Cliff's soft mid-section, working to wear him down. When Cliff tried to protect his body, Johnny shifted the blows to his face.

A looping right hurt Cliff, and he flinched back, hooking a boot heel in a half-dug post hole. He fell on his back in the mud of the seep, the water spraying out with the *smack* of his fall and rolling back to drench him.

Again, painfully, stubbornly, Cliff maneuvered to his feet. His broken nose had started to bleed. His right eye was beginning to close. Muddy water streamed from his soaked clothes as he slogged out of the seep.

He turned his head till his eye fell on a shovel rammed into the ground, left by one of his men who had moved back safely beyond the perimeter of battle. Cliff yanked up the shovel and swung it to striking position as he charged after Johnny.

The rifle bellowed in the clear morning; the shovel was torn from Cliff's hands and flung yards away.

It fell in the sand by two Long S 'punchers, but they made no move to retrieve it. They were careful to make no move at all. The sunlight glanced eloquently off the long, silvered streak on the rusty blade.

Lottie coolly shifted the rifle to bear on Cliff's broad chest. "The next one," she said clearly, "won't be aimed at what you're holding."

Cliff made a snarling sound and lunged at Johnny, hoping to bear the small man down by weight and surprise. Johnny danced away, slashing again and again at Cliff's face and belly. Seeing the torpid drag of exhaustion in Cliff's movements, he knew the fight was won. He stepped in and brought up a left hook that traveled no more than ten inches. Cliff went down on his back. His right leg flexed, it straightened, but otherwise he didn't move again. Breath bubbled through his nose.

Johnny looked up sharply as a horseman started down the rise beyond, a stocky, white-haired man who looked born to the saddle.

"That's Jim Baylor, Johnny," Lottie said, her voice shaky now that it was over. "Town marshal at Moreno."

Baylor pulled up his dancing horse, his agate-hard eyes

43

falling to the unconscious man, then lifting to Johnny. "Looks as if you beat me to him, young man."

Baylor went on to explain that a dead man had been found in the alley by the town hall about an hour ago. A stranger, he'd been dead for hours. No one knew him till Judge Hasker identified him as the fighter from Frisco that Cliff had brought in. Looked as if—according to the coroner—his head had been caved in with the barrel of a gun.

Cliff was sitting up now, staring from glazed eyes at the marshal. "What's that got to do with me?" he asked.

"The judge says you was the last one to be seen with Kendricks," said Baylor. "Says you trailed him out of the hall last night, mad as blazes because Kendricks refused to go through with an arranged fight between him and Angus Horne's man. The judge figured you might've pulled Kendricks into the alley to argue with him. Then you lost your temper when you couldn't talk him around. So you hit him with your gun. You didn't know the blow killed him, so you let him lay. Sounds reasonable to me, Sanders. If a jury thinks so, too, you're facing a manslaughter charge."

He pulled his revolver out and cocked it. "Get on your horse, son."

Cliff rose and trudged, muddy and beaten, to his horse, after sending a single darting glance of hate at Johnny Green.

Bull Munson growled suddenly to Johnny: "You done this! If it wasn't for you. . . ." Munson's gorilla-like arm twitched down. He jerked out his gun, and fired.

Johnny felt a bursting flare of pain in his head and felt himself falling. He heard Lottie scream. The marshal cursed as he spurred his horse around toward Munson. Then sight and sound ribboned off, pin-wheeling into blackness.

VI

Much later at the ranch Dr. Lane finished bandaging Johnny's head. "Just a crease," the medico said as he packed his bag. "That thick skull of yours wasn't damaged. As usual."

Johnny gingerly felt the bandage with one hand. Lottie stood by his chair, a hand resting on his shoulder. Angus spoke anxiously from his cot.

"No ill effects, son?"

"You can judge that," Johnny said with a wry smile, "when I tell you this. I didn't mention it before, but my memory's returned."

Lottie gasped. Doc jerked in surprise. Angus whistled. "Was it Munson's bullet?" he asked.

"Could have been. Anyway, I remember everything. Who I am, why I came to Arizona. I've been trying to get it sorted out."

Angus remarked, for Doc's benefit: "Said all along that we should have lambasted you in the first place. Quickest cure."

"Be quiet, Angus!" Lottie said urgently. "Let Johnny talk."

Johnny told it tersely, swiftly, because he knew she had waited to hear this. First he gave his real name, Bill Loesser. He'd grown up in a San Francisco slum. His father had died years ago, and his mother had eked out a living as a washerwoman. When Johnny was eighteen, her health had broken under overwork and the dank, fog-drenched air of Frisco. The doctor had said her only hope was a dry climate. Arizona would be best.

Johnny had quit his mill job and had set about to get

45

the necessary money to move her here in the fastest way possible—in the prize ring. He'd hated doing it. But his natural strength and reflexes were those of a fighter; he'd risen quickly from obscurity. Meanwhile, he'd read up on Arizona, burrowing out every scrap of information on his future homeland. He'd had almost enough money, when his mother died quietly in her sleep. That had been two years ago. Angry against everything that society stood for, he had continued to fight.

"No wonder Kendricks was afraid of you," Lottie whispered.

Johnny continued. He'd never forgotten Arizona. When the sorrow of his mother's death had blunted enough for him to take a long look at himself, he'd decided to leave the fight game for good. He'd gotten off in Moreno with the intention of hiring a horse and riding to look over the country that had become so close and familiar through his reading. At the corral, Munson and the others had pulled their trick. He'd been battered senseless when the horse threw him and his past was wiped from his mind.

Now he looked at Angus and Lottie with a wry smile. "I don't guess it was much of a loss."

"Maybe it wa'n't," Angus said gently. He reached out a corded hand to grasp the young man's arm. "You can forget it all over again. Johnny Green's our man. Yours, too."

Johnny felt Lottie's hand move on his shoulder, and he looked up, meeting her smile. Then her lips bent to his.

"Welcome home, Johnny," she murmured.

A Time to Fight

Sun City sprawled like a great dry bone in the otherwise unbroken symmetry of undulating prairie. The main street was a dusty road flanked by warp-walled, unpainted buildings, several with false fronts, marking them as business buildings. Lawyer Mainwaring, a slight man of thirty in black broadcloth, left one of these buildings on this bright morning, descending the rickety stairs from the second floor, where his office and quarters were located.

Standing on the board sidewalk, he glanced downstreet toward the jail that held Tate Siringo. *Taking Tate on as a client was a foolish thing,* he thought.

Mainwaring smelled the dust lifting off the street in the wake of a passing wagon, and the strong cattle smell from the now empty stock pens, and decided that there was nothing like proximity to a Kansas cow town to rob it of glamour. In the glowing reports of fresh opportunity, the colorful lithographs sent out with town-promotion literature to the innocent back-Easterners, there lay a vast difference from the harsh reality of this sun-scorched, treeless avenue of dust.

Mainwaring saw Sun City through bitter and disillusioned eyes. Two years ago he had come here as one of the innocent back-Easterners, thinking that, in a land new to law, a man

47

could pioneer in legal practice. He knew now that he'd been wrong. In the early 1880s men like cattle baron Josiah Winterfield still wielded power that trampled roughshod over hypothetical law.

The federal government had granted every alternate section in a ten-mile strip to the railroad, and the railroad knew that settlement of this land meant produce, and hence commerce over their line. So they sold great land grants at the lowest prices possible. This meant unusual opportunity for the little man. But Josiah Winterfield had long been the power here. With the first influx of new settlers, he began a series of small persecutions designed to discourage them and drive them off their grants. These persecutions were at first restricted to a mild hoorawing in town, or pulling down fences and letting cattle into fields to forage among a nester's crops.

The nesters could take it. Winterfield had come to see this, and his next play to scare out newcomers was to frame a nester for murder. That was the man Mainwaring must defend tomorrow in court.

His gaunt face etched with the grimness of his thoughts, Mainwaring angled across the street to Rosemary Gilchrist's café. Rosemary waited on him.

She said unsmilingly: "Do you drink your coffee black, now that you've gone tough on us, Jeff?"

"Don't start on that again," Mainwaring said wearily. "I'm no fighter, and you know it."

"No, but you've been acting like it," Rosemary said primly. "You're practically rattling a saber under Winterfield's nose by defending Tate Siringo. Winterfield's a big man in this country, Jeff. You're a struggling lawyer. At this point, he can make you or break you . . . and you know it."

"You're not saying anything I haven't said to myself a hundred times."

"Then why do you fly in the face of something you know you can't lick? I'm out of humor with you, Jeff."

Mainwaring sipped his coffee, eying her over the rim of the cup, a small girl with a thin face framed by raven-black hair drawn to the back of her head in a smooth prim knot. Like himself, Rosemary and her father were newcomers to Kansas from a far more sedate land, and, like himself, they understood the ways of this harsh country only a little.

At least, Mainwaring thought, he hadn't understood them at first. He had since learned that a man could not give mere lip service to his principles; he must stand ready to fight for them. Perhaps women lived less by principle than by emotion, Mainwaring thought, for he and Rosemary, who saw eye to eye on so many things, could not agree on this. She wanted him to pull out of this nester/cowman feud, and made no bones about it.

He said now: "A month ago I asked you to marry me, Rosemary. Have you decided it was a bad bargain?"

"I didn't say that. I only want you out of this."

"There might be a certain wisdom in it," Mainwaring agreed dryly. "But look, honey. It isn't as though I were going out to face Winterfield with a gun in my hand. I'll fight him, but in my own way, in a courtroom. Whether I win isn't altogether the important thing. What matters is what I'm fighting for, Rosemary, and I can't turn my back on that . . . and still make this the kind of town you want to see it become."

"I'm sorry, Jeff. It's just that I'm afraid for you, and wondering what you can really accomplish."

"I don't know, but I can do *something!*" said Mainwaring.

Mainwaring paid for his coffee and left. Pausing on the sidewalk for a moment, he decided to head on to the jail and question Tate Siringo again. As he walked, Mainwaring reviewed the facts. Siringo was a Missourian who'd come to Sun City only two short months ago. He'd immediately bought up a quarter section from the railroad at two dollars an acre, thrown up a soddy for himself and his family, and started to plow up the good earth which till now had been only graze—for the buffalo once, and more recently for Josiah Winterfield's cattle.

Winterfield's cowhands gave Siringo a typical nester hoorawing, which came to nothing. Siringo was a horn-handed, slow-witted man, gaunt and stooped from years behind a plow, and never very strong for all his hard work, but with an inner core of toughness that made him stubborn as a Missouri mule. He drove Winterfield's hands off his land at shotgun point, and, when some of Winterfield's cattle got in his fields, he shot them and dragged the carcasses off his land with his team.

"That nester better use that plow to dig his own grave," folks said. "If he gets old Josiah worked up, he'll need one."

It might have been a prophecy. Early last evening, Joe Murchie, the hostler, had found Siringo sprawled unconscious in the alleyway between Lou Bentwick's saloon and the adjacent feed store. He was reeking of whisky. Murchie then noticed the side window of the saloon, which opened into the alley off Bentwick's office.

Nearly all the glass had been smashed out of the window frame, and Siringo's body was sprawled directly under the window. Curious, old Murchie glanced into the office, and had seen Lou Bentwick lying contortedly on the floor by his desk, in a litter of playing cards. Murchie hadn't paused to see more; he'd headed at an unwieldy run for Sheriff Billy Lowe's office.

Mainwaring had been chatting with Lowe in his office

when Murchie burst in and rattled off his story. The three had gone to the saloon. Bentwick was dead all right, strangled to death. Reviving Tate Siringo, Billy Lowe had questioned the man for an hour. Siringo had insisted he'd had only one drink at Bentwick's bar and had left. As he'd passed the alley, he'd been struck over the head and knew nothing more until he'd come to just now.

But Billy Lowe formed his own opinion of what had happened. Everyone knew that Siringo had occasional games of penny-ante poker with Lou Bentwick in Bentwick's office. For all his dullness, Siringo was a sharp man with the cards, and Lou, who'd been a professional gambler in his day, enjoyed these poker sessions.

Lowe said that Siringo must have been drunk when they'd started playing this evening, and perhaps had been accused by Lou of cheating. In a drunken anger, Siringo had strangled Lou, then tried foggedly to get out by way of the window. He must have plunged through the pane and then dropped, unconscious, into the alley outside, and been too stunned and stupid with whisky to rise.

Josiah Winterfield had been standing by, listening, as Lowe had voiced his opinion aloud to the small crowd gathering around Bentwick's office. Seeing the faintly supercilious amusement on Winterfield's face, Mainwaring had known then, with a sudden conviction, that Winterfield had wanted this, that he might even have maneuvered Siringo into a frame-up.

It was then, on the spur of the moment, that Mainwaring had announced to the room at large that he'd defend Tate Siringo in court, for nothing. He hadn't missed the immediate warning anger that flashed over Winterfield's face at his announcement. But at the moment, swayed by outraged principles, Mainwaring hadn't cared.

51

Now, as he knocked at the door of the sheriff's office, the lawyer knew a queasy misgiving. As he'd told Rosemary, he was no fighter, and as such he couldn't wholly avoid being touched by the incubus of fear in which Winterfield held Sun City. He didn't have the spirit for the kind of fight that Winterfield would bring to his doorstep.

"Come in," said Billy Lowe's sleepy voice.

The sheriff was sitting at his desk, brooding over his day book, a paunchy man with the tired and unassuming face of a sheep. He looked as if he might bleat when he opened his mouth. Officially he was an honest lawman who went too much by the book. Unofficially he was Mainwaring's best friend.

"How's the prisoner this morning?" Mainwaring asked.

"Still holding to his story," Lowe said sadly. "You want to talk to him, I suppose."

At Mainwaring's assent, Lowe led the way to the cell-block, unlocked the door of Siringo's cell, and stood by as Mainwaring entered it.

"Well, my drunken friend," Mainwaring said with a forced smile, "how're they treating you?"

Tate Siringo grinned stiffly as he sat up on his bunk, but his face bore a haunted look. "All right, Mister Mainwaring. I'm just marking time till you get me out of this."

"That depends on whether you tell me the truth all the way, Tate."

"By grab, sir, I told the truth last night. Someone's trying on purpose to make it look as if I killed Lou."

"That's how I figure." Mainwaring glanced obliquely at Lowe. "You know who really did Lou in, don't you, Billy?"

Lowe scowled. "As the law in Sun City and county, I have to walk the middle of the road, Jeff. You know that. Lou Bentwick was murdered last night, and Tate was found under the broken window of his office."

"Which proves nothing except that Tate was found under the broken window of his office," Mainwaring said dryly. "The bartender told us he didn't see Tate enter or leave Bentwick's office last night."

"Which proves nothing," countered Lowe, "except that the bartender didn't *see* Tate enter or leave the office. A bartender's a busy man. He didn't see anyone else enter or leave the office either, but someone got in there."

"Tate said he only had one drink in Bentwick's. The bartender corroborated that, and said Tate was sober when he left the saloon. According to your theory, Tate would've had to be blind drunk when he passed out in the alley. That is, if he weren't hit over the head, like he said."

"You smelled that whisky all over him yourself," snapped Lowe. "And he could've had a bottle stashed away under his coat, and started in on it after he left Bentwick's, then come back later."

"Then he was drunk," Mainwaring said. "But if he were so drunk he passed out afterward, how'd he find the strength to strangle Lou? There's no sign of a struggle in Lou's office, and Tate isn't overly strong. It would take a mighty strong, mighty sober man to hold Lou Bentwick still while he strangled him."

"Look," shouted Lowe in a harassed voice, "this isn't a courtroom! If you can convince a jury of all this when the time comes, more power to you! But Tate's presumed under suspicion on such evidence as we have now, and he stays in jail until proved otherwise." He added in a lower, worried voice: "Jeff, for your own sake, if you're right about Tate, I hope Win . . . I mean, the man who got Bentwick . . . doesn't add you to the list."

"I know what I'm up against."

"I wonder if you do," Lowe said with a shake of his head. "Well, good luck, anyway."

Mainwaring left the jail, judging that if he were to find evidence to free Tate, it was best to start at Bentwick's office. The saloon was across the way, and he bent his steps toward it, taking only fleeting notice of the two cow ponies racked in front. The barroom was big and shadowed and musty cool, and empty except for the bartender and two men drinking at the bar.

Hardly glancing at them, Mainwaring nodded to the bartender and said: " 'Morning, Harve. I'd like to take another look at Lou's office." He headed for the office door at the rear without pausing.

As he reached it, the voice of one of the two men at the bar brought him up short in his tracks. "That's him now, isn't it, Mister Winterfield?"

The other man said: "It is, Robert, and now is as good a time as any."

With something like a lump of ice in his stomach, Mainwaring turned to face the two men, of whom he'd taken little notice. Now he saw that they were Josiah Winterfield and Bob Landers.

Winterfield was a whiplash-lean man with a profile that a Roman senator might have envied. His clothes, conservative and cultured, matched his voice. Bob Landers was the antithesis, a big, brutal man, unshaven and dirty, in rough, much worn but little washed clothes. All Mainwaring knew about this was that he was new to Winterfield's service and had a position that was indefinable. He was a kind of trouble-shooting handy man.

The two seemed to be waiting, Mainwaring observed with a sudden panic. He fought this feeling down silently and gave his attention to Winterfield's words.

"I understand you're representing Tate Siringo legally."
The lawyer nodded.

"I don't think you will," Winterfield said with a soft threat incongruously sheathed in the gentle culture of his tones. "I think you have more sense than to mix in this, friend. You're too sharp a lad to fight a lost cause."

"Maybe you think I'm sharp enough to find more than Billy Lowe did," Mainwaring said. "Maybe that worries you."

Menace laid suddenly bare and flat in the rancher's wintry eyes. "Lay off. You've got a wildcat by the tail. Lay off, Mainwaring."

With a cold confidence he would never have thought to find in himself, Mainwaring said: "Don't pressure me, Winterfield. You may have been born to give orders, but I wasn't born to take them."

"You'd better shut up," Landers said slowly.

Winterfield lifted a hand. "No," he said. He was smiling. "Let him talk, Robert. He's a shyster. He likes to talk."

"I'm finished," Mainwaring said.

"Well, now, that is a pity. Take him, Robert."

The command followed so casually on the heel of the idle comment that Mainwaring did not recognize it for what it was until Landers hunched his shoulders and began moving in toward him with a primordial exuberance.

Mainwaring put his back to the wall, feeling the quiet panic rising in him again, knowing that he was hopelessly out-matched. Mainwaring saw Landers's first punch coming at his belly; he tried to block it, and Landers shifted his attack and landed his first blow high on Mainwaring's temple. The world seemed to spin away, and Mainwaring knew Landers had a weighted object clutched in his fist to give his blows more impact.

Dazed, in no condition to defend himself, Mainwaring tried to close with Landers, but the man circled carefully away from his reach, while he systematically chopped the lawyer down. In one minute, Mainwaring could hardly stand, and could no longer feel pain, only a sodden thud of blows. He went down on his knees.

Landers stepped back now, and Mainwaring began to climb to his feet again. He saw the disgusted pity in Landers's brutal face.

"Give it up, feller," Landers said. "You don't want any more."

Mainwaring came up on his feet then, and Landers moved in to finish it. Mainwaring saw the blow coming, tried to duck, and failed. He never knew when he hit the floor.

"Feel better, Jeff?" Billy Lowe asked.

Mainwaring answered wryly: "Physically."

They sat at a corner table of Bentwick's, Mainwaring holding a wet cloth to his bruised head. His face was cut and swollen; he knew that without having to look at it.

"Better get some rest," Lowe said. "I'll see you to your room."

"That's all right, Billy. It looks worse than it feels."

The bartender, who had summoned Lowe after Winterfield and Landers had left, came to the table and handed Mainwaring a tumbler of whisky. "It's on the house, Mister Mainwaring. Sorry this happened in our place. If Lou were still here, it wouldn't have."

"Forget it, Harve. There was nothing you could do." Mainwaring downed the drink, feeling its angry warmth curdling with the sick rage in his stomach.

Lowe was silent a moment, then said: "If you want to swear out a warrant for Landers, I'll serve it on him, Jeff."

"A warrant would only get Landers."

"That's how it is, boy. Sorry."

Mainwaring got gingerly to his feet. He said: "I'm going to take a look in Bentwick's office."

"What do you expect to find there?"

"Something we might have missed last night. I know now that Tate's innocent, Billy . . . because Winterfield was feeling guilty enough to have me beaten up."

"I'll join you," said Billy Lowe.

In Lou Bentwick's deserted office, Mainwaring paced between the four cramped walls like a caged animal, his eyes questing restlessly over every detail of the room. Pausing by the window, his shoes crunched on broken glass. He poked absently at splinters and shards with his toe, then stopped. The one flaw in Billy Lowe's theory of Siringo's guilt stabbed home to the lawyer with the cold sharpness of an icicle.

He turned to the sheriff, who was lounging against the doorjamb. "Billy, you figured the way Winterfield wanted you to."

"What?"

"You figured Tate strangled Bentwick in drunken anger, then broke the window to escape through it, and passed out when he went through. Assuming that, Tate would have had to break the window from the inside, and the glass would've fallen outward . . . and not inward to the floor of the room!"

"Why . . ."—Lowe scratched his head—"reckon that's so. And if the glass was busted from the outside. . . ."

"It could mean that someone got in this way from the out-side, strangled Lou, then left the same way, slugged Tate and dragged him over under the window, then doused some whisky on him to make it look as if he was drunk. But one thing's sure. If Tate were having a card game with Bentwick, he didn't *enter* the office by way of the window. And he didn't break the window in leaving. The glass tells us that."

"I reckon you can get Tate acquitted, all right." Lowe said, scratching his head again. "It kind of figures, at that. I happen to know Lou had some outstanding gambling debts on Winterfield. Maybe Winterfield killed him and rigged it on Tate to get two birds with one stone. Too bad, but I guess that finishes it. You can't touch Winterfield without concrete evidence."

But it's not finished, the lawyer said to himself. Not yet, not while there remained something for Mainwaring to find out about himself.

Mainwaring slept the rest of the morning and late into the afternoon. By five o'clock he woke, his face stiff with a raw, steady ache. But his head was clear, and he was ravenously hungry. He washed and put on a clean shirt and string tie. Before leaving his rooms, he strapped on a .38 in a shoulder holster that was hidden when he buttoned his coat over it.

At Rosemary Gilchrist's café, he found the counter empty at this hour. Rosemary gave a gasp of shocked dismay at sight of his face. He told her what had happened in a few spare words, unconsciously unbuttoning his coat as he spoke. Rosemary glimpsed the gun.

"Jeff," she said haltingly, "what's that for?"

Mainwaring glanced down and cursed himself silently for exposing the gun. "For Bob Landers, maybe."

"You're going to kill him!"

"Rosemary, Rosemary," he chided gently, "did I say that? Did I?"

She was silent a stubborn moment. Then she said: "You're going to threaten him with it, then . . . which comes to the same thing. You've taken to wearing a gun to prove you're a man."

"Maybe that's it," he said, watching her steadily. "There's

time for you to run, you see, and a time to fight. I didn't really see that till today. I told you I wasn't a fighter, and that always seemed all right, because a man who isn't big enough to back down now and again isn't big enough to live with his fellows. Only if you back too far, it starts going in reverse, and you get smaller instead of bigger, and finally you're standing on your knees. And no man . . . *no man* . . . can live on his knees. This is one thing I can't fight in court."

"You talk as if you're rehearsing for court," she said coldly.

"Rosemary," he said softly, "you must let me be a man."

"I won't argue, Jeff," Rosemary said in a steely voice. "Either give this up or give me up."

Mainwaring stared at her, then shrugged in acceptance. "I can't talk sense till you're ready to hear it."

He left the café and headed for a saloon to start the rounds of a search for Bob Landers. It was Saturday night, and Landers would be in town, now or later. Winterfield had to be taught a lesson on his own ground—force—and the way to do it was through Landers, the rancher's instrument of force.

He thought with a sudden scathing anger at himself: *Now who are you fooling? If he shows his teeth, you'll spook.*

Yet as he forced his steps into the saloon, he had a full, sudden conviction that he'd lost Rosemary anyway, and there was nothing left to lose. With this thought a dead fatalistic calm came to him. *With nothing to lose, why worry?*

A heavy burst of laughter rolled against his ears as he moved into the barroom. He was in luck, Mainwaring thought, in meeting Landers now, before he had too much time to think about it. Landers was one of a group of laughing, carousing cowhands grouped about a table toward the rear.

Mainwaring headed for the table and came to stand by

Landers's chair. "Bob," he said gently.

Landers glanced around, frowning. His face cleared when he saw who it was, and he laughed outright as he took the cigar from his mouth.

" 'Evening, Counselor. You look pretty banged up. Have a shot of pain-killer." He poured a glassful from the bottle of whisky at his elbow.

"When I take anything from you," Mainwaring said, "it won't be offered."

"Come on," Landers said, laughing, and handed the lawyer the glass.

Mainwaring took it and threw its contents in Landers's face. The man started up from his chair, rubbing at his eyes, cursing. Mainwaring suddenly drew his .38 and rammed the muzzle into Landers's stomach so hard he sat down.

"Is that how you dosed Tate with liquor when you killed Bentwick and framed him for it?" Mainwaring asked softly.

"You're crazy! I never . . . take that damned gun away!"

"Tate didn't strangle Bentwick, Bob. It would have taken a strong man to do that . . . as big and strong as you."

Landers's eyes narrowed. "Walk soft, Counselor."

"I've walked soft for a long time, Bob," Mainwaring said, and smiled. "Now I'm going to stampede a little. Stand up."

Landers came slowly to his feet, and the lawyer brought the barrel of the .38 hard alongside his head. A long, dark welt sprang across Landers's jaw and temple, and he staggered but didn't fall. Mainwaring shifted the gun to his left hand and hit Landers with his closed fist. The man sat down heavily in his chair, and his backward impetus carried the chair over with a crash.

The cowhands, on their feet now, made a concerted stir of movement toward Mainwaring, but he looked at them and something very ugly in his face stopped them. Their voices trailed to mutters.

Mainwaring looked now at Landers, sitting on the floor and holding a hand to his bleeding face. "Now you know how it feels. And tell Winterfield this. Tate will be freed. The law can't touch Winterfield yet, but his days are numbered. Tate and the other little men are here to stay. And tell him this, Bob. No matter what happens, we're not afraid of him . . . any of us."

Mainwaring pivoted and walked from the saloon, leaving a dead silence in his wake, and not noticing it for the wild, exultant lifting all through him. It was that easy, he thought. You've been afraid of Landers and his kind for two years, and it was that easy to talk back to them.

Much later that evening, Mainwaring sat in his office, working at preparing a brief of Siringo's case with a quiet contentment marred only by the thought of how Rosemary was bound to take this.

He supposed it was inevitable that a sedately bred girl could hardly understand about how things could go so badly that force was the only answer.

There was a knock at the door. At his—"Come in."— Rosemary entered and closed the door swiftly behind her, then turned to look at him. She said in a faltering voice: "Jeff. Oh, Jeff."

He came to his feet in swift alarm, circling the desk to grasp her arms. "What's the matter?"

"Nothing, only that people have been coming in and out of the café all evening . . . merchants, farmers, railroad men, even Mayor Phipps . . . all of them going out of their way to tell me how proud I must be of you, telling me how much courage it took to do what you did to Winterfield's bully-boy, telling me that it will make a big difference for all of them.

They're all proud of you. Jeff, I didn't see how it is out here, how it is with the people. I have so much to learn about them, about you. Just be patient with me."

Mainwaring smiled, in spite of the hurt it caused his cut mouth, and the smile was gentle. "Learning about people, and about me . . . I guess we'll be learning together, Rosemary. I just started today, myself."

The Ambush

Corporal Ben Griffith, C Troop, U.S. cavalry, sprawled on his belly behind a boulder and peered out to view the rocky slope, devoid of moving life. Somewhere up there, the Apaches were poised like vultures, waiting for the three men to rise from their covert. You couldn't see the Apaches, but they were there. The three knew they were there, because several minutes before Trooper Kirkwood of Boston had raised his head tentatively above his boulder and had received a bullet through the face.

Corporal Griffith twisted his dark head to view his two remaining companions, likewise sprawled prone behind sheltering rocks. There was Lieutenant Vindig, thin features knit in preoccupation as he gripped his carbine and peered cautiously around his rock. His immaculate blue uniform was wrinkled and dusty. The other man was Sergeant Flagg, a man who had seen more Indian campaigns than all the shavetail subalterns in the U.S. cavalry. He had a heavy, bluff, weather-beaten face. His powerful shoulders were hunched to the ground.

The body of Trooper Kirkwood lay as it had fallen, sprawled behind the boulder. The bodies of the men and horses of C Troop strewed the rocky floor of the cañon. At the crest of the walls, the Apaches waited to pot the remaining three troopers as soon as they raised their heads.

Ben Griffith had no sympathy for the hostiles. At the age of twelve he had seen his entire family—mother, father, and three brothers—killed outright or tortured to death by White Mountain Apaches. He had escaped only by dropping to concealment behind a clump of mesquite where he had laid, paralyzed by terror, watching the hideous orgy. The experience was as indelibly branded on his mind as though seared there by one of the white-feathered bolts driven into his family.

He glanced again at Lieutenant Vindig. He would have hated to be in the young Pointer's boots. The detachment had been two days out of San Carlos, guarding a pack train of ammunition and supplies for the garrison at Fort Mac-Dermott, nearly a hundred miles to the south. Overriding the advice of Sergeant Flagg, veteran of a dozen campaigns against the Utes and Mescalero Apaches, Vindig had driven mules and men through the narrow cañon.

It was, after all, a foolhardy move. Even a dub like Ben Griffith knew that the Apaches would be aware of their passing and would, if opportunity presented itself, ambush them at arroyos, ravines, or dry washes. Any abrupt declivity or break in contour was a natural trap for cavalry or foot soldiers, for the Apaches could find cover in places which the white man would disregard as unfeasible.

There was more open country to the east, and it would have taken them but a few miles and a negligible amount of time out of their way, but young Lieutenant Vindig, fresh from the Point and up-to-date, viewed with contempt the unhurried languor of the Southwest. A little efficiency would eliminate hours, and the military precision of C Troop, he had found, was at an all-time lackadaisical low. That was what Lieutenant Vindig had told Sergeant Flagg. After all, how the hell could a gang of siwashes large enough to do them any harm hang out in the death-like stillness on the rim of the cañon in the blazing heat of the midday sun, without making some betraying movement? For a good mile now, they'd had a clear view of the rocks up there as they approached the cañon, and there had not been a sign of life. Lieutenant Vindig had yet to learn that patience, a quality of mind that he had already shown himself to possess in the minimum, was a fine art with the Apaches. On the war trail, heat, thirst, and what other diverse discomforts may be thrust across an Apache's path are as naught.

And so Lieutenant Vindig had ridden into the cul-de-sac. The wily hostiles waited until the last man was in the narrow confines between twin walls of rock, and until the pack train had been driven entirely through. Then a landslide of rocks had been loosed from above at an overhang of rock that now protected them from gunfire from above. As yet, they had scarcely caught a glimpse of their savage foes, but their cries had left no doubt as to their identity.

It was no easy task to fathom the thoughts of Lieutenant Vindig. He had unwittingly and obdurately led his entire command into the jaws of an Apache ambush. Because of him, the rest of his troop had been wiped out—strewn along the cañon floor for its entire length. All horses were shot down for the Indians took no chances on the few survivors making a break when darkness came. It was possible, after all, although not simple, for a horseman at a fast gallop to ascend either of the little avalanches of rock that now blocked both ends of the cañon.

Sergeant Flagg, a taciturn man by nature, had said nothing to Lieutenant Vindig since the ambush. Like other tough old non-coms, he had long since found that many young subalterns heed the voice of but one mentor—experi-

65

ence. For one man's folly, other men died—and the officer had learned his lesson, but what good would it do now? Ben felt almost patronizing toward the lieutenant at that moment. Griffith was even younger than the lieutenant, and, like Vindig, this was his first close encounter with the foe, but he had gone on numerous reconnaissance patrols in the past year, and he knew that the wisdom of the veteran of numerous campaigns was never to be sneezed at.

"Flagg!" said Vindig.

Ben noticed that the lieutenant's tone had lost not an iota of its peremptory arrogance.

"Sir?"

"What's our chances?"

"To be honest, sir, maybe one in a thousand, and I reckon that's putting it a little to our favor, sir."

Vindig grunted. "Anything else you'd like to say, Flagg?"

"Why, no, sir."

"You're lying." Vindig's voice was rising. "You're thinking. . . ."

"I'm not thinking anything, sir," interrupted Flagg sharply, "except that we don't stand a chance of getting out of here before nightfall."

"My God! It's six hours to sunset. We can't last that long in this heat." Vindig wiped perspiration from his forehead with a dusty blue-sleeved forearm.

"Darkness is our only chance, sir."

"We'll never last it, Flagg. Our only chance is a break now."

Ben Griffith, a silent listener to this intercourse, realized abruptly that this stupid young man was again deliberately overriding the veteran's advice. Men had died, and the lieutenant had not yet learned his lesson. Ben remembered Trooper Kirkwood of Boston and felt violent, wild grief that caused a sudden anger to flame in his gentle soul.

He twisted furiously toward Vindig. "Damn you!" he gritted. "You heard the sergeant once. . . ."

"Shut up!" bellowed Flagg in a voice that silenced him instantly. Flagg added in a quicker tone: "You know a soldier's place, Griffith."

Ben turned his eyes upward toward the rim of the cañon above and kept them there, fighting down the rage that bled on the verge of violence. His knuckles were white under the pressure of his fingers gripping his rifle stock.

Without looking, he was aware of Vindig's intent gaze turned on him.

"Kirkwood was your friend?"

The lieutenant's voice held a humility that surprised Ben and affected him to the extent where his consuming anger was somewhat cooled. Still, his fingers gripped the stock more tightly until they ached, and not once did he remove his gaze from the rim.

"Yes, sir."

The lieutenant raised himself on one elbow, opening his mouth to speak again, and in so doing exposed himself to possible fire from the enemy. But Ben was alert. His gaze went to the rim; he saw immediately the rifle barrel and giveaway forearm exposed to view over the rim above, as a foeman drew a bead on the lieutenant's exposed head.

Ben made no effort to warn the lieutenant, although he alone was cognizant of his danger. Instead, he waited deliberately for the marksman above to expose more of his body to draw a bead. As he had expected, the Apache drew one eye into view so that he could sight along the barrel. Ben took a minute to aim and pulled the trigger. His carbine roared a second before the Indian's weapon.

He saw the Apache's fingers relax on the smoking rifle,

and the exposed face, no longer to be identified as a face, slid slowly outward over the edge of the rim and fell clattering over the rocks clear down to the base of the cañon.

The lieutenant clenched white-faced behind his rock. The hostile's bullet had whined off the boulders scarcely an inch from his head. If Ben's shot had not broken the Apache's aim a split second before the latter fired, Vindig would have died.

But Flagg was not pleased.

"Corporal!"

"Yes, Sergeant?"

"What kind of foul play was that? You saw that savage long before he fired, did you not?"

"Yes, sir."

"Don't 'sir' me. Instead of warning the lieutenant immediately, you took the obvious risk of waiting for a clean shot, and took your sweet time about drawing a bead on the savage. The lieutenant might have died for your folly!"

"Yes . . . Sergeant."

Ben said nothing else. He knew that he deserved to be reprimanded—but then Vindig thrust his oar in.

"Griffith, I can understand your feelings. Naturally you wish to kill as many hostiles as you can. So do we all, but not to a foolhardy extent. I am deliberating now whether to report you to Major Kline . . . if we get out of this alive."

Ben said nothing, didn't even glance at him. He was aware only of a burning fury that he had to fight to control, and for a moment his limbs trembled like a palsied man's, his fingers aching from their clutch on his rifle. Flagg defended the idiot who was responsible for the wiping out of one of the finest troops of fighting men in the U.S. cavalry not an hour since!

Time dragged by. The three men were assailed by a torturing thirst, but there was no water—except in the canteens on the saddles of the dead horses, which they could not reach. The heat was severe and punishing, and it steadily sapped their strength with a draining energy that was almost fierce.

But Vindig spoke no more of a break. He was content to let the wisdom of such matters rest with Flagg. Ben felt that he had helped to put this fact across to the lieutenant, and it made him feel like a martyr.

The next hour of the afternoon came, which was between two and three o'clock, and compelled them to be immobile while the moisture was sapped from their bodies and their tongues began to obtrude with thirst. The three men found it even agony to breathe through dust-clogged and contracted nasal passages. The rocks among which they laid were as red-hot iron, another factor to preclude shifting their cramped limbs, and the barrels of their rifles might have been vulcanized.

Water. Even the creatures of iron waiting above might slake their thirst with a hot rancid, unpalatable liquid from a primitive canteen, fashioned perhaps from a horse's intestine —but still real life-giving moisture. The white men, children of a pampered race, could only suffer on without even that meager benefit. Ben thought of his childhood when his migrating family had crossed the Missouri, of how he had sworn with childish vindictiveness when his spooking roan had pitched him into the churning water. There had been other rivers later, but nothing like the Missouri, and it had been mildly swollen with the spring thaw at the time, so that Ben, caught in the heaving current and no swimmer, had been half frenzied and half frozen before his father, leaning down from horseback, looped a rope under his armpits and hauled him unceremoniously ashore, where he had laid for a half hour, gagging and spitting out "half the Missouri," as his father had jocularly put it.

The Missouri. It was framed as clearly in his mind's eye as though he had only yesterday watched its sullen torrents seethe by. The Missouri. Incalculable tons of water rushing to augment the mighty Mississippi. Tons of water surging on toward the ocean, untasted, unappreciated by those who had never known thirst. Fresh water rolling to waste . . . water . . . water. . . .

"Easy, lad."

The voice was Flagg's; it was Flagg's hand extended to grasp his arm with an iron reassurance as though intuitively knowing. Then a *spanging* rifle bullet caused both to duck flat.

On wore the afternoon. It was to Vindig's credit that not a whimper of complaint escaped him. His jaw was set in a way that made Ben think of a little boy about to cry. Eventually they would join their dead comrades, Ben knew. Now or later —what was the difference? Better to jump up and die fighting than suffer on in an agony of discomfort that could have but one ending.

Again it seemed that Flagg might have read his thoughts, for again his arm was grasped by those hardy, great-knuckled fingers. Once more Ben subsided.

The shadows, lengthening, cast elongated figures over the silent cañon, shadows that fell mercifully across the ugly tableau of fallen men and animals. Ben forced himself to watch the shadow that crawled with agonizing deliberation across Tom Kirkwood's upturned face, touching his fair hair with a shade darker than the congealed blood. Ben bent his face in the dirt and retched.

Somehow the burning thirst and cramped discomfort and wearying heat passed into oblivion, and he dozed. Yet it seemed almost immediately that a hand was shaking his shoulder and Flagg's voice was whispering: "It's time!"

Time for what? Ben thought idiotically, then saw that it was pitch dark. The moon was just topping the silhouetted rimrock.

"Now's our only chance," whispered Flagg, "and they may have the same idea about getting us. So we'll move fast. Take off your boots."

Ben sat up, feeling suddenly alive as his cramped limbs eased. As he pulled off his boots, he wondered what they could do even should they escape the cañon, on foot without water, and with no known white habitation within miles. At any rate, they could spot an Apache against the rimrocks if one should show his head, whereas even the keen Apache eye could discern nothing against the fathomless blackness in the cañon. How to deceive the equally keen Apache ear was another thing, even walking in stocking feet. And there would surely be guards at the exits of the cul-de-sac.

Flagg had anticipated even this. Ben could hear a faint scrape of rock. Then Flagg said: "Wait till you hear the stone hit. Then move toward the left. Leave your rifles. You won't want them."

There was a stirring sound, and Ben saw the stone, flung by Flagg's powerful arm, arc up against the sky and fall, far downcañon to the right, setting up a small rattling. He understood then. The sound would pull the Apaches' attention to the right while they went through the left exit.

Flagg went first, then Vindig, with Griffith bringing up the rear, all three carrying their boots, moving silently in stocking feet that made a bare whisper over the rock. Once Ben bent down to pull a full canteen off a saddle and bring it over one shoulder. He located it easily in the dark, since he had had coveted eyes on it all afternoon. Over the blocking pile of rubble they picked their way. There would be a guard at the

71

cañon mouth, Ben thought, and they came upon him suddenly as a darker figure sprang from the cover of a boulder, an upraised knife gleaming in the moonlight. Flagg, always anticipating ahead, clubbed the Apache down with a ready pistol. The man fell without an outcry.

Vindig chuckled softly. "Stupid barbarians."

"Quiet!" hissed Flagg. "And don't ever underestimate a 'Pache. This one must have been a fool young buck."

Free of the cañon now, they pulled on their boots, and Flagg led them in a wide, circuitous route around behind the Apache encampment on the river. Finally they paused in the shadow of a boulder.

"Listen," panted Flagg. "We must have horses, and we must have them before they find out we're free. There's only one way." He paused "The Apache remuda."

"Can I volunteer to get them, sir?"

"Not 'sir,' Griffith, and you may not. You know horses, but I know Apaches."

Flagg moved away into the darkness toward the Apache camp.

"Damn it, man," Vindig said.

Flagg's voice floated back quietly. "I must do it alone, Lieutenant, sir. I'm the only one who can."

Ben heard no more then, save for the brief sound of Flagg's laborious breathing as he wended his way up a slope behind the Indian camp.

Ben settled back to wait with Vindig. Flagg would have to creep in close to the wary Indian ponies, and must depend more on speed than secrecy, for no white man could hope to deceive an Indian in a matter of stealth, and, when the Indian ponies caught his strange scent, they would warn their masters instantly.

There were shots from above the slope that brought both

Vindig and Griffith to their feet. The thundering of countless hoofs started from the slope, and then the surging remuda hove into view with Flagg, clinging like a burr to the back of the foremost.

"Get horses," he roared at them, "as they go by!" Then he was carried on by the vanguard of the rushing herd.

Vindig and Griffith waited, backs flattened against the boulder as the ponies surged on by, then Ben sprang forward to seize one of the stragglers with a rope on his snout. Ben swung to the bare back and caught the rope, Vindig performing the same with another straggler. Before either could make another move, Ben distinctly caught the released *twang* of a rawhide-string mesquite bow and a solid thud as a quartz-tipped arrow struck. Then he saw that Vindig had received the shaft in his shoulder, and was slowly slipping from his pony's back.

Ben reined in instantly and supported the lieutenant with one arm, at the same time turning to look up the slope. Plainly in the moonlight crouched the wiry frame of a breechclout warrior in the act of necking another arrow to his bow—the man left to guard the ponies. Ben pulled his Colt and shot once, instinctively. The guard spun wildly and pitched forward down the slope.

Ben caught up the rope of Vindig's mount and, again holding Vindig in his saddle, set out unhurriedly after Flagg and the other ponies. Then he heard the yells of the Apaches as they swarmed over the crest of the slope. There were shots then, and one took his hat away. Another pierced his sleeve.

"You've . . . got a . . . chance," Vindig gasped. "Take it . . . leave me."

"No, sir," Ben said blandly, and turned in his saddle to shoot again. A horse and rider bulked ahead in the moonlight, and Ben raised his pistol.

"It's me. Flagg. Lieutenant hurt?"

"Yes, sir."

Flagg sighed. " 'Sir' again. Come on, Griffith. We'll get out of here, then look to his wound. The 'Pache remuda's scattered to hell-and-gone, and they're left afoot. They won't follow us tonight anyway."

The first gray hint of the aurora in the east saw three tired, dirty, and unshaven cavalrymen on three nondescript Apache ponies well on their way south to Fort MacDermott.

"It seems we'll make it, after all," Flagg said. "Thanks to that canteen of water Griffith thought to bring."

"He ties a good bandage, too," Vindig said sheepishly, touching his shoulder bound with strips torn from his undershirt.

Vindig had come out of this a changed man, Ben decided, but at what a cost! The U.S. Army might as well disband, he thought bitterly, if the lives of so many good enlistees must always be the price for the making of one good officer. Vindig had said he would give himself up to a court-martial at MacDermott. Could a thousand courts-martial bring back Tom Kirkwood, or a single other man of C Troop? The bitter knowledge of the answer settled over Ben bleakly, and he rode in the gray, depressing dawn in silence behind the others.

Flagg reined back to his side, again seeming to know. "Things have a way of smoothing out, Griffith," he said mildly.

"Yes, sir."

"Do I have to say it again, damn it?" Flagg said wearily. "Griffith, you don't 'sir' a non-com."

But glancing at Flagg, Ben saw a faint, wry humor touch the tough old sergeant's wide mouth.

Tenderfoot

Vern Brady stepped off the train, placed his suitcase on the weather-beaten station platform, mopped his perspiring forehead with a white silk handkerchief, and surveyed his surroundings with noncommittal interest. This was Cactus Junction, a typical Arizona cow town with its weather-beaten, warped edifices and false fronts, and Vern Brady, fresh from New York, was not inclined favorably to it at first glance.

He looked around and saw no one; the street was deserted. He looked at his watch and frowned. He had written Sid to meet him on June 15th at 3:00 p.m. Could he have gotten the dates mixed? That would be a hell of a note! He was wondering what to do, when a voice hailed him to one side. "Say, are you Vern Grady?"

Vern turned to view the author of the voice. He saw a buckboard, and then he stopped, blinked, looked again, and swept off his hat.

"Pardon me, miss. This is a very pleasant surprise, but I didn't expect to meet a . . . a young lady."

The girl nodded. "I hope you're not disappointed."

She descended in one lithe movement from the buckboard and walked toward the platform. She had short brown hair bound neatly at the back of her neck, arched, aristocratic brows, sharp, clear, gray eyes, and a smooth complexion, tanned by sun and wind. She had no hat. She wore a white blouse, half-length boots, and a tan divided riding skirt that did not hamper her free stride, or conceal the grace of her slender figure. This was a girl of the open. There was a free virility about her that proclaimed that. She was more than pretty. Her beauty was not classic, but it was plainly a product of nature and not of artificiality.

She ascended the platform and reached down to take his suitcases. Vern blushed and quickly seized his luggage first. She smiled at that, for the first time, and the smile did justice to her features.

"I'm not disappointed, miss," said Vern awkwardly, "but where's Sig, my brother? He was supposed to meet me. . . ."

"Oh, Sig's down the street. He's getting supplies at the general store. He'll be along in a minute. I'm Judy Wallace, his fiancée."

"His fiancée? But he never wrote me. . . ."

The girl gave a low, melodious laugh. "We've scarcely been engaged a week, Mister Brady. But I've known Sig for nearly a year. He told me a lot about you."

She held out her hand. Vern set down his suitcase and took it. Her hand was slender but strong. Verne had never met a girl like this before. Her frankness and lack of affectation was thoroughly refreshing to his jaded Easterner soul. He was unaware of his own admiring gaze until she blushed and said: "Can I have my hand back, Mister Brady?"

It was Vern's turn to redden, and he did as he released her hand. At that moment, he heard a shout: "Vern! How's my big brother, the merchant of Broadway?"

Vern turned and saw Sig, running down the street toward them. He vaulted to the top of the platform and embraced Vern with one arm—the other was in a white sling.

"Well, howza boy, Vern?" exclaimed Sig with swift, undiminished ardor.

"Fit as a fiddle, kid. But your arm . . . ?"

"Ah, it's nothing, Vern." Sig brushed the remark aside, but Vern, observing him keenly, saw some of the humor leave his eyes to be replaced by a darkening of his brow. "I'll tell you about it later," Sig added. He put an arm around Judy Wallace's shoulders. "I see you've met my girl, big shot. Isn't she something?"

"She certainly is," responded Vern gravely.

Judy looked at Vern and smiled, and Vern smiled back.

It was not difficult to ascertain the relationship between Vern and Sig even if one had no knowledge of their affinity. They had the same blond hair with darker eyebrows; they had the same conformation of wide brow, long noses, and firm chins. Vern's face was leaner, however, and Sig's was heavily tanned from exposure to the elements. Vern was nearly a head taller than his brother, and had always been by nature the stronger, although Sig's hard, rigorous life on the Western plains for the past two years in contrast to Vern's position as a dry-goods merchant could probably now render him more than a match for his brother. Vern wore a dark, conservative business suit, while Sig affected cowboy garb. He looked like a hard-riding cattleman.

"Come on," said Sig, "we'd better get out to the ranch. There are a few things I'd better tell you on the way, Vern. The sooner you know, the better."

From his brother's sobered mouth and the heavy Colt he wore at his hip, which seemed to Vern significant that he divined trouble. A newcomer to the West, he did not realize that the packing of a sidearm was quite common on the frontier and quite essential to the continued pursuit of life, liberty, and happiness.

Seizing up with his good hand one of the bags Vern had set down, Sig jumped from the platform, tossed the piece of luggage into the back of the buckboard, and swung up to the seat. Vern deposited his other suitcase in the back and turned to help Judy into the seat, but she smiled and swung up quickly without aid. Sig took the reins, clucked to the horses, and laughed as Vern seated himself.

"You'll have to get used to that, Vern. Jude never lets a man help her."

Judy laughed. "He'll become adjusted."

Vern liked that low, melodious laugh. It struck pleasant chords on his ears. The high, silly giggles of coquettes with secrets always irritated him. "I intend to become adjusted," said Vern, "to a lot of things."

The ride to Sig's ranch was long and dusty, but it gave Vern an opportunity to see this new land at first-hand. His first unfavorable impression was altered as he looked across the dry, baked plain to the undulating line of purpled mountains in the distance. They did possess a rugged beauty, he thought, and the lure of them came upon him. Farther to the south, he could discern a series of green, wooded foothills.

As they rode, they talked, and Vern became friendly with Judy. Sig kidded them. It was evident that he was pleased to see the two people closest to him hitting it off. Vern learned that she was an orphan like Sig and himself and that she lived with her guardian, Zach Morley, an old, reclusive prospector in a cabin five miles along a wagon road from Sig's ranch.

Vern had come out West half willingly at his brother's invitation after his own dry-goods business had failed. He had laughed at what he had considered his brother's harebrained scheme, but he was now constrained to admit that

Sig had invested his share of their father's inheritance the more wisely.

As they neared Sig's Bar S spread, Sig began to divulge his present state of affairs. "Things are bad, Vern," he said bluntly. "These cattle thieves . . . rustlers, they call them . . . have made a hell of a depletion in my herd in a month. I can't post all of my boys as outriders at night. They've got to work in the daytime, too, and they need their beauty sleep."

"I can see they gave you a little memento, too," said Vern, indicating the wounded arm.

Sig nodded with a grim smile.

At that moment, they topped a gently swelling rise, and Sig halted the team.

"Look there, boy," he said, pointing dramatically.

Ahead, silhouetted darkly against the final rays of the Arizona sunset, was the ranch.

"Your first view of the Bar S is at its most impressive moment, Vern." Judy smiled.

When they reached the ranch house, Sig jumped out and pulled Vern's luggage down.

"I'll take care of this," he said. "I've got a mess of things to take care of, Vern. Will you drive Judy home? She'll tell you the way."

Judy smiled and took the reins. "I'll drive," she said, "since I know the way. Vern can drive back all right."

They set out for the cabin where Judy lived. She explained that it was three miles straight across the plain to where a winding trail entered the grove for two more miles where old Zack Morley and Judy resided.

Vern surreptitiously regarded the girl's clean-cut profile in the fading light.

Suddenly she said: "Now that you're here, you and I can help Sig. He needs help badly. He's learned Western ways fast and has made a success out here, but he's frustrated by this rustling business."

Vern asked: "You're being married soon?"

She nodded. "I know I can steady him then, and we can clear this up."

"You'll stick by him to the finish, eh?"

Again she nodded simply. "A girl sticks by her man."

"That's the way it should be," said Vern.

Vern set out to adjust himself to range life. This new, raw environment presented an unparalleled fascination for the young Easterner. He had always lived clean, *sans* petty dissipations; that was in his favor; nevertheless, there was a considerable difference between the continual straddling of a mettlesome broncho and a weekly canter in the park on a docile high-stepper. Vern was aware of this and knew he was in for a rough time.

The morning after his arrival, Sig informed him at breakfast that he would have to assume the responsibility of bookkeeping.

"The accounts are in a muddle," he admitted. "You know what I think of headwork, Vern."

He took Vern out to the bunkhouse after breakfast and introduced him to the boys. He met Prescott, the foreman, a big, dark, surly man slovenly attired. A few of the cowboys were a trifle too effusive in their greetings, which made Sig grin, for he knew from experience that these would be the ones to make life semi-unbearable for the tenderfoot with poker-faced humor and practical jokes.

The baiting of the boss' brother started when Vern said he would like to take a ride on a rather gentle horse, since he had not ridden for a year. Tacit winks were exchanged, and a lean creature with a shaggy mane was roped with difficulty, led into a small enclosure at one end of the corral, saddled, and bridled.

"Try Thunderbolt, boss," said a facetious 'puncher, putting an undue emphasis on the last word. "Gentle as a lamb. Why, after you been on him one second, you'll agree it's like sailin' through air."

Vern obligingly scaled the corral fence, eyed Thunderbolt dubiously, then leaped from the top of the corral to his back. Immediately the gate to the enclosure was swung open, and Thunderbolt leaped out. Vern felt one violent jolt, and then the promise of the 'puncher was fulfilled as he was wafted gently through space and deposited not so gently on his face in a pile of loose sand.

Vern came to his feet angrily, but unhurt, while a roar of laughter was evoked from the watching cowboys. The anger drained from him, and then he smiled good-naturedly, as he realized that this was an essential part of his "conditioning."

Prescott growled to the men to quit fooling around and get to work. It was evident from their sullen acquiescence that Prescott was far from well liked.

The days passed swiftly after that. The cowboys came to like Vern thoroughly, because of his cheerful, easy-going nature and his earnest desire and effort to learn Western ways. He rode with them; his aching muscles attained a wiry toughness that they had never previously possessed. In the evenings he straightened out Sig's accounts, which were not so muddled as behind in date.

Judy visited when she could spare the time, and, when she did, Vern liked to ride with her. Sometimes Sig rode with them, but more often he did not, because of his other duties.

Vern was surprised himself, for girls had never previously interested him. The bond of friendship with Judy strengthened. Vern had to remind himself constantly that this girl was engaged to his brother, and each time it became harder to remember.

Vern was already a good shot with rifle and revolver. He had practiced back East, in idle moments, shooting at inanimate objects thrown into the air, so he devoted his attention to mastering a piece of recalcitrant horseflesh. He practiced unceasingly on a tough little roan and presently mastered him. On that day the boys were not working, and they spent most of the day sitting on top of the corral fence cheering Vern caustically. They groaned and whistled whenever he was thrown, as he always was. Being bucked off was becoming so commonplace, he was rather inured to it.

"Ride 'em, cowboy!"

"Don't take no water, boss!"

"Hold on thar, New York!"

These and other spurious comments only goaded Vern, so that before the end of the afternoon the roan was beaten. Immediately all the boys stood in line to shake Vern's hand.

The next day he felt himself prepared to tackle Thunderbolt, the brute that had first thrown him. He roped Thunderbolt and herded it into the little enclosure. To Vern's eye it appeared that this morning Thunderbolt was leaner, its mane wilder, its coat shaggier, and its eye wickeder than ever before. Indeed, it did present a sinister aspect with quivering muscles, and its upper lip writhed back from its teeth. Vern quelled his uneasiness and swung astride.

Once in the corral, Thunderbolt erupted beneath his rider like a miniature Vesuvius. Immediately Vern was thrown. He had more or less learned to land in a manner that would mitigate possible injury, but this time he had no chance. He was thrown harder than ever before, and he landed as heavily.

For a moment he lay stunned. It was strange how at this moment he was aware of nothing but purely physical sensations

—the hot ground under his back, the warm, dusty air, the whirling blue of the sky above which seemed out of focus, and the thump of the black gelding's hoofs as it galloped off across the desert to temporary freedom. Suddenly he saw Judy, running toward him and calling his name. In an instant, she was bending over him, her lovely face close to his, anxious with concern. Her cool, slender hands were lifting his head; he could smell the warm, clean scent of her skin and hair.

Then his vision cleared, and for just a moment he was gazing straight into her eyes and an expression of guilt passed between them. Never before had they been so close together.

She would have drawn back then, but Vern could not have stopped himself. His arms went around her and pulled her down to him. Her hot, quivering lips came against his, and he kissed her hard, savagely. For an instant, she resisted him fiercely, her strong young arms pushing his shoulders back, and then, with a gasp, she gave in, and her hands encircled the back of his head and pulled him closer. Her kisses were hot on his lips.

With an exclamation, she tore away and came to her feet. "No, Vern, no. . . . It's wrong . . . it's all wrong."

He stood up and caught her by the shoulders in a fierce grip she could not dislodge. "I love you, and you are engaged to my brother . . . but the hell of it is, you don't love him . . . you love me!"

She gasped. "Oh, God, I don't know. . . . Let go . . . please! You're hurting me!"

He released her slowly, the passion dying from his eyes. "You're . . . you're right, Judy . . . it's wrong . . . all wrong. We'll forget it."

He turned away and walked toward the ranch house, leaving the girl there, hands pressed to her cheeks.

Vern entered his room and sat down on a bench. That

which he had feared had finally happened. He felt no regret, only weariness and disgust at himself. He knew that he was terribly, thoroughly, and wretchedly in love with the girl who was to marry his brother. He wondered dimly if all life was a lie and a sham.

The following morning Sig came to breakfast with a lowering brow. Vern was afraid for a moment that his brother had learned, but Sig only growled: "Lost fifty head of cattle last night, and one of the guards was killed."

"Good Lord," said Vern, shocked by this seemingly brutal statement of the uncertainty of life on the frontier. "Who?"

"Bill Evans. The rustlers must have stampeded the herd, and Bill tried to lead them off and his horse tripped in the path of the cattle. Anyway, we found him this morning. The whole herd must have gone over him."

"God. Can't we do anything?"

"What?" Sig asked sourly. "The damn' thieves are miles away into the badlands over lava ground where only an Indian could trail 'em."

After a while Sig seemed to recover a little of his good humor, but he was still melancholy. Vern could not blame him. The rustlers were spelling his ruin bit by bit.

Another week rolled by. Vern became moody. He lost his good nature and became touchy and surly, and Sig became more melancholy. The men were accordingly affected by their bosses' moods, and a pall of gloom settled over the Bar S.

"At least I can be sure of Judy," Sig confided to Vern once. "She'll stick by me, no matter what happens."

If you only knew, kid, thought Vern bitterly. *You don't even have Judy.*

One evening Vern was in the bunkhouse playing cards

with four of the men at the rude table. The room was fitfully illuminated by several lamps. The game was placid until Prescott, the foreman, walked up to the table, scraped back a chair, and commanded them in a loud voice to deal him in. He seemed to have lost a portion of his habitual surly reticence. The boys dealt him in, and for a while the game continued in silence.

Suddenly Vern said: "Damn it, Prescott, if you have to cheat, don't be so obvious about it. Anyone could see how you're marking these cards with your thumbnail."

Prescott scowled and shuffled to his feet. "You're one to talk," the foreman sneered. "Everyone on this ranch except the boss knows what's going on between you an' that Wallace trollop. . . ."

Vern hit him squarely with all the force of his arm and shoulder. He felt a gratifying tingle of pain run the length of his arm as his knuckles cracked solidly into Prescott's mouth. It was a powerful blow, perfectly timed and deftly administered. It carried an element of surprise against the slow-thinking foreman. It split Prescott's thick lips open, but to Vern's immense surprise it did not budge the bulky foreman an inch. For the moment he stared at the young man only half comprehending, blood flowing from his mouth, before the full enormity of what had happened burst upon him. With a bawl of rage, he lunged.

Vern was the taller by several inches. Prescott outweighed him by twenty pounds or more. Vern automatically sank into a boxer's crouch and side-stepped the huge foreman's wild lunge. Then he laid open Prescott's jaw with a straight left. In a blind fury, Prescott drove into Vern's solar plexus, his impetus and weight carrying them both back into the tin stove that went over with a crash. The stovepipe clattered to the floor, deluging the adversaries with powdery soot.

They came to their feet.

"Stop it."

The voice was low and toneless but it bore a note that brought the two antagonists to a standstill. All eyes turned toward Sig, standing in the doorway. His face was pale, but his light blue eyes held a chilly glitter that Vern had never seen there. The erstwhile combatants stood facing the young rancher awkwardly. Begrimed from head to foot with stove soot, they presented a ludicrous spectacle, but somehow nobody felt like laughing.

Sig stepped into the room and, without removing his gaze from Vern, jerked his head toward the doorway.

"Get out, Prescott. You're fired."

Prescott's eyes widened. "But, boss . . . ?"

"I heard what you said. Get out." Sig spoke in that same inscrutable tone.

Realizing the futility of further argument, Prescott choked back an epithet, and turned to his bunk to collect his belongings.

Sig glanced at Vern with a thin smile of irony on his white lips. "You had me fooled, Vern," he said slowly, with no inflection in his voice. "You and Judy . . . ?"

"Sig. . . ."

The latter shook his head with a trace of irritation. "No explanations. I've known it for several days. I got these in town this morning."

He reached in his pocket and handed two pasteboards to Vern, who accepted them wonderingly.

"Your tickets for the East-bound train tomorrow," continued Sig quietly. "It pulls out at two-thirty. I want you to be on it . . . you and Judy."

There was a note of bitterness in the final words that he made no attempt to conceal. Then he twisted and walked out, disappearing into the cool darkness of the evening, leaving Vern staring helplessly at the tickets in his hands.

"Vern! Vern! Wake up!"

These words aroused Vern from a tormented sleep. Still groggy, he swung himself slowly to a sitting position. He had been sprawled fully dressed. As he awoke entirely, he realized not more than an hour or two had elapsed since he had fallen asleep. Judy was bent over him, shaking him by the shoulders. He could barely see her features in the dim moonlight filtering through the window.

"Vern, you must listen."

"I am listening," he replied in a dispirited voice.

"Vern, my guardian is the leader of the rustlers!"

That brought Vern to attention. He came to his feet and grasped her by the arms. "Are you sure?"

"Yes, yes. I was in my room at our cabin. I should have been asleep, but I couldn't sleep. Then I heard low voices in the next room. I was puzzled and surprised, because no one ever comes to see Zach Morley. I listened at the door and realized from their talk that the men visiting Uncle Zach were the rustlers and that Uncle Zach is the leader. And I recognized the voice of Prescott, Sig's foreman! He's one of the gang, too, and he was terribly angry about something. He insisted that they make a big raid on the Bar S cattle tonight and clean Sig out! The others finally agreed. I got dressed, climbed out my window, took one of the horses they'd left outside, and came here to warn you."

"Good girl. Come on, we've got to warn Sig."

But Sig was not in his room.

"He must be on duty guarding the herd tonight," snapped Vern. "Come on . . . we'll warn the boys."

They ran to the bunkhouse. Vern swung the door open

and shouted a cryptic warning into the darkness that brought the muttering, abruptly awakened cowboys to their feet with sundry scuffling.

"You stay here," Vern snapped at Judy, and ran to the nearby hitching rack where Judy had left her horse.

Vaulting into the saddle, he seized the reins and spurred the bay to a gallop in the direction of the herd.

The main herd was concentrated about a mile away. Before Vern had covered half the distance he heard sudden shots. With a groan, he bent lower in his saddle and spurred his mount to a still greater speed.

Ahead he soon saw the dim silhouettes of riders and the tossing horns and milling bodies of hundreds of steers. The yells of the rustlers, the roars of their six-shooters, the bawls and thundering hoofs of the cattle were deafening. Without slackening his pace, Vern headed for the mêlée. He drew his revolver and fired at the nearest riders. Some turned in surprise and returned his fire.

There was a sudden burst of pain in his left temple. He gritted his teeth and fought for consciousness, but it slid from him, just as he was now sliding from the back of the flying mount. Down he fell, and, as he struck the ground, he heard above the din a mocking laugh. Then roaring blackness took possession of his senses.

Once again a voice was calling him: "Vern, wake up!"

Consciousness returned slowly as he opened his eyes. His head ached horribly. He put one hand to it and found it bound with a bloody bandage. In the gray light presaging the dawn several hours away, he saw Shorty Davis bending over him, his thin, homely face anxious.

"Gosh, boy," he said, "you had us all worried."

"I'm all right, Shorty." Vern struggled, with Shorty's aid,

to a sitting position. He saw some of the 'punchers standing around. "The rustlers . . . ?"

"We fixed 'em," explained Shorty. "Your warnin' saved us . . . we took 'em by surprise. Circled around, ambushed 'em from some rocks. They didn't have no chance. We killed some and took some prisoners. As far as we can figger, three of 'em got away. An' Vern, they took. . . ."

"Never mind!" said Vern impatiently. "Where's Sig?"

"He's . . . wounded. Maybe dyin'. . . ."

"No! He couldn't be. Let me see him."

"He's unconscious. Come this way."

Vern arose with difficulty, and Shorty escorted him to where Sig laid, limp and motionless, on some blankets several yards away. He didn't deserve this, thought Vern. With everything else, he didn't deserve this. He bent beside his brother and called his name. There was no response.

"Best let him sleep," said Shorty.

"All right. Where's Miss Wallace?"

"That's what I tried to tell you before, Vern," Shorty replied slowly. "They took her . . . the three fellas that got away."

Vern leaped to his feet, an ugly light in his blue eyes. "And you let them get away? You didn't follow them?"

"Cripes, we didn't have a chance. We'd left Miss Judy at the bunkhouse. When those three fellas went past it, they musta seen her, put her on a hoss, an' taken her with 'em. She was gone anyway, when we looked for her, an' by the light of a lamp we found the tracks of four hosses headed toward the south. It was too dark to follow 'em."

"Give me a horse!" snapped Vern.

"Vern, it's still too dark, an' you're in no condition to ride."

"Are you going to get me that horse?" asked Vern truculently, although he swayed a little with dizziness.

"All right, but let some of the boys go with. . . ."

"I'm going alone," interrupted Vern in a voice that brooked no opposition.

Without another word he ran past Shorty, leaped into the saddle of a standing horse, seized the reins, turned the animal's head, and galloped away toward the south.

The silent cowboys watched the receding figure disappearing in the gray dawn.

"Shorty, why'd you let him go? We better follow him," said a 'puncher.

Shorty hooked his thumbs in his cartridge belt and looked thoughtfully after the disappearing horseman. "No, boys. He's got two battles on his hands, and the biggest one's with himself. Let him fight it."

The half gleam of dawn had given way to a gleam of light from the east, so Vern had less difficulty than he had anticipated picking up the clearly defined trail of Judy and her three abductors. By mid-morning he could see rugged foothill terrain ahead. He judged that they would be expecting pursuit and would not slacken their pace. He was certain, however, that the relentless pace at which he had driven himself and his mount had begun to tell favorably.

He slowed up now, threading his way around crags and shoulders of rock. The ground was stony here, and a novice like Vern would find it impossible to track over it. However, he found a poorly defined trail and indications along it that those whom he sought had passed over it.

The ground sloped upward and grew more irregular. He had to dismount to lead his horse. Then the rocky slope ended suddenly, and he could see nothing beyond except blue sky. His heart beat with anticipation as his head topped the ridge. Then he stopped, as he saw before him a rocky hollow and four people, picking their way across it. They were not more than a few yards away. Now they had stopped. He pulled his rifle from the saddle scabbard and threw himself prone behind a low boulder. On top of it, a straggly bush had found lodging for its tenacious roots in the seamed surface, and through this bush he could plainly scrutinize their movements without fear of detection.

One of them was a small, hatchet-faced fellow with nervous, beady eyes. There was Prescott and a short stocky man with a seamed visage and long white hair that hung to his shoulders. He was hatless and was bald at the crown of his skull. He saw Judy, her head drooping listlessly. "What if Brady tries to follow?" growled Prescott.

"Which Brady you mean, Lenny?" asked the white-haired man with sour humor.

Prescott laughed harshly. "It sure as hell won't be Sig, Zach. I put a bullet through his middle."

Morley, thought Vern. The white-haired man was Zach Morley, the leader. His eyes turned to the hatchet-faced man. This man said nothing; he apparently paid no attention to the others, but Vern suspected that he was far more dangerous than either of the others. His face and its cruel, warped mouth were expressionless, but his small, beady eyes roved ceaselessly.

Prescott turned to Judy. There was no sign of fear about her, as Prescott leered at her. "You an' me will get along fine, sweetie," he said. "I paid Zach my share of the cut from our raids just for you. Ain't that flatterin'?"

There was scorn and loathing in the girl's eyes as she backed away against a rock. Prescott laughed as he reached her and put an arm around her slim waist. As he pulled her to him, she was suddenly galvanized to furious action. She fought so that his vile kisses missed her lips.

Morley shifted uneasily. "Lenny, we've got to be moving."

Prescott grinned and released the girl.

She pulled away from him, panting, her eyes flashing hate. Her gaze shot to her guardian. "You! You sold me to this . . . ?"

"Let's go," snarled Morley, avoiding her eyes.

Leading their horses, they set off down a rocky trail, the hatchet-faced thief first, then Judy, Morley, and Prescott. In a moment, Vern saw, they would be lost to his view around a rocky turn.

With sweating palms he lifted his rifle out and trained it on Prescott. He could easily drop all three of them from this distance. But, as he took aim, a chill clutched his heart. God help him, he couldn't pull the trigger. He was not a product of this untamed West. He could not murder in bold blood.

Then there flashed in retrospect before him the white, still face of his brother, who was dying, or dead, by this time. He saw Judy, helpless in the clutch of Prescott. He saw him drunken, beating her. These and other hideous pictures passed through his mind and, like a flash within him, died forever. The veneer of generations of civilized intuitions fell from him, leaving only primitive hate, hot, bared, quivering. There was a light in his eyes that New York society had never seen. Disgusting? Bestial? Perhaps, but bears interpret their natural instincts honestly. It is only man, tainted by the greed and false luster of civilization, who twisted them into something ugly and sordid.

The crack of the Springfield-Allison echoed across the cañon. Prescott stopped, staggered, and slumped against a rock from which he slid to the ground. Morley turned, swinging his rifle to a level. He must have located Vern, for his bullet whined off the rock so close that it sent stinging splinters into the young man's face.

With cold, deadly precision, Vern turned his rifle and fired, killing Morley in his tracks. He swung his rifle then toward the small, hatchet-faced man, and terror clutched him, for that one had caught Judy around the waist and was holding her before him as a shield while he edged toward the rock that would conceal him from Vern. Judy struggled frantically, and it was only with difficulty that the man held her, for she was as large as he was.

Suddenly she broke free and threw herself to the ground, leaving the outlaw exposed to Vern's rifle. The man drew his revolver, but, before he could use it, Vern fired. The hatchet-faced one wavered and crumpled.

Judy rose to her feet, her face white, and Vern walked down toward her. She came into his arms, and he held her wordlessly.

It was well after nightfall when they arrived at the Bar S. It was only when they had finally reached the deserted corral and dismounted that Vern spoke.

"I'm leaving on the next train, Judy. You . . . can work this thing out with Sig."

The hurt in her eyes was eloquent. She took a step toward him. "Oh, Vern. . . ."

"Don't, Judy," he told her quietly. "That will only make it worse."

"I couldn't help it, Vern! I do love you! I loved him. He's . . . the type of boy you want to . . . well, you want to take and mother, but I never respected him as a woman should a husband. It's just the way I feel."

"But you can't leave him now, Judy," said Vern inexorably. "He repudiated us both, out of pride. It's true, but he still loves you. Unless you go to him, it may kill him."

She lowered her head as though under a blow. She barely nodded in agreement.

Footsteps aroused them. Someone was approaching in the moonlight. It was Shorty. His quick gaze took them in.

"So you're back safe," he said. "The outlaws . . . ?"

"Dead. All three of them," said Vern quickly. It was something he wanted to forget.

Shorty nodded. "I'll tell Sig you're here."

He disappeared toward the ranch house. Vern and Judy were silent. There was nothing more to be said. Shorty returned in a few minutes and jerked his thumb toward the house.

"He wants to see you. Both of you."

They entered Sig's dimly lit bedroom. He was propped up in bed, apparently little the worse for his wounds. They stood side by side in the doorway as though awaiting his judgment.

"Come on in," he said tonelessly, and they mechanically obeyed. "I could hear what you said out there from my window," he continued. "Voices carry quite a way on a still night."

"So?" Vern asked through stiff lips.

"So I love you both too much to let you ruin your lives for me," Sig said calmly.

They stared, and he smiled.

"Oh, I meant what I said before when I said it. All day, I've been thinking I wanted to hurt you both for this, the way I was hurt, but I know how you couldn't help what happened . . . either of you. I'm the only one who was wrong."

It was possible that Sig was assuming more of the blame than was his due, but neither Vern nor Judy thought of that as they turned to regard each other.

"Well, kiss her, big shot," said Sig. "Isn't that what you want to do?"

It was, and he did.

End of the Trail

Branch Cutler rode out of the mountains into Cain Valley as the sun began to wester behind the far peaks. He paused on a pine-laced slope to let his hard gaze sweep the vast meadow below, to where it edged on a lake. Branch Cutler was a big man, in a land where big men were no exception. He stood six-four in his stocking feet, and there was a solid breadth to his shoulders and upper body.

His clothes were colorless with caked dust. His unshaven whiskers had begun to form into a curly black beard. Absently he scratched his knee through a rent in his trousers, his elbow knocking the obtruding butt of the heavy Dragoon pistol at his hip. This valley might hold the end of his search. Cold-eyed, he considered that, then nodded slightly to himself.

Below was a single settler's cabin, sprawling among its outbuildings on the bottomlands of the lake. There would be food there, and a night's sleep. Suddenly Branch Cutler was aware of his hollow-bellied hunger and his dragging exhaustion. He put his horse down the slope, and in a half hour was riding into the yard.

A girl of seventeen or eighteen was scattering feed to a bustling flock of chickens. The golden haze of sunset turned her tangled wealth of hair to fire. She shook it back from her face, glancing up suddenly to see the stranger. Then she became motionless, watching him like a wild thing on the verge of flight.

Without taking her startled eyes from him, she called softly: "Pa."

A white-haired man limped out on the porch, a small man bent from hard labor whose face was tired and seamed and guarded. One of his horny farmer's hands rested on the shoulder of a tall young man. The young man's face was cheerful under its tangled shock of blond hair. The contour of his jaw and mouth was like the girl's, and his hair of an identical shade to hers. Cutler guessed that they were twins.

"Light down, stranger," said the old man, regarding Branch Cutler with guarded friendliness. "I'm Bryan Westover. That's my daughter Sue Ann, there, and this here's my son Will."

"Branch Cutler."

The young man suddenly shifted his feet in the stillness, and Branch glanced at him mildly. But Will Westover's face appeared as open and cheerful as before. Branch swung down, and the old man told Will to take care of his horse, then motioned him inside.

Mrs. Westover was a hefty, raw-boned woman, inches taller than her husband. She greeted Branch with the same ready neighborliness of the father and son. The family had eaten, she said, but she made the stranger sit down, and dished up steak and potatoes and strong coffee for him.

The old man eased himself into a chair opposite Branch and thoughtfully watched him eat. "Did you ever hear of a man named Mark Caslon, Mister Cutler?"

Branch chewed slowly for a moment. He glanced at the girl, Sue Ann; she was leaning against the fireplace, the leaping light and shadows playing over her fine, straight-limbed body. Unlike the mobile faces of her family, her features held a quiet repose, unperturbed and impassive. Her eyes were fixed on him in a look he could not interpret. It embarrassed him, and he looked down at his plate. "Not that I recall," he said.

The old man grunted and seemed to relax. "Just wondered. I thought you might be coming to work for him."

"I'm drifting."

Bryan Westover seemed to mull that over; then his words came in natural loquacity. "Caslon is a rancher. He came into this valley years ago, before any of us. He claims he owns it, and that he'll drive us out if he has to bring in hired gunnies."

Branch understood then. It was the old story—man and land. "And you thought I might be one of them?"

Westover hawked in embarrassment. "Well, you look like a man used to taking care of yourself."

"I am," Branch said dryly. He stirred in his chair, and his gun butt bumped the table. "But I don't hire out to any man."

"I don't mind telling you that's a relief," Westover said frankly.

He leaned his meager frame back with a gusty sigh, and began to talk. It was good land here; the Lord had given him his work, and he had a family. It was a mortal sin, Westover said, that this beautiful land must be spoiled by the greed of a few people like Caslon.

Branch listened respectfully to his host, silent except for an occasional word of agreement. The Westover family consisted of simple pious folk, he decided, and the place to find the man for whom he was looking was not among these salt-of-the-earth settlers. Westover had said, though, that this Caslon was taking on hired gunnies. That might be a fruitful field for the search that had brought him this far.

He was slacked in his chair, in the drowsy lassitude that follows a good meal, smoking and half listening to Westover, when the noise of shuffling hoofs and the rattle and creak of harness sounded from the yard. Will Westover piled in through the door, breathing hard.

Westover came to his feet, limped to the wall, and lifted down a shotgun from its rack. Then he went to the door and stood with the weapon slung carelessly under his arm. His son got a rifle that was leaning in the corner, and followed his father. Without raising his voice, the older man spoke into the dusk.

"All right, Caslon, say your piece."

"Step out here." The voice in the yard spoke in the quavery cracking of an old man.

The two Westovers moved onto the porch. Branch rose quietly, patted his lips with a pocket bandanna, and followed them. He took up a position by the door, leaning there with casually folded arms. He could see only the shadowy hulks of seven horsemen.

"Who's that?" the quavery voice asked.

Inside the house, Mrs. Westover turned up the lamp so that its full light spilled through the windows and open doorway, flooding the yard. Branch Cutler saw the seven riders clearly now. There were five tall young horsemen, cowhands, with one older man, also in range clothes—a man who must have been six feet in height, but who was so thick-bodied he looked like a squat barrel. He flanked a black-suited figure, an old, old man, not really small, but wasted by age, his face shrunken under his fine black Stetson. This must be Caslon, who had spoken.

"It's a stranger who's staying over," Westover said.

"Keep out of this, stranger." Caslon's old voice was like cracking steel.

"It's not his affair," Westover snapped. "Quick now, what do you want?"

"To give you an ultimatum. This is it . . . you will move out tomorrow, with your family and household goods. I want your word on it. I claim all the land to the center of the lake by riparian right. I'm through coddling you squatters."

"We never asked for coddling," Westover said gravely. "We do not look for trouble with any man. We ask for nothing except God's grace and the right to put down roots on His land."

"*My* land," Caslon rasped, striking the air with a claw-like hand. "You fool, this is cattle country. You farmers'll starve out."

Branch looked over this old, old man sitting on his splendid copper-bottom bay like a wizened monkey and chuckled softly. "The Lord cuts a mighty poor figure lately."

Caslon pointed at him with a trembling taloned finger. "Stranger, I warn you." He shuttled his still-young, still-fierce eyes to Westover. "That is your answer?"

Westover's comment was clipped. "You have it."

"Bruce," Caslon said tersely to the barrel of a man siding him.

This man stepped laboriously from his saddle, with a heavy creak of leather. He tossed his reins to a young cowhand and waddled to the porch. His face was thick-featured and bloated in the lamplight.

"Pop," he told Westover, "pass me the gun. Your boy's, too."

Westover pointed the shotgun dead center on Bruce's burly chest. "Get back on your horse, Slattery. Don't force my hand or you may be sorry."

Bruce Slattery's brutal face did not alter. "Now, pop, if there's shooting, your womenfolk're likely to catch a bullet.

99

We wouldn't want that, would we?"

"No, we wouldn't." Branch Cutler had spoken, pushing away from the wall, his arms unfolding. He moved to Will Westover's side with a casual grace. "You look like a big man, Bruce. You talk like a bigger man. Let's see how big you really are."

Slattery's face gathered into a fixed scowl. "What're you driving at, broncho?"

"We can settle this without guns . . . just you and me."

"Bruce!" It was Caslon's high warning rasp. "We didn't come to brawl."

"Not with anyone his own size, anyway," Branch gibed. "He didn't expect anything like that."

Slattery made a growling sound and swung his gorilla-like arms at his sides. "All right, broncho. You come ahead." Clumsily he unbuckled his gun belt and dropped it. Branch had shucked his own before Slattery had finished speaking.

Westover roughly swung his shotgun in front of Branch as he began to step from the porch. "You will not fight our fight, Mister Cutler!"

Gently, but firmly, Branch pushed the gun aside.

"Call it a private bout then, between Bruce and me."

Slattery rushed in. Branch side-stepped his first blow by turning his shoulder and letting it slide off, then he belted Slattery's jaw with a hard right. The big man shook his head as though at an annoying insect bite, and bored in. He was used to swarming over smaller opponents by sheer weight, but he had only about twenty pounds on Cutler. Branch met him solidly, lifting his shoulder into Slattery's belligerently out-thrust face, then sinking his fist deeply into Slattery's belly. He had expected a muscle-taut resistance, but to his surprise he had found Slattery's weak spot.

The big man grunted and bowed with pain, but rallied

100

quickly, battering Cutler's face and body with wind-milling blows. Under the fury of his attack, Branch gave back step by step.

He heard the riders reining their mounts away as Slattery's onslaught carried him backward. It was not until his back came solidly against the tool shed that he realized they'd battled clear across the yard. He knew that, by giving him no opportunity to press an attack, Slattery hoped, through his clumsy yet effortless power, to batter Branch into insensibility. Branch let Slattery hammer him back against the shed, then, as one of Slattery's blows smashed his chest, he dropped his guard and began to sink down as though stunned. Dimly he saw the giant shift his weight for the finish.

As Slattery's swing began traveling toward his unprotected face, Branch moved his head—only a few inches—and Slattery's fist burgeoned past his ear and crashed against the shed planking. Slattery stepped back, cuddling his broken hand. But his anguished howl trailed off in a wheezing grunt, as Branch came inside his guard and again sank a solid blow into his vulnerable stomach, then clubbed both fists in a short hammering arc to Slattery's neck.

Slattery was down, and he did not move. Branch stood over him spraddle-legged, then walked toward Caslon, hauling up a couple yards from him and gesturing toward the shrunken rancher.

"You're through here for the night, Caslon. Pick him up and clear out. And, maybe, I'll be seeing you."

Caslon's eyes burned like live coals in his shrunken monkey's face. "You will be seeing me." It was a promise.

With Slattery supported in his saddle between two 'punchers, the group rode out. Branch Cutler watched them go, wondering how much this meant, and what might come of it. The voice of the girl, Sue Ann, broke across his thoughts.

"You've been hurt. Please come inside."

He started, and saw that she had come to stand beside him. Beyond her, by the porch, the other three Westovers waited for him. He could feel the warmth of their gratitude folding him into their midst, and instinctively rebelled against it, although feeling its pleasantness.

He sat in a chair while Sue Ann bathed his battered face, aware of her warm, strong hands and her nearness, and listening to Westover. "We'd be obliged if you'd stay on a while, Mister Cutler. You could live with us and work with us. It's not only that we need a man like you in these bad times . . . though most certainly we do, as we found tonight . . . it is, I think, that you've been a friend to us, and we owe you some return. I feel that God in His wisdom guided you here for our sake . . . and perhaps for your own."

Branch twitched uncomfortably. He said roughly: "You don't know me. You owe me nothing. And if you knew why I'd come to this valley, you might think it was the Lord's enemy who was leading me on."

"The Lord moves in strange ways," Westover said serenely. "We do owe you much. And all that is written in a man will not be found in his history."

Cutler stared out the window, watching the land blur and sink until it was swallowed in the deep well of night. It was a long time before he spoke.

"I'll try."

Will Westover took Branch on a tour of the country surrounding the lake the next morning. Will talked as they rode, explaining the state of things in Cain Valley. By virtue of past experience in range feuds, Branch Cutler was able to sift Will's biased settler's views and come up with a fairly objective picture of how matters stood. Caslon had his side, too,

Branch knew; that very old man had pioneered this valley, had taken all the hard knocks, and now was asked to stand aside for late-comers who would gnaw away his great range-land piece by piece. Even Will reluctantly conceded that point.

"But this valley's more than one king-size ranch could use even in one man's time," Will added, "and Caslon's life is nearly finished. It isn't as if we're laying claim to anything he really needs. This is just some drained-off bottomland with rich soil. Good farmland's pretty expensive in this country. It shouldn't be wasted on grazing cattle. Look here, Branch."

Will pulled up his horse and lifted a brawny arm in a sweeping arc. "That's really choice land there, along the south shore of the lake. Caslon's headquarters for his Hour-glass spread is up there. His fenced range covers a fifteen-mile strip. It wasn't until outsiders began coming into the valley that he felt he had to start claiming everything outside his fence, too. Why, there's room for plenty of settlers to come in along the south shore, and still leave Caslon's ranch intact for a hundred years to come . . . not that he'll need it. And when the marsh here is drained. . . ."

Will made another motion of his arm to describe the perimeter of the marsh. Then Branch Cutler stopped listening. His gaze riveted on Will Westover's outstretched wrist, no more than a foot from his face. He saw the little, white, crescent-shaped burn scar revealed when Will's movement pulled his sleeve back from it.

They rode on, Branch Cutler with a chaotic mind deafened to Will's voice, to the sights and sounds of the morning. Silently Branch kept denying it to himself, for he liked Will. He thought of Will's family, and, achingly, of Sue Ann. Still, he knew now—knew beyond doubt. He had come to Cain

Valley to kill a man. Will Westover was the man.

Branch's black, moody silence was a heavy thing in the room, as he dined with the Westovers that night. The elder Westover's usual loquacious outbursts were futile efforts tonight, and supper was finished in a grim quiet.

Will's discomfort was such that he asked to be excused before the meal was over, then he quickly left the table. Sue Ann helped her mother clear the table, and, vaguely, Branch felt her eyes on him constantly.

Finally, with a muttered excuse, he ground out his cigarette and went outside, walking as far as the corral. He leaned on a corner post and stared unseeingly at the night, its sounds a bitter cadence to his thoughts.

When he heard the light footsteps approaching, it was a thing expected, a thing he knew must be faced squarely, no matter how hard it would be.

"It's a lovely night," Sue Ann's voice said in the dusk by his elbow.

"Is it?" he asked in a brittle tone, because he knew that she was strongly aware that something was wrong, and he was in no mood for sparring.

"Branch," Sue Ann said, "is it Will?"

"What makes you think so?" He did not look at her. He did not dare to, because this girl was the one person who might undo his resolve.

"We're twins, Will and I. I know his mind almost as well as my own, and I could sense that the trouble is as deep in him as it is in you. You started this black-mood business, so he must be the object of it. Am I right?"

He was silent for a while. Then he said: "You're right."

Hesitantly she touched his arm. "Why, Branch? Tell me." His arm muscles grew tight under her touch, and, sensing his stiff aloofness, she dropped her hand.

"Did your brother go north last year, maybe on a cattle-buying trip?"

"Why, yes. After we'd been here a while, we found that Cain Valley, except for the bottomland, isn't much as a farming land goes. It's really cattle country, as Mister Caslon says . . . and a lot of valley graze is going to waste, unused. Pa thought we could start running a small herd and learn the cattle business from the ground up. So he sent Will up to one of the northern ranches to dicker for a few head. When he came back, we all pestered him to tell about the trip. It's funny, but he didn't want to talk about it. Will just isn't that way. He's open and eager. He seemed almost afraid of something."

"I imagine he was," Branch said coldly. "Listen here. One day last year a young fellow stopped at my father's ranch up north. He said he wanted to buy any extra stock Dad had on hand. My youngest sister, Jenny, took quite a shine to this young feller. They went outside after supper, and neither of 'em came back. But it wasn't till next morning that the folks found Jenny was missing. Her bed hadn't been slept in. First off, they thought she must have run off with the stranger. She was a flighty, flirty sort of kid, given to daydreams about every drifter that stopped over. They were all shining white knights to her." Branch paused, drew a breath, then let it out hard. "They found her body that morning, back of the barn."

"Oh, no," Sue Ann cried softly.

"Jenny had a bad heart. The doctor had told the folks any undue excitement or strain might make it give out. It looked as if this stranger had molested her, and, when he saw she was dead, he got out fast. He left his saddlebags behind, showing he was in a hurry. It was a long time before I heard about it." Guilt touched Branch's voice. "I reckon Jenny and I were alike in that. I couldn't stand the humdrum life around the ranch. I ran away when I was sixteen and joined a trail herd. I fell in with some hardcases from Texas, learned how to use a gun, and generally lived pretty hard and wild. A couple of months ago, I got a yen to see the old place again, and the folks. I'd sown all the wild oats out of my system, broken with the tough crew, and was thinking about settling down to steady work. But as soon as I got back, they told me about Jenny. Well, it was a matter of family honor. I had to find that stranger, even if he was months gone.

"There was not much to go on. Dad has poor hearing, and hadn't caught the man's name. There was no clue in his saddlebags. All Dad could tell me was that he'd come from the south. He gave me a general description that wasn't much help. The only sure identification was a little crescent-shaped scar Dad had spotted on the inside of the stranger's right wrist. I couldn't go on yanking back the sleeve of every man I saw who was about twenty, blond, had blue eyes, and was of medium height. But I set off south."

"Will has a scar like that," Sue Ann whispered.

"I saw it this morning. And I remember how he looked, for a second yesterday, when I introduced myself. The name Cutler rang a bell."

"But Will wouldn't molest a girl! He's terribly shy of girls. If you'd only talk to him, he could probably explain."

"Then why did he run away?" Branch asked bleakly. "Anyway, it doesn't matter now. I'm leaving here . . . tonight."

"Leaving?" It caught her off guard.

"Yeah. I can't hurt Will because . . ."—he hesitated—"I can't hurt anyone dear to you."

"Branch," she faltered.

"It has to be this way," he said harshly. "Do you think I can stay on here, knowing what I do, seeing Will every day? I couldn't answer for what might happen. Go up to the house, get my gear, and bring it to the stable. Make up some excuse to your folks. It would be best if you wouldn't tell 'em the real story." His voice lowered on the last words, then sharpened again. "Do as I say!" He turned her and pushed her toward the house.

She looked back for a moment, her lips parting as though seeking words. Then she walked slowly toward the house. Branch watched her for an aching moment, then pivoted and headed for the stables.

He groped in the gloom for the lantern hanging from a post, and found it gone. By feel, he located the saddle pole and his own hull, which he swung down. Then he paused with it in his hands, listening.

There were the usual night sounds—insects and the croaking of frogs by the lake shore. But his plainsman's ears picked out another sound that did not fit the pattern, and he stood in silence to catalogue it.

Finally he picked out the muffled hoofs of horses, then the muffled voices of men beyond the walls of the stable. Among them were the heavy growling accents of Bruce Slattery.

"We'll fire the stables, then spread ourselves around the yard, out of sight. When the Westovers see the fire, they'll come boiling out of the shack, and we'll catch 'em in a crossfire."

"Mind now, Bruce," came the aged and failing voice of Caslon, "no shooting at the womenfolk. I'll not have that."

"Sure, sure," Slattery said irritably. "You hear him, boys? Get to your places, fan out around the shack. I'll set the fire."

Branch heard the men dispersing and hazarded a mental reckoning of their numbers—half a dozen or more. This was Caslon's big play to drive out the Westovers. And only Branch Cutler could stop it.

He eased the saddle to the floor and drew his Colt. He slipped toward the rear doorway to the building and let himself out, then began working around toward the side where he had caught the voices beyond the thin walls.

He picked out Slattery's dark, lone hulk there as he turned the corner and paused. Slattery was crackling dry brush as he piled it against the wall. He struck a match. It guttered and went out, and he cursed. As he fumbled for another, Branch moved out beyond the building.

He called firmly: "Bruce!"

Slattery pivoted clumsily, coming to his feet. Branch waited till he caught the faint light glint on Slattery's drawn gun, then fired. Slattery grunted at the impact, swayed as though in indecision, then toppled with a crash into the stacked brush heap.

"Bruce!" shrilled Caslon, somewhere by the house. "Bob, Lacey, get back there. See what happened to Bruce."

Shooting broke out. The Westovers had been warned. Branch ran past the fallen Slattery to the front corner of the stable, and waited till he saw the two shapes of running men detach themselves from the far shadows and come toward the stable.

One of them hurdled over some stacked posts and was outlined against the cabin lights. Branch fired and saw the man flung around and falling across the pile, setting the posts toppling and rolling. As the man reached the opposite side of the stable and shelter, he snapped a shot at the man and missed.

There was a renewed outburst of firing from the house. A window broke in a jangling shower of glass. The lights went out inside, and Westover's shotgun roared.

The family was putting up a game fight, but Branch could not go to their aid, with the second Hourglass man waiting by the far wall to shoot him when he moved into view. Branch set his teeth, and began to work back, around the rear of the building, hoping to catch the man from behind.

As he moved past the rear door, which he'd left open, he heard the grate of boots on the clay floor, and knew that his man had circled to the rear and ducked inside, to ambush him from the cover of darkness. Branch swung his gun around, knowing in that aching moment that he would be too late. His muscles tensed to meet the impact of a slug.

Then there were the sounds of a thudding blow, a groan, a body hitting the floor. Branch stood motionless, straining his eyes into the darkness, his gun held ready. Will Westover stepped out into the moonlight.

"You," Branch Cutler said stupidly.

"I hit him," Will said. "There's no time to waste." He was holding the gun of the man he'd slugged. "Let's get up to the house."

Branch nodded, then put a hand on Will's arm. "Listen."

The shooting had ceased. It was silent by the house. Then a light went on, its pale wash flooding the yard. They saw Pa and Ma Westover on the porch, holding guns on four cowed Hourglass hands. Bryan Westover lifted his voice in a bellow.

"Will! Branch! Are you all right down there?"

"All right, Pa!" Will called. When they reached the porch, they saw Caslon's diminutive body crumpled at the base of the steps.

Will said eagerly: "Is he dead?"

"Yep," Bryan Westover said grimly. "But not by a bullet. He led a charge on the house, and, just as he reached it, he folded up." He paused and added in a sonorous tone: " 'Vengeance is mine, saith the Lord.' "

Branch nodded toward the four cowhands, who were sullen and silent and watching. "What about them?"

109

"They gave up, too," Bryan said contemptuously.

The biggest 'puncher took a hitch in his pants. "The old man's dead. There's nothing to fight for now, is there?"

"Was there ever?" Bryan asked softly.

The 'puncher shook his head. "Mister, that's a question." He added diffidently: "Can we leave?"

"If I have your word you'll clear out of the valley. We want to fill it up with honest settlers, not hardcase gunnies."

The four men nodded agreement, and forked their horses. When they'd left, Will said: "There's one man down in the stable I knocked out, Pa."

"And two more I had to gun," Branch interrupted. "Bruce Slattery was one of 'em."

"Slattery," said Bryan. He sighed and shook his head. "I wish I could say I was sorry. I'll see to them. Mother, fetch a lantern."

Ma brought the lantern, and Pa took it and headed for the stable. Branch took Will's arm and drew him away from the porch so his words wouldn't reach Ma, who was helping Sue Ann clean up the broken glass.

Branch asked: "You saved my skin back there. Why?"

Will hesitated. "I was in the stable, trying to think things out in the dark, when you came in," he said sheepishly. "I thought you were looking for me, so I hid in one of the stalls, taking the lantern with me so you wouldn't light it and see me. When the shooting started, I saw that guy duck inside, and figured he was waiting for you. So I came up from behind him and. . . ." He made an angry gesture. "Damn it, I couldn't let him murder you."

"You knew I was looking for you, then?"

"I could guess, from your name and the bad looks you've been giving me all day. You're Jenny's brother. But I didn't figure you'd hear out my side of it, so I didn't see

110

the use of saying anything."

Branch looked up. Sue Ann stood in the doorway, and she was listening. "I'll hear you out," Branch said finally. "I owe you that much . . . now."

"Your sister followed me out to the barn that night," Will said, "when I went to my horse. Right off, she got excited and wanted me to take her away with me. She said she was sick and fed up with her father's ranch, with coddling him in his old age, and so on. I was scared. I tried to tell her as nicely as I could that I didn't want any part of such a thing. She got real mad, and started to dress me down in some pretty mean language. Then she started choking for breath, and just sort of crumpled down and didn't move. I was really scared then. I tried to wake her up, and then found she was dead. I could see how it would look . . . me a stranger in the country, and no witnesses. I panicked, saddled up, and cleared out, hoping I wouldn't be traced. I knew that was wrong, but what would you have done?"

Will had found his courage now; he faced Branch Cutler unflinchingly, waiting for his judgment.

Branch shook his head slowly. "I don't know what I'd have done," he said musingly, "but I did know Jenny, and that sounds like her, right enough. It could have happened at any time, with anyone, I reckon. It was just bad luck that you were the one."

Will let his breath out hard. "Glad you see it that way, Branch. You don't know how glad I am."

Sue Ann came quickly down the steps and laid one hand on Branch's arm, the other on Will's. "You both did well tonight," she said softly. "And now, Branch, will you stay?"

Branch felt no indecision this time. "I'm going up north to see Dad and tell him the whole story. The thing's been riding him, and I think the truth'll give him ease. Then I'll come back, Sue Ann . . . to you."

Deadline Day

Old Aaron MacKane strode wrathfully in the office of his nephew, Lane "Scotty" MacKane, stomping goutily at every other step, his massive white mustaches bristling truculently, startling against the crimson anger adding to the natural ruddiness of his portly face.

"Lane, ye no good son-of-an-Englishman!" bellowed old MacKane, that being the choicest epithet he could put his tongue to on a moment's notice. "I'll have a word with ye!"

"Have two," invited Scotty beamingly. He was leafing through a batch of reward posters, tilted back in his chair, feet propped on the desk, musty sunlight through the single window gleaming on the sheriff's badge on his worn cowhide vest. He was a lengthy, slender young man with a battered hat pushed to the back of his dark, curly head. His thin, handsome face and mild blue eyes seemed to hold a latent goodnature—too much perhaps.

"Aye, and as many more as I damn' well please!" roared MacKane, gouting it over to Scotty's desk to stand over him menacingly. "I ask ye again . . . what're ye going to do aboot the widow MacGregor? Ye knew that blood-sucking leech Sunderson forecloses today."

"Ah, ah . . . my father's brother," said Scotty, wagging a

finger. "Sundy has to live, too. 'A man's a man for a' that, and a' that, and. . . .' "

"Dinna spoot thae molly-coddlin' poetry at me, ye incapacitated imitation of a law, ye! Sit in here and draw a salary fer naethin', an' read poetry. Ooh! Ye're old man would turn in the grave could he know that thae last oov thae fightin' clan hae deteriorated into *ye!*"

Scotty closed his eyes, sighed, and opened them again. "One," he intoned, "this is the American frontier, not the merry Highland. Two, this is the Nineteenth Century, not Robert Bruce's era. Three, dear old Sundy's methods may resemble those of Eddie the First, but there happens to be a small matter of law which I am sworn to uphold. . . ."

MacKane snorted.

"And Sundy operates within the law. Four, no true son of the Highland would deny Burns."

"Hoot! I'm not denyin' him, ye jackass. But Bobby Burns would rise from thae dead could he see a spineless fish like ye sworn to uphold the down-trodden, an' join naethin!"

"Pardon me while I flutter my gills," grinned Scotty. "Look, though, Unc . . . the law comes first with me, and Sunderson stays inside it. I can't reach him."

"Bah! What oov thae homesteaders he scared off . . . an' I understand he's cleaned the Navajos out of water rights?"

"Both irrefutable facts . . . but the homesteaders was too scared to talk, and the Navajo business is for a U.S. marshal to investigate. Besides, I can't do anything without proof. I'd like to help. . . ."

MacKane snorted again. "Ye mought call in a marshal, an' ye mought try to get proof. Dae that ever occur t'ye?"

"Well. . . ."

MacKane waved a massive hand. "Noo excuses, lad. Ye're plain lazy, an' that's it. Naethin' kin drag ye oot o' the office, it seems. Now'll I'll tell ye what ye're going to do, as ye're next o' kin." He paused for a breath. "Yere damn' law is all ye think oov. Weel, there happens to be a right and a wrong t' this McGregor matter. But t' ye, black's white, an' white's black . . . ye cae nae who wins soo long as yere damn' law is abided by. Only now, I'm goona make ye see two sides. Git up! Ye're going to look into thae matter."

Scotty only grinned and didn't move. MacKane raised a foot and kicked him in a leg. It chanced to be his gouty foot, and for fifteen ensuing seconds he did a one-legged Highland fling around the desk to a piper's tune of lurid profanity.

Scotty came slowly and reluctantly to his feet, feeling gingerly of his calf. "You've convinced me," he said to his uncle ruefully.

"I wonder hou!" snorted MacKane. "Weel, doan' stand there! Get ye out to the MacGregor place an' start collectin' evidence on the divil, Sunderson."

Scotty looked down at MacKane helplessly, towering a head over the old man. "How do I go about it?"

MacKane's jaw dropped, then he closed it and sighed lengthily, and patted his nephew gently on the arm. "Ah, noo, that's the question, lad. Well, ye bein' the law hereabouts, ye tell me!"

He stomped out of the office, pausing outside the door to view the small, black-lettered sign, **Sheriff's Office**, over the door. Old MacKane laughed outright, said—"Sheriff! Hah!" —to the sign, and stomped on down the street.

Scotty sighed deeply, and slouched out of the office toward Walt's place. He shouldered inside; it was shadowy and cool inside after the sunlight and dust of the street. The big relic was empty except for Dusty Kellam, sitting at a table, feet on it, a bottle and an empty glass on it, too. He was propped back in his chair, hat tilted over his eyes, and listening to Walt rattle off a tune on the tinny piano.

Scotty walked over and nudged him. Dusty pulled his ancient Stetson back and said: "Well, our teetotal sheriff. A sarsaparilla man . . . the way I am." He snickered. "Howsa boy? Have a drink."

"Shut up," Scotty said mildly. "Sober up, too. I am hereby deputizing you. Stand up."

Dusty stood up, swaying a little, a sandy-haired young man of Scotty's height and age. "Ha." He snickered. "You can't deputize a drunken man, boy."

"Of course not," Scotty agreed amiably, and went over to the door, returning with a glass of water, and flinging the contents into Dusty's face.

"That better?" Scotty asked gently.

Dusty cursed, needless to say, but Scotty finally got him sworn in, and they stepped together out into the warm sunlight.

"What now?" asked Dusty Kellam, late town loafer, now deputy sheriff of Trail's Corner.

"I need you to show me the way to the MacGregor place. Go get us a couple horses at the livery," Scotty directed. "Tell you about it as we ride."

Fifteen minutes later, jogging southeast out of town, Scotty was explaining wryly: "Public opinion is against Sunderson, and for the Widow MacGregor. I've got to make the voters happy."

Mr. Kellam scratched his head. "Seems like there might be a right an' wrong to it, like ol' Aaron said."

"Right or wrong, hell!" said Scotty, who seldom swore. "Wipe the law out, then talk of right or wrong to me. Sunderson works inside the law, and I represent the law. His mortgage on old lady MacGregor's lease falls due today, and

I have to enforce that mortgage if she balks at moving off.' "

Dusty nodded thoughtfully. "Pretty rough place for you to git caught in."

An hour's ride brought them to the brow of a rise overlooking a rolling swale. Grassland thrust a broad expanse beyond. In the swale nestled a small, one-story frame house, complete with roses and rambling vines. The few neat outbuildings were strategically isolated from this domestic edifice.

MacKane hooked a leg around his saddle horn, tilted his hat back, and gave a low whistle.

"Never been here before, huh?" Dusty commented. "You got more than one surprise coming." He snickered slyly.

They reined into the yard, dismounting.

"I see what you mean," murmured Scotty, as a tall, auburn-haired girl stepped out of the house.

"Missus MacGregor, I'm Sheriff MacKane, and must admit I had no idea. . . ."

"Miss," the young lady corrected serenely. "My mother is inside, Mister Sheriff. You did want to see her?"

"Up to now, I . . . ," Scotty began, but Dusty cut him off hastily.

"That's right, Dawn."

"Hello, Dusty," Miss MacGregor said sweetly. "My, are you a deputy or something now?"

"Or something, I guess." Dusty grinned. "Meet Scotty, Dawn."

Scotty took her proffered hand, noting that her callused little palm was rougher than his own. He mumbled some amenity, feeling deflated.

Turning with a graceful swish of her worn, wash-faded skirt, Miss MacGregor led the way inside the cool little bungalow, a faint gleam of amusement in her eye. Mrs.

MacGregor was a white-haired, frail-looking little woman, moving her rocking chair back and forth in the middle of the tidy front room. There was the same utter serenity in her face as in her daughter's.

"Mother, this is Sheriff MacKane."

"Hello, Sheriff. And you, Dusty. Sit down."

They sank into chairs, Scotty a little dazed at the tart resonance of her voice.

"You, Dawn. Fetch some coffee. Now what can I do for you gentlemen?"

Scotty looked uneasily at her, twirling his hat between his fingers. This woman shared few of the symptoms of a person about to be dispossessed. As he searched for words, Dusty arose idly and sauntered into the kitchen to help Dawn with the coffee.

She was pouring it into cups as he entered.

"Close the door, Dusty," she said and, as he did so, added: "I want to talk about your sheriff."

Dusty grinned hugely. "Ain't he something?"

"*Something* is right," Dawn murmured. "Just what sort of a . . . a man is he?"

Dusty looked hurt. "Why, Dawn, he's real high-class. I figured you'd like him, bein' a schoolteacher. The other gents 'round don't seem to have enough culture fer you, but Scotty, he talks poetry you kin 'preciate. You oughter hear him! 'Breathes then the gent wif soul so daid, who never to hisself has sayed. . . . ' "

Miss MacGregor looked pained. "That will do, Dusty," she said gently, "and will you help me with the coffee, please?"

As they returned to the front room, Mrs. MacGregor was saying: "I did not arrange this mortgage, Mister MacKane. My husband did three months before his death, a month ago." She paused as though debating. "Since you are the law, I can confide in you. I advised him against putting our property in any such jeopardy as this, especially to Sunderson, though it was a hard winter and heaven knows we needed the money."

Scotty said slowly: "So now for lack of a trifling sum, you lose a ranch worth thousands. No note extension?"

Mrs. MacGregor shook her white head. "Sunderson won't grant it. Angus was a shrewd businessman, but headstrong. I knew the danger of liens. My family lost all their property in Louisiana from such. Recently someone robbed our safe here at night, and took the savings that would have paid the mortgage. I don't see how they did it. It was a combination safe. Well, Angus could have put the ranch back on a paying basis in time to meet the deadline, but I cannot supervise even a little crew from here, and my foreman is shiftless. Dawn"— she glanced at her daughter—"quit her teaching job to come here and do what she can, but she knows nothing of ranch affairs."

Scotty downed his coffee hastily and stood up. "Well, I was wondering if I could do something," he said lamely.

"I'll bet you were," Mrs. MacGregor said tartly. "I heard you weren't much of a man, Sheriff. I can qualify at least part of that! You have not the merest inkling of initiative."

Her candor rocked Scotty back a little. "What would you suggest, ma'am?" he asked humbly.

"Sit down, young man."

Scotty sat.

"There was a peculiar circumstance to my husband's death. I presume you know how he died?"

Scotty fidgeted uneasily. "Uh . . . no."

"It's your business to," snapped Mrs. MacGregor. "He was crushed under a landslide of rock while trailing some strays up a cañon. He was half buried under the rubble and dead when . . . but let Dusty tell you."

Scotty glanced in surprise at his friend. "You?"

"Sure, I found him."

"How come I didn't hear about this?"

"I figured you knew, Scotty. Hell, everyone else does. Pardon me, ma'am . . . Dawn. . . ."

"All right, Dusty," said Dawn tranquilly. "I fear our sheriff has taken even less trouble to be informed on such matters than we realized."

Scotty knew painfully that this was true. He didn't even pay attention to common gossip.

Dawn said: "Dusty was working here, then, Sheriff. He was out on the range with Dad when it happened. Go ahead, Dusty."

"Well, I was working . . . a ways behind the boss. I heard the landslide upcañon but didn't make nothin' of it. Only when Angus didn't come back, I took a *pasear* after him, an' found him buried up to his middle under the slide. He was layin' on his belly. A big rock had hit him square in the back. It looked, mind you, I say, it looked . . . like he'd scratched something in the dust with his finger before he died."

Scotty leaned forward. "What was it?"

"A local cow brand, or part of a brand. An R with the lower half of a circle. A-course it could 'a' been done by someone else after MacKane was dead, leavin' it incomplete, making it look like Angus died 'fore he could finish."

"The Circle R." Scotty looked sharply at Mrs. MacGregor. "My Uncle Aaron's brand . . . but he couldn't have done it!"

"Of course not," said Mrs. MacGregor flatly. "He was Angus's best friend. If I'd thought he had, I would have said so a month ago. As it is, that brand business has been mentioned to Aaron himself. Someone else did it to throw the blame on Aaron. The same person who rolled our safe."

"Of course," murmured Scotty as he got up, stalking thoughtfully around the room, "Sunderson had a reason. If he could wreck your chances of meeting the mortgage. . . ."

"Obviously, young man," snapped the Widow MacGregor, "but you waited a little too long to do anything about it."

"Perhaps not." Scotty reached for his hat and set it on his head. "Come on, Dusty."

They started outside and had covered half the distance to the horses, when Dawn said from the doorway: "Just a minute, Mister MacKane."

Scotty paused and turned to face her as Dusty walked on to the horses. She came up to him and wasted no words.

"Mister MacKane, I think you are approximately the laziest, most shiftless. . . ."

Scotty raised a hand. "All right, lady, sure," he said tiredly, "I'll try to get evidence on Sunderson. That's the best I can do now."

"But don't you see?" she asked in a quietly passionate voice. "You've waited too long. If there was a chance of proving that Sunderson attempted to seize our property by crippling us with my father's murder, it's gone now. You have five hours to work. Six o'clock tonight is the deadline. It's too late now."

"Ma'am," Scotty said patiently, "you'll not help matters by detaining me."

She breathed deeply and stepped back. "All right, Mister MacKane. But think this over. Perhaps you believe that greater education and supposedly higher culture give you some claim to a superior status. In actuality, you are an entirely useless parasite in an office where you have no business. Even Dusty, loafer or not, works for what he gets. Briefly, you are the most despicable man it has ever been my misfortune to meet."

She turned, then, and stalked back toward the house, but before she reached it, the sound of an approaching horseman down the slope caused her to turn back. A rider reined into the yard.

"The honorable banker Sunderson," she said dryly.

"Hello, Dawn," Sunderson said mildly, dismounting. He was a tall, flaxen-haired, deceptively gentle-looking man in his mid-thirties. "I was wondering if you had it, yet."

"We haven't, as you well know," Dawn said evenly, "and won't, as you know equally well."

Sunderson straightened his wide shoulders in his tailored coat of black broadcloth and regarded her idly. With a faint smile and, speaking as though he were commenting on the weather, he said: "You can save the place for your mother any time you want, you know, Dawn. I outlined the terms."

"You did," she said thinly. "You wouldn't find me a very tractable wife, George. Neither would my mother retain the ranch on those terms."

Sunderson smiled in a polite, obscure way and glanced at Scotty. "Just leaving, Sheriff?"

"He was," Dawn said flatly, "and so were you. It isn't your land yet."

Sunderson chuckled gently, and fell into pace with Dusty and Scotty as they started up the slope. At the crest, they paused.

"I'm glad you're around, Sheriff. I have anticipated trouble in moving the MacGregors off. Apparently they have no intention of so doing. They haven't even begun to assemble their belongings."

"*¿Quién sabe?*" said Scotty dryly. "As Miss MacGregor

said, it isn't your land yet."

Sunderson grinned a little and lifted one shoulder in a meager shrug, turned, hit the saddle, then put his mount toward town, saying: "Good day to you, gentlemen."

Scotty's gaze, abruptly wintry and decisive, swiveled to Dusty, giving the latter a small shock. "Dusty, you worked for MacGregor . . . he have many enemies?"

"Naw. Everyone's friend . . . wait a minute. There was a homesteader name of Metzgar. He set up a shack near MacGregor property and begin 'propriatin' mavericks. MacGregor warned him to quit or git burned off. That was just a while before Angus was killed."

"Metzgar! Charley Metzgar?"

"Yeah."

Scotty nodded slowly. "He used to be cashier at the bank. Sunderson fired him for confiscating funds so he's switched to cattle, hmm? Was this before the MacGregor safe was robbed?"

"Yeah . . . the safe was robbed a week after Angus was killed, but what . . . ?" He broke off then, seeing Scotty's point. A bank cashier, familiar with safes and combinations, could likely make a potential safe-cracker.

"Where's Metzgar now?" Scotty asked.

"Still homesteading, an' runnin' MacGregor calves. We going there?"

"I'm going there," Scotty corrected flatly. "Give me directions."

Dusty sighed. "Five miles due east from here. Metzgar's taken over an old shack. Look, Scotty, I better. . . ."

Scotty shook his head. "I've got to finish this myself. I can't explain, Dusty. You go back down to the ranch. Stay there, and, if Sunderson comes back to try pushing them off before I'm back, shoot him."

Dusty's face lightened hopefully, pleasurably, at this assignment, and he started back down the slope. Scotty set off due east. As he rode, the stinging weight of Dawn's words struck him anew. Before this, people had criticized his shiftlessness; he had merely grinned it off. He wasn't grinning now. It had suddenly seemed the most important thing in the world that Dawn MacGregor tell him that she had been wrong about him, and was sorry.

But was she wrong? Was her mother wrong in saying he had no initiative? Scotty himself wasn't certain; he could only find out by catching MacGregor's murderer himself, and saving the MacGregor Ranch. It was why he refused Dusty's help, and now with a twinge of uncertainty he wondered if he was good enough. In a sudden rare moment of self-searching, he saw that Dawn was right about his parasitical ways and about the neglectful inadequacy with which he handled his office. All he could do now was show that the potential was in him, and change his ways accordingly.

Metzgar's place was by a drift fence on the far boundary of the MacGregor land. There was the line shack itself, a tool shed, a small, rude corral of naked cedar logs, and an ancient well. Metzgar himself, a small, stoop-shouldered, sandy-haired man in greasy overalls, came out of the tool shed. He didn't look so tough, but there was something raffish and shifty to his slovenly manner and unshaven face in contrast to the immaculate figure cut by the young bank cashier whom Scotty remembered that made him wish he had brought a gun.

Metzgar smiled uneasily as Scotty stepped down. "The bank ain't finally sicked you on me, have they, Sheriff? They said they'd forget it if I stayed out of town."

Scotty shook his head negatively, not speaking. Metzgar offended his sensibilities, and his olfactories.

Metzgar nervously ran his dirty fingers through his shaggy hair. "Must be old lady MacGregor, then. Her old man said he was gonna oust me. Hell, I ain't bothering nobody over here."

"How about nobody's cattle?" Scotty asked dryly. "Mavericking isn't appreciated around here . . . or didn't you hear?"

"Now, Sheriff," he said, trying to look benevolent through dirt, "I'm minding my affairs."

Scotty said tiredly: "You're a purple liar, but I didn't come about that. I want to take a look around your place."

Metzgar seemed relieved. "Look ahead."

Scotty walked over to the well and looked down. It was so old that the stone wall was crumbled, rotting in places and with great gaps in the sides where chunks of rock had fallen out. Far below he could see the opaque water gleaming darkly. Metzgar hovered around and seemed relieved when Scotty turned away and headed for the tool shed. Metzgar followed.

"What you looking for, Sheriff?"

"The money from MacGregor's safe."

"Now did somebody rob them?"

Scotty didn't trouble to answer. He stepped into the dark, dirt-floored, warp-walled shed, and paused. Within was a heterogeneous collection of worn harness, paint, and other miscellany, even some unnecessary gardening tools. He walked around the rather spacious interior, examining the equipment on wooden wall pegs. He tripped over something half buried in loose sand. Bending down, he picked it up—a new branding iron. He examined it off-handedly, then his eyes widened in a sudden stunned realization.

He wheeled toward Metzgar to snap a question, then realized too late that Metzgar had seen and interpreted aright his excitement. He turned just in time to see the mattock in Metzgar's hands downswinging at his face. He tried to twist away, but still it caught him a glancing blow on the temple. He was falling then, pitching onto the dirt floor.

"It's fifteen minutes to six," Sunderson said, tucking his watch back into his waistcoat. "Wouldn't you ladies like to start moving out?"

The MacGregor women only regarded him steadily. The sun's dying light illuminated where they stood before the house, Mrs. MacGregor at the bottom of the steps, Dawn beside her, Sunderson standing by his horse, Dusty squatting negligently on a step, a gentle and beatific smile on his face as he kept his .30-30 trained on the banker.

Some of Sunderson's inveterate patience was commencing to fray. "The sheriff rode off and not to Metzgar's place. He'll keep riding till he's in the next county, and he'll stay there until this affair blows over. The entire range will be up in arms against him, and he knows it."

"We'll wait till that happens, then," Dusty said with a placid grin.

Sunderson cursed him.

"The MacGregors are ladies," Dusty reminded him with a gentle smile, as he idly fingered his rifle, but there was no humor in his mild gaze, and Sunderson stopped quickly.

It was then that they all heard it, and four heads swiveled toward the east and the sound of fast-nearing horses. Shortly afterward, the horsemen came into the yard. One was Metzgar, tied by his wrists to the saddle horn, his face battered almost beyond recognition. Only the fact that he was tied to the saddle prevented his swaying frame from toppling. The other was Scotty, hatless, with dried blood and dirt on his head and several bruises, and one eye almost entirely closed. His damp, shapeless clothes were caked thick with dust. One big, raw hand grasped Metzgar's reins.

He swung off, saying in a grating whisper as he pointed to Sunderson: "Dusty, keep your gun on him. He's a killer." Then he pulled a dirty wad of greenbacks and papers from his belt and handed them to Mrs. MacGregor. "Pay him off out of that, ma'am . . . it's your money . . . not that he'll be needing it."

Mrs. MacGregor fumbled through the papers with shaking fingers. Her voice broke a little. "It *is* ours. All of it. I was very wrong, Sheriff."

Dawn stared disbelievingly at the money, then at MacKane. "But what does Metzgar have to do with this?"

"He murdered your father at Sunderson's orders. Also rolled your safe. I'll start at the beginning."

Still holding Metzgar's reins, Scotty sank tiredly onto the step. "I searched Metzgar's place, looking for the money, but I found something else . . . an iron for the Rocking R brand."

"Rocking R? But I never heard of it."

Scotty nodded. "It's Metzgar's private brand. It's also the brand that your father scrawled in the dust before he died . . . not an uncompleted Circle R as Dusty thought."

"Dog-gone me for a knock-kneed knucklehead!" said Dusty.

Scotty grinned. "Granted. Well, when Metzgar saw I was onto him, he knocked me over the head, tied me up, and threw me in his well."

"Holy smoley!" ejaculated Dusty. "I seen that well of his. How'd you get out?"

"I'd still be there," Scotty said wryly, "but he tied me with rawhide, and you know what water does to rawhide in water. I was half drowned by the time I got loose, but it wasn't hard climbing out . . . the wall was broken and fallen in. I was almost to the top when I accidentally dislodged a rock. The money and papers Charley stole were hidden behind it. Very clever. Once out, I took Charley by surprise and persuaded him to tell the whole thing."

"Yeah," Dusty remarked, glancing at Metzgar's battered visage. "I noticed you did."

"Well, once he was convinced, he was eager enough to speak out. It seems that after MacGregor threatened him on that maverick business, he bore a bad grudge against the old man. Charley had worked for Sunderson and knew that Sunderson wouldn't pull back on scruples. He also knew, of course, that Sunderson wanted this ranch bad and would do just about anything to keep MacGregor from meeting that mortgage. So he made a deal with Sunderson, and rigged that landslide to finish off Angus. Only Angus saw him and had just time to leave that one clue. A week after, Sunderson learned that Missus MacGregor had enough money to meet the deadline, after all, so he tipped off Metzgar about the safe, and hired him again. Charley's share, including what Sundy already owed him for doing away with MacGregor, was all the cash in the safe. Sunderson was just satisfied to kill the possibility of payment on the mortgage."

Scotty glanced up at the MacGregors, seeing a slow admiration touch their faces, and felt a kind of humble thankfulness.

"Well, I thought I knew men," said Mrs. MacGregor. "And I was certainly wrong about one."

"You weren't wrong when you said it, ma'am," replied Scotty with a sheepish grin.

"But I was, young man. If it hadn't been in you all the time, nothing could have brought it out."

"Mount up," Dusty directed Sunderson. "You lads are takin' a ride . . . short and one way."

As Scotty stood up, starting back to his own horse, Dawn touched his arm. "Hold on," she commanded. "You need to clean up first. And I apologize, Mister Sheriff."

"Not too soon," Scotty cautioned with a grin. "Every bad egg has one good spot."

"Maybe," she said, "but you'll have plenty of time to prove otherwise."

He looked down at her gravely. "Why, yes," he agreed slowly. "The rest of my life."

Killer's Law

Tom Vickers, attorney-at-law, stood at the dingy window of his second-floor office, staring down into the hot, dusty street of Maguey. A gangling young man in a shabby, ill-fitting suit, his thin face was etched with the bitterness of his thoughts.

His uncle, Sheriff Steve Vickers, hadn't told all the story when he'd written Tom that there was opportunity on the frontier for a young lawyer wanting to make a start. With this advice from his only living relative, Tom Vickers, having just passed his bar examination, had packed his bag with his meager belongings and taken the first train West.

Tom smiled wryly as he looked around the room and its bare, battered furnishings of a desk, two chairs, and a filing cabinet. Uncle Steve had gotten him this low-rent office and had gone out of his way to introduce Tom to the leading citizens. That was something, anyway.

Tom had collected a few dollars in fees for drawing up legal papers. It was enough to keep a roof over his head and food in his belly, but still a damned inauspicious beginning for the high hopes that had carried him out here. Yet all this was incidental to the true reason for his discontent, and he reluctantly admitted it. Back East, a man didn't have to rub elbows with dozens of rough characters who looked ready at the slightest provocation to put a knife or a bullet between his ribs. Back East, a man wasn't jerked nightly from a sound sleep by gunshots beyond his window, as someone let off steam or settled an argument. Tom Vickers was an orderly young man who felt out of place among people stripped to the elemental passions, in a land where he was convinced that the only enforceable law was killer's law.

He'd bitterly told his uncle as much last night. "But don't you see, son," old Steve had argued, "that's where your opportunity lies? It's the men who pioneer in the making of a land who'll be remembered. It's high time for your kind of man to move in and help the rest adjust to a changing West. It'll be rough, with the very people you're trying to help fighting you hardest. But nothing worth having comes easy."

Tom's attention was drawn to a rig rolling down the street. He noticed that a young woman held the reins, and he was mildly surprised when she pulled up before his own office building and descended gracefully from the high seat. He saw one of the two JJ men lounging against the bank wall nudge his companion and nod toward the girl.

They watched attentively as she went into the building. Then both men quickly rose, pitched away their cigarettes, and entered the bank. Tom was idly wondering about that when he heard a soft tap on his door. When he opened it, the girl stood there.

"Mister Vickers?"

"Yes, ma'am," Tom said, running a hand through his carelessly combed dark hair, and adjusting his tie. "Won't you come in?"

She took the chair he indicated. She was a tall girl, he saw, as he sat down at his desk, a tall girl with pale gold hair and delicate but faintly sunburned features. Her calico dress was clean but worn, and neatly patched in several places; her

130

hands were reddened and work-worn. He mentally cata-
logued her as the daughter or wife of some hard-scrabble
nester.

"How can I help you, Miss . . . or Missus . . . ?"

"Dunbar. Sharon Dunbar. And it's Miss. I do need help
very badly." Her hands twisted nervously in the folds of her
skirt. "Not for myself, but for my brother Webb."

This might, Tom thought, have the makings of a sizeable
case, the kind on which a lawyer could build a reputation. For
a moment he was heartened enough to forget his bitter reso-
lution to return East. From the girl's appearance, there would
probably be little or no money in it, but that was of secondary
concern.

"Go ahead, Miss Dunbar. Suppose you start from the
beginning."

"Two months ago, my brother filed a homestead claim
east of town, in a fork of Deering's Creek. I don't know if
you're familiar with the place."

Tom shook his head. "I'm new to this country, Miss
Dunbar."

The name of Deering's Creek was familiar, though. Tom
tried to place it. Then he remembered that his Uncle Steve
had told him Jeff Jaffers claimed all the richly grassed open
range north of Deering's Creek. South of the creek was an
unwatered, desolate area of clay and sand hills, useless to
either ranchers or sodbusters.

The girl had started to go on when Tom interrupted: "Is
your brother's claim north of the creek?"

"Yes."

Her eyes were a clear gray that seemed to reach into his
thoughts. Tom's throat was dry with his inkling of what was
coming. He had to observe the courtesy of hearing her out,
but his enthusiasm had abruptly gone stale.

Sharon Dunbar's story was about what he might have expected from what Steve had told him, and from such rumors and gossip as were circulated among the towns-people. Jaffers's hands had tried their usual tactics on Webb Dunbar, but Dunbar's spine was stiffer than the usual run of settlers who had so far opposed the JJ spread. Dunbar wasn't dismayed by having his cabin shot up in the middle of the night, or by having his fences torn down and JJ stock driven through his newly plowed and seeded field. He had fought back. He had repaired his fence and re-sowed his field, then had sat up with his rifle for three nights straight, until Jaffers's men had returned to repeat their previous carnage. When they'd ridden off, the fence was still standing, but three JJ horses were dead and two JJ hands who'd returned Dunbar's fire were bleeding from various wounds.

The next day, Webb Dunbar had ridden into Maguey to buy some supplies, some fresh Winchester ammunition, and a new Colt .45 with a shell belt. After loading his wagon, he'd gone into Bourne's saloon to have a drink.

Some of the JJ riders who'd raided his homestead were at the bar when Webb entered, and they'd eyed thoughtfully the defiant jut of the new .45 strapped to Webb's hip. Farmers and pistols didn't mix traditionally, and they'd judged that this was a chance to repay the cocky sodbuster for the night before. One, Roy Bonner, had started taunting Webb about "that shiny new hog-leg," wondering if he could use it as fancy as he wore it. Bonner had found out, but never knew it. Webb's first bullet took him in the heart.

Sheriff Vickers had found Bonner face down on the saw-dust-covered floor, clutching a drawn but unfired six-shooter. The witnesses—the JJ men and the bartender—had already given testimony that Webb Dunbar had made the draw first.

Tom shrugged slightly. "The verdict seems cut and dried, Miss Dunbar," he said uncomfortably.

"But suppose Bonner provoked the fight, and drew first?"

Tom smiled patiently. "The witnesses. . . ."

"Are liars," Sharon interjected. "Webb told me that Bonner drew first. JJ could be expected to lie with their hands on a whole stack of Bibles. Their only religion is hating nesters. They had a grudge against Webb anyway, after he shot them up, and it was their bunkmate he killed."

Tom said gently: "The fact that he's your brother wouldn't make your opinion slightly prejudicial, would it?"

A touch of anger flickered in her gray eyes. She drew herself up stiffly in the chair. "Webb has never lied to me. He wouldn't lie now, even to save his life."

Tom regarded her uneasily. Her earnest conviction impressed him, despite his reluctance, but he didn't want to get embroiled in a legal fracas that would pit him against JJ and all its power.

"Exactly what do you expect of me, Miss Dunbar? To defend him in court?"

"Yes."

"But do you seriously think there are sensible grounds for a court defense? It seems useless, with all the sworn testimony against your brother. Without proof. . . ."

"Then get it, Mister Vickers. Find proof."

"I'm sorry, Miss Dunbar." His tone was cold. "If you want an official investigation, I suggest you appeal to my uncle, the sheriff."

She stood up, facing him levelly. "And not to a timid lawyer? I see. Good day, Mister Vickers."

The door had closed behind her before he could reply. He sat motionless, his face burning with shame. She had seen through his sparring like glass. For a moment, humiliation and angry pride overbalanced fear, and he almost got up to call her back.

Stay out of it, he told himself flatly—strictly out. He had thus dismissed it when someone knocked at the door—a loud, arrogant rap of knuckles, by contrast with Sharon Dunbar's diffident tap.

At his—"Come in."—three JJ men pushed into the room, bringing the smell of cattle, sun-tanned leather, and the open range with them.

Jeff Jaffers was an aging man whose gauntly mournful face was half hidden by a spade beard. His hands were thick and rope-scarred, looking out of place with the neat dark business suit that was uncomfortably cramped across his wide shoulders.

"I'm Jaffers," he announced, standing with an arrogantly wide-legged stance in the center of the room. He added, almost as an afterthought: "These are Pliny Willet and Toby Creagh. They work for me."

"What can I do for you, Mister Jaffers?"

Jaffers slacked into the visitor's chair, looking Tom over in a measuring way. "Maybe I can do something for you, son. It depends on how you play your cards."

"I always aim to oblige, sir," Tom said carefully.

Toby Creagh gave a soft, contemptuous chuckle at this. He was a swarthy man with close-set eyes full of a vinegary meanness. Pliny Willet was a blond, lank scarecrow of a youth about Tom's age. He grinned blandly, rolled a tobacco cud in his cheek, looked about for a spittoon, found none, and let go at the floor.

Tom felt a sudden, raw tightening of anger that he didn't attempt to analyze. It was even stronger than his fear.

"I'd like to throw some business your way," Jaffers said. "Maguey needs better legal representation, and I'd like to see our young lawyer off to a decent start."

"That's kind of you, Mister Jaffers."

Jaffers took out a cigar and waved it. "Not at all. And knowing how hard it is for a young professional man trying to make ends meet, I'd appreciate it if you'd accept a small gratuity as a personal favor from me to you."

"I see," Tom said, his mouth dry. "A loan."

Jaffers hunched forward in his chair, lightly tapping his cigar on the desk to punctuate each emphatic word. "A gift, Mister Vickers."

He means a bribe, Tom thought. And then, in sudden shame and anger, he added to himself: *He thinks he can buy a man like he'd buy a stallion.* This feeling carried into his voice.

"I can't accept such generosity, Mister Jaffers."

Jaffers bit off the end of his cigar, and spat it out. "Did Dunbar's sister convince you of his innocence?"

"Let the authorities decide," Tom said with a shrug. "I'm not in it. I told Miss Dunbar as much."

Steel edged Jaffers's tone suddenly. "See that you stay out of it. You're standing on quicksand, boy."

Tom stood up and leaned his fists on the desk, carried along unheedingly now by his anger. "Mister Jaffers, I can't be threatened. Understand that."

Jaffers flung the cigar to the floor and also stood, his eyes wicked. "You're the one who doesn't understand, Vickers. Toby, Pliny, show him."

Creagh and Willett swiftly circled the desk from opposite sides. The maneuver had been pre-arranged. Tom knew as he scraped his chair back with his heel. He threw a wild punch at Creagh's head, and the man fell back a step, taken off guard by the lawyer's unexpected offensive.

It put Tom's back to Willett, and Willett whipped a rabbit punch under his ear. Dazed, Tom began to swing around, only to catch Creagh's hard slam in his short ribs. Tom was driven to his knees by a rain of blows on his head and back. A vicious neck chop with the edge of a calloused palm spun Tom into unconsciousness. He sprawled, face down on the floor, not feeling the savage kicks directed at his head and shoulders.

He came to, his feet tangled in the rungs of his chair. He disentangled them and maneuvered painfully to his feet, holding to the edge of his desk. Breathing shallowly because of the soreness of his ribs, he hobbled to a wall mirror. His face was scarcely marked—that would attract too much attention to a beating that had been a mere warning. An exploration of his bruised body with probing fingers told him that no ribs were broken. He gave a sigh of relief. As he buttoned his shirt, a cold fury rode him. He'd been willing to let well enough alone, but JJ had not.

Five minutes later he was telling his story at the sheriff's office. His uncle, Steve Vickers, was a small, white-haired man, deeply burnt by sun and wind. He wore clean, well-worn range clothes with a quaint, neat dignity that gave him more the aspect of a quiet merchant than the restlessly energetic lawman he was.

He listened attentively, then took a cold pipe from his mouth and shrugged slightly. "You can sign a warrant, of course, and I'll serve it. But. . . ."

"I know," Tom said dryly. "It will get only Creagh and Willet, not Jaffers."

"Jaffers is smart enough not to do his own fighting. He'll have them out on bail shortly."

"Judge Waring is chief magistrate. Can't you ask him to refuse bail?"

Steve Vickers's thin lips were a bitter line. "Waring is a

close friend of Jaffers's. For that reason, Waring and I aren't very friendly."

"You told me that Jaffers has most of the elected officials under his thumb," Tom said slowly, "but it's hard to believe."

"He paid for their campaigns, or bought their loyalty with favors after election, if they refused his help before. Jaffers has a way of buying a man so subtly that his personal integrity is not affronted. He's under obligation to Jaffers before he knows it." Steve smiled wryly now. "I've had to look sharp to keep my own ethics intact."

"He tried it on me," Tom said. "But when it didn't work, he didn't hesitate to have me worked over."

"He counts you as small potatoes, son. No one is going to shed tears over a poor, uninfluential shyster."

Tom said musingly: "Steve, how thoroughly did you investigate the killing of that JJ man, Bonner?"

The sheriff's shrug was expressive. "It seemed open and shut. Dunbar swears that Bonner made the draw, that the whisky Bonner had taken slowed him enough to permit Dunbar to pull his gun and get off the first shot. It sounded reasonable. The coroner said Bonner had been drinking heavily. And Dunbar hasn't given an inch on his story. But five witnesses say otherwise."

"Dunbar sticks to his story," Tom said. "His sister, convinced of his innocence, comes to me and asks me to investigate the shooting. Immediately afterward, Jaffers offers me a bribe to lay off. When that failed, he had me beaten up. That means he's afraid I'll learn something. There's a loophole in his frame-up. I have to find it."

The sheriff peered sharply at his nephew. "You mean you've changed your mind about taking Dunbar's case?"

Tom felt a flush mount to his face. "I thought Miss

Dunbar was blinded by loyalty to her brother. And . . . I'll admit it . . . I was scared. I knew I'd meet violence if I opposed JJ, and that's not in my line."

Steve Vickers's smile was slow and warm. "You aren't scared now?"

"More mad than scared, I think." Tom shook his head in a baffled way. "If I left Maguey now, with this thing hanging fire, I'd always wonder if it was because I was afraid of Jaffers. No matter what the outcome, I have to see this case through."

Steve nodded approvingly. "It's a man's privilege to be scared. Running away is something else." Then his smile faded. "But you're set on going back East afterward?"

"Don't get me wrong, Steve," Tom said levelly. "I told you this isn't my kind of country. I haven't changed my mind about that. Can I see Dunbar?"

Steve Vickers sighed and scooped the big key ring off the wall. "His sister's talking to him in his cell now. I'll take you there."

He led the way to the cell-block at the rear of the court-house. Sharon Dunbar was standing before a cell door, talking to its inmate. Seeing Tom Vickers, her lips parted in surprise. Tom sheepishly touched his hat to her as the sheriff unlocked the door.

"Here's your lawyer, Dunbar," Steve Vickers said.

Webb Dunbar was a lanky young man, handsome in a rugged, weather-worn way, with his sister's hair and eyes. His handclasp was hard and solid, his glance direct and forth-right. It *was* hard to believe that this man could lie, even to save his life.

To Tom's questions about the story he had been told, Webb could add little. Yes, the JJ witnesses were lying, but they hated him enough to stick to their testimony come hell or high water. Jaffers would have no concern on that score; he

138

knew his men. Yet, Tom insisted, Jaffers feared a leak somewhere.

"What about the bartender?" he asked Webb.

"Charley Bourne? He's for the cowmen, and has never made a secret of the fact."

"A good citizen, though," Steve Vickers put in. "It's hard to believe he'd perjure himself where a man's life is at stake."

"A good citizen," Sharon Dunbar echoed bitterly. "A good scared citizen . . . like everybody else in Maguey. I'm sorry," she added quickly to the two Vickerses.

"No apologies, miss," Steve said grimly. "That's so close to being true, it hurts. Tom, if you could uncover a JJ frame-up, it might arouse a lot of people in this town from the corner Jaffers has worked them into. A lot of people resent JJ's high-handed ways, but they've all been just a little too scared to speak out openly against them. Charley Bourne's personal sympathies aside, he's decent enough. I think Miss Dunbar's right. JJ cracked the whip, and Charley jumped."

"Bourne's our best bet, then. Maybe I can needle his conscience," Tom said. He shook hands again with Webb and left the cell.

As Tom walked from the courthouse, headed for Bourne's saloon, he heard Sharon Dunbar call: "Mister Vickers, please wait!" She hurried up to him with a flushed face. "You didn't give me a chance to thank you."

He touched his hat gravely. "No thanks are necessary."

"But you changed your mind. Why?"

Tom told her about the beating. "That was Jaffers's mistake. It proved to me there was more to this case than met the eye."

Her flush deepened. "I'm sorry I misjudged you."

"I'm not sure you did, when you made the judgment. I was scared then. Maybe I still am."

"Isn't that real courage . . . when a man's afraid, but swallows his fear to do his duty?"

Steve had said almost the same thing, but Tom felt oddly better for having heard it from Sharon. He was aware of a quickening excitement as he watched her, a girl who was bearing a cross of courage for her brother and herself, yet had reassurance to spare for him.

His gratefulness showed through his formal: "Thank you."

"Good luck," she said.

When he reached the door of Bourne's saloon, he looked back and saw her still watching him.

Charley Bourne was mopping the deserted bar with a damp rag. His hand paused, motionless, as Tom walked in; his eyes grew wary. He was a paunchy, balding man in a soiled apron.

He said: "Howdy, Counselor. First customer of the day gets one on the house."

He poured it, and shoved it across with pudgy hands that trembled slightly. Either Bourne had sampled too much of his own wares, or he was nursing a justifiable nervousness, Tom thought. He gave his thanks with a lift of his glass, and tossed off the drink. Then he leaned his elbows on the bar, crossed his arms, and came to the point. "Mister Bourne, I'm representing Webb Dunbar. Is there no question at all that he drew on Bonner?"

"None," Charley Bourne replied too quickly. "Chuck was making some pretty proddy talk, I'll admit, but there was no call for Dunbar to go for his gun. Chuck Bonner was considerably under the weather. You expect a drunk to be mouthy."

"Granted," Tom said, "but if Dunbar drew and fired right away, in a temper, it's odd that Bonner got his gun out at all, drunk as he was."

Bourne wet his lips. "Chuck was pretty fast, drunk or not."

"Maybe," Tom said casually. "But what really happened in here that day, Bourne? What happened that was enough to make Jeff Jaffers have me beaten up for fear of my finding out?"

Bourne said in a badly shaken voice: "Lay off me, Mister Vickers. Please lay off me."

"Not with a man's life at stake!" Tom hammered his fist on the bar. "You have to come clean, Bourne!"

Bourne said: "If I tell you more, I'm dead with Dunbar."

"It's been riding hell out of you, or you'd never have said this much," Tom said. "I don't think you can let it go, Bourne. I don't think you're that kind."

"Listen." Bourne leaned forward, his voice a harsh whisper now. "I can't go through with it if it means testifying in court. I haven't got the gumption. But I'll tell you this much. There was a *sixth* witness."

"What!"

"That's gospel truth, Mister Vickers. That old derelict, Clayt Holden, who swamps out in here for drinks, was coming through the back door to mop up, just as Bonner started prodding Dunbar. He saw the whole thing. I reckon young Dunbar was too occupied to notice, but I saw Clayt. So did the JJ men. Toby Creagh collared the old man right after the shooting and warned him not to breathe a word of what he saw. But Clayt doesn't threaten worth a damn. He's nothing but the town drunk now, but he used to be a mountain man, and he has rawhide for guts. He told Creagh to go to hell, then walked out, so he wasn't there when the sheriff came in. But Jaffers himself must have gotten hold of the old man as soon as he got wind of what happened. Jaffers came in here and told me to give Clayt all the liquor he wanted, and put it on the JJ tab. Clayt doesn't scare, but he'll do anything for whisky."

"Where can I find Clayt Holden?"

"He'll be sleeping off last night in the loft of the livery." Bourne's eyes were pleading. "If you get Clayt on the witness stand, Jaffers'll be wondering where the leak was."

"I'll say that Clayt came to me of his own accord," Tom said, pitying the man.

This is another black mark against the frontier, he thought disgustedly as he left the saloon. Weak-spined men like Bourne could survive only by swallowing their pride and knuckling under to the lawless strong. The frontier turned the strong into tyrants and the weak into worms.

He scanned the tie rail in front of the bank and saw that the three JJ horses were gone. He saw them hitched a block down, in front of a saloon. Jaffers had completed his business at the bank and was having a drink before leaving town. That was good. His two men would be joining him at the bar, not waiting on the street. Tom didn't want to be spotted while going to the livery.

In the stable, a hostler directed him to a rickety ladder that led to the loft. Tom ascended it gingerly. There was a small, withered man snoring on a straw pile in a corner, his whisky-livid face half obscured by long, lank, white hair. The lawyer squatted and shook the man by the shoulder.

"Wake up, Holden."

The old man stirred, groaned, and sat up in the straw, blinking his rheumy eyes. He sneezed and scratched his beard stubble with one scrawny hand.

"What might you want, son?" he asked irritably.

"My name's Vickers. I'm a lawyer, representing Webb Dunbar. I want to hear from you exactly what happened when Chuck Bonner was shot."

A shrewd gleam touched Clayt Holden's bleary eyes. He didn't say anything. He fumbled under the straw and drew out a half-empty pint of whisky, took a tremendous slug, then slapped the cork back with the heel of his palm.

"Even the sheriff didn't know I saw it. If you know that much, I reckon there's no reason for me to try to bluff you about what happened. And now you want me to blab it to a judge and jury. Nothing doing."

"Not even if it means Webb Dunbar's life?"

Clayt's leathery brow corrugated. "A damn' nester kid!" He spat with a mountain man's disgust. "Wrecking the country, cutting it up with fences and plows. Too many people are moving in. There's no elbow room. We ought to poison all of 'em like coyotes."

Tom was hitting a blank wall. He rocked back on his heels, his face thoughtful, and tried another tack. "I wonder how long Jaffers will be willing to humor your thirst, with you possessing information about how JJ bribed you and perjured themselves to frame a man for murder. If it got out, it would wreck all Jaffers's prestige, not to mention most of his business enterprises. I wonder how long it will be before Jaffers decides to shut you up for good."

The old derelict blinked. He set the bottle on the floor, his furrowed, unshaven jaw working. "I never thought of that."

After that it was only a matter of a few minutes' persuasive talking to convince Clayt Holden to appear as a defense witness for Webb Dunbar.

"Do you want to take me to the calaboose now?" Clayt asked humbly.

Tom thought for a moment. Steve would lock Clayt up at his request, but would bars and brick shield Clayt from all the means by which JJ would try to silence the old man before the trial? You couldn't keep a thing like this quiet.

Clayt sensed the lawyer's dilemma. "Look, son, I lived for years up in the mountains yonder, before the damn' country got over-settled and the pelts were all trapped out. I know those mountains like you know your lawyer's foolery. If you give me some provisions, get me to the mountains, and turn me loose there, not a man alive will find me till you come to fetch me down for the trial."

Tom eagerly seized on this solution. Descending from the loft, he told the hostler to saddle two horses. He and Clayt mounted up, and Tom gave the old man hurried directions.

"We don't want to be seen leaving town together. You ride out first and wait for me by that dead cottonwood just beyond the lumber mill. Meanwhile, I'll buy a grubstake for you. That will take ten minutes or more . . . then I'll follow."

Clayt nodded his agreement and rode from the stable, jogging out of town on the road east to the foothills. Tom waited a minute, then slipped out and headed for Hopkins's General Store.

While he was dickering with the proprietor, Sharon Dunbar entered the store and caught his eye. He walked quickly over to her.

"I've been watching," she said. "You've been running from one place to another. Did you learn something?"

In a low voice, Tom swiftly summarized what he'd found out, and watched relief flood her face. "I'm glad," she breathed. "I'd almost thought it was hopeless." Then a new worry clouded the clear gray eyes. "You're insuring Clayt Holden's safety, but what about yours?"

Faint surprise touched him; he smiled. "I hadn't thought about it."

"Don't you think you'd better? You're organizing Webb's defense. What do you think your life will be worth when Jaffers knows you're onto something? When he learns that

Clayt's disappeared, he'll guess what you've been up to."

"I suppose so," Tom said wryly. "But I can't hide out with Clayt. There's too much to do, preparing a case."

"At least buy a gun and carry it with you. Don't go around defenseless. If anything happened to you, I . . ."—she bit her lips—"we, Webb and I, would feel responsible."

"All right, if it'll make you feel better."

He nodded gravely to her soft—"Be careful."—and watched her leave. Then he walked to the gun case and selected a short-barreled Colt, which he stuck into his trousers. He concealed the weapon by buttoning his coat. He paid for the gun, a box of shells, and the food, and left the store carrying the supplies in a flour sack.

At the livery, he secured the provisions to his saddle, mounted up, and rode down the street at a casual gait. As he neared the saloon where the JJ horses were still hitched, he felt a quick flare of alarm. Toby Creagh was leaning on the batwings inside, with a glass in his hand, raking the street with an idle stare.

How long had Creagh been standing there? Had he seen Clayt ride out? That alone should ignite no suspicion in Creagh's mind. But now, seeing the lawyer follow ten minutes later, with a bulky sack tied to his saddle . . . ?

Tom thought bitterly: *Damn the luck!* He started to rein in, hoping to pull around before Creagh saw him. Too late. The JJ man's idle gaze stopped on Tom, fell to the sack of provisions. Creagh's jaw dropped, and the glass slipped from his fingers and crashed on the boardwalk. He whirled back into the room, shouting Jaffers's name.

Now it comes, Tom thought with a sinking heart as he kicked his horse into a run. Within moments, he was in sight of the cottonwood where Clayt Holden waited.

"We'll have to run for it! They know!" he called to Clayt.

Without question, the old man wheeled his horse and followed him. Their lead was short-lived, Tom knew. A lawyer and an old man could not hope to outride cowmen who lived in the saddle.

"You know the country!" Tom shouted at Clayt as they raced stirrup to stirrup. "Where can we hide? We can't outrun them."

"Just hold the road till we touch the foothills, son," Clayt replied imperturbably. "We'll leave the horses and take to the brush. No cowhand can fox old Clayt on foot."

The road wound tortuously through boulder-studded country. Time and again, Tom threw back fleeting glances, but saw no sign of Jaffers and his men. It puzzled him, and worried him, too, for their lead was not great. JJ should have closed the gap rapidly. It was hardly likely that Jaffers would make no attempt at pursuit; he must have an unknown ace up his sleeve.

This cold suspicion caused Tom to pull swiftly to a stop. Clayt reined in, too, eyeing the lawyer questioningly. "This road does a lot of winding," Tom said. "Suppose Jaffers took a short cut from town, a straight beeline, and cut us off down the road."

Clayt groaned and slapped his forehead. "Cuss me for a whisky-addled old fool, he might at that. I forgot. They's an old game trail that cuts over this steep timbered ridge and hits the road just ahead. They built the road around the ridge because the grade yonder was too steep and stony to grade for wagon traffic. A horseman, though, could cut his time in half by coming over instead of going around. Jaffers would know that . . . and it's not likely he'd forget."

Tom wheeled his horse in a tight rein. "There's no time to lose. Let's backtrack . . . and fast. They'll be waiting ahead."

The high ringing crack of a rifle punctuated his words.

Clayt grunted and folded up in his saddle, then began to slide to the ground. The origin of the shot was lost in the slap of echoes, but Tom placed it high up the timbered slope of the ridge that rose away from the roadside.

Jaffers must have spotted them on the road long before they reached it. Seeing them stop, he must have realized he was outguessed. It was a long-range shot, even for a rifle. It was just bad luck that Clayt had been hit.

Tom knew the JJ men would spur a breakneck pace downslope to reach them and finish the job at close range. The brief panicked thought touched the lawyer that he could save his own neck by leaving Clayt, but he dismissed it quickly.

He tumbled to the ground by Clayt's horse, catching the old man under the arms as he toppled sideways. The mountaineer was a limp burden as Tom carried him to the shelter of a huge boulder at the roadside. Then he returned for the horses and tied them up in thick scrub pine back from the road.

He crouched behind the rock near Clayt. The old man was unconscious, and his breathing was harsh and labored. Tom's mouth tightened as he jerked the Colt from his belt and checked the loads with a remembered dexterity. This surprised him; he supposed that it was an unforgettable skill. His father had loved guns, had made him practice frequently as a boy. "Guns are great for sport, son, but not to use on men," his father always used to say.

Tom grimaced. He'd thought of himself as taking after his father in all ways, yet here he crouched, gun in hand, waiting without tremor or regret to shoot at men. Then he forgot everything except the three riders who poured out of the thinning timber up the slope, spurring their horses recklessly.

Tom braced his pistol across the rock and triggered two

fast shots. Instantly the three riders split up and headed for cover behind the rocks that studded the treeless lower slope.

Firing as they appeared had been a mistake, Tom knew regretfully. They'd believed him to be unarmed, and he should have waited till they were close. Now theirs was the advantage. They were three against one, and they had rifles.

Toby Creagh was nearest, and now he began working in, racing daringly from rock to rock. Tom thought shrewdly: *he's feeling sassy because he thinks he's up against a shyster who never held a gun in his life. All right, let him think so.*

Tom moved to a side of the rock that would give him partial shelter from Jaffers's and Willett's covering fire, and placed a couple of shots in Creagh's direction. They went well wide of their mark.

Creagh gave a taunting laugh and moved boldly into the open, starting for a nearer rock. Tom rested the Colt across the rock, lined up the sights, and squeezed off the fifth shot very slowly.

Creagh stopped in mid-run, jerking with the slug's impact. Then he folded his arms across his belly and fell forward. His body rolled loosely down the slope until it lodged against the rock he'd failed to reach.

Willett gave a shout of rage and opened up with blistering rifle fire. Tom crouched down under a shower of flying rock splinters. Jaffers's laugh boomed from above.

Tom saw the rancher leave cover and come bounding down the slope. Tom had expended his last bullet, and Jaffers knew it.

With feverish haste, Tom broke the loading gate and fumbled for a fresh cartridge among the loose ones in his coat pocket. He jammed it at the empty chamber too hastily, and dropped it. Jaffers was only feet away. Tom palmed another shell and slipped it in.

Too late! Jaffers was on the other side of the rock, his eyes glaring malignantly down at Tom's. He swung his heavy arm back and forward to slam the bullet home. Suddenly Tom heard a shot—a high, clear rifle explosion. Jaffers twisted slowly and fell limp.

"Throw away your guns, Willett! Step out with your hands high!" That was Steve Vickers's voice.

Willett offered no argument. He emerged from a jumble of rocks with his hands clasped at the back of his neck. While the sheriff stumbled down the uneven slope with his prisoner, Tom examined Clayt's wound. It was not serious.

To Tom's question, Steve replied that Sharon Dunbar had seen Jaffers ride from town hard on the heels of Tom and Clayt. She hadn't lost a moment in telling the sheriff.

"I remembered that old game trail, too," Steve observed grimly. "I figured Jaffers would use it to cut you off, so I used it to come up on him from behind. Miss Dunbar is coming by the wagon road." He paused, eyeing Tom keenly. "If you return East now, after the start you've made, then I've made a wrong guess about you."

Tom nodded thoughtfully. "I'm staying, Steve. As long as I was observing things from the sidelines, I couldn't understand the country or the people. When I saw Clayt shot in the back, I was mad enough to shoot back, and then I was in it myself and knew why I had to meet violence with violence." He gave his uncle a quizzical look. "You figured I would react that way."

"Sure," Steve said calmly. "If you hadn't had a yen for excitement, 'way down, you'd never have come West in the first place." The sheriff glanced down the road. "Here's Miss Sharon. I suggest you tell her what you just told me. Somehow I think she'll be very glad to hear it."

Midnight Showdown

When young Cole Haven stepped off the train, he knew he was home. Standing on the crude platform in the gray spring twilight with cold winds chilling him to the marrow, he took a deep breath of the lung-searing, frigid atmosphere and felt clean for the first time in a year. Down Red Rim's single street, two irregular wheel ruts of frozen slush flanked by false-fronted frame shacks, windows were warm with orange rectangles of oily light. The town was just sliding out of its customary winter lethargy.

Standing on the platform, a tall, thin, dark figure in ragged Levi's, Haven lifted his tired gaze to the towering, snow-mantled slope of Razorback Hill with its backbone of black spruce, looming back of the town. This, at last, was home, as he had envisioned it. A year working in Eastern mills had not done him any good, he reflected wryly. Well, if his health and vitality were gone, his strength and youth remained. He belonged to this country—he had learned that, although it had taken him a foolish jaunt to realize it.

The wind carried a thin, stinging sheet of snow into his face. He hunkered farther into his Mackinaw and looked again at the warmly lighted windows downstreet, and he was now aware of a groaning hunger and a growing weariness that drew his eyes to Red Rim's single hotel. He picked up his bag and started to step down from the platform. He stopped in his tracks at the sound of a woman's voice, low-pitched and angry, off to one side.

At the opposite end of the platform were four people—two of them women who had evidently just stepped from the train and were waiting for someone. The other two appeared to be cowhands who had intentionally accosted the women.

"Now, now," the bigger one was chuckling with a liquored slur in his voice.

"Drunken cow nurse!" she hissed, and brought her handbag down with a *splat* against the man's skull.

The blow did little more than anger the big man, as might the sting of a mosquito, and he started after her.

All this, Haven's swift gaze telescoped in a few seconds. Then he dropped his bag and sprinted down the platform, colliding with the big man and knocking him away from the woman. Their bodies, falling entangled together, caught the other 'puncher just below the knees, knocked him off balance, and brought him down with them.

The collision knocked the breath out of Haven, whose wind had suffered along with his health during long months in a stuffy downtown city tenement. But the two 'punchers were on their feet almost immediately, and each of them caught one of Haven's arms and hauled him up with them.

"Let him go!" cried the woman with the handbag that she was wielding vigorously at the head of the big 'puncher.

The man cursed. "Give this joker the rush, Al . . . then we'll take care of these wildcats."

Holding Haven upright and helpless between them, the two broke into a run for the opposite end of the platform. When they reached it, they halted abruptly, bracing themselves and, without breaking Haven's forward momentum,

151

pitched him outward. He felt himself hurtling through cold air, then he hit on his rear in the ice-rutted street. His traveling bag followed, striking the ice in back of him and skidding into him.

He heard the big 'puncher bellow after him: "That's what wise rail bums get around here!"

As Haven pulled himself painfully erect, another man, towering and hawk-visaged, was angling across from the opposite side of the street. As he reached Haven, he stopped and helped him up. "All right?"

"Fine," Haven said wryly.

The towering man nodded, strode purposefully on, and, reaching the platform, stepped onto it and confronted the two 'punchers.

"You two tramps know who this is?" he snarled at the thugs as he jerked a thumb toward the woman with the handbag. "Miss Maylin. Get off her or I'll boot you off."

The smaller one's mouth fell open. Then he turned and bounded off the platform and scrambled down the street. The big man looked uncertain.

"Move, Tolliver," murmured the towering man.

The other's eyes flickered wickedly, but he moved, and moved without more hesitation, following his companion.

The towering man turned to the woman, who threw herself into his arms. "Cass," she cried hysterically, "thank God you're here."

"I'm here, Kit," said Cass Farrell gruffly as he patted her back awkwardly.

Kit recovered herself abruptly and drew away, a white-faced decorum asserting itself in her. Haven, still standing where he had fallen, thought with awe that he had never seen such a picture of regal beauty. Her tall, graceful form was set off by a plain-belted, woolen coat, her hair framing her pale face in auburn clusters. About her was an intangible measure of unconscious dignity.

The other girl was perhaps ten years younger, in her late teens. She was small and frail, flushed with cold, her blonde prettiness reduced almost to drabness by the royal loveliness of her companion.

"Hello, Julie," Farrell said very gentle to this girl. "Grown up, I see."

"You're the same, Cass," said Julie shyly.

"He never changes, Julie," said Kit. "Just like when he was a kid."

"Now, you two make me out an old man," said Farrell aggrievedly.

"I just mean you carry your age well, Cass," said Kit with a faint smile. Her gaze wandered to Haven, still standing where Farrell had helped him up. "Boy," she said, "are you hurt?"

Mildly irked, Haven said: "No."

"Good. And thanks."

"Don't mention it." He picked up his suitcase and began to hobble gingerly away.

"Wait." Her voice stopped him in his tracks. "Are you looking for a job?"

Haven turned, saying—"Yes."—cautiously.

"You've got one."

That was Cole Haven's introduction to Kit Maylin, her niece Julie, and Cass Farrell, foreman of Doubletree.

Besides Cole Haven, there proved at present to be only one other cowpuncher employed at Doubletree, George Mack. From Mack, Haven learned of the feud of long-standing between Doubletree and Ralph Payton, owner of the adjoining Blackjack spread. Payton had pressed Kit to marry him for years until she had moved East, partly to get away from him, taking John Maylin's daughter Julie, who wanted to go to school there, with her. That had been five years ago. Two months ago, John Maylin had been murdered by an unknown assailant, and now Kit Maylin had returned to the ranch, half-owner with Julie. The two troublesome 'punchers at the station were both Payton's men.

Haven threw himself enthusiastically into the range life, and his weight and health returned quickly. Even post-hole digging, a job which he had always hated in common with all 'punchers, he now tackled with a will, and George Mack soon found that he could foist a portion of his own chores off on his new friend.

Then there were the occasional rides with Julie, for which Mack and Haven vied. Kit, on the other hand, spent most of her time in her uncle's office, trying to straighten out the ranch books, her uncle having been no bookkeeper. It was all too fine to last, Haven thought, and he was right. One afternoon at the corral, he was assisting Julie to mount her horse, when her foot somehow slipped in the stirrup, and she fell into his arms. The next thing he knew, he was kissing her. Then he released her swiftly, a little scared.

"Cole," she said softly, "didn't you mean it?"

"More than anything," he said a little dismally, then, being a forthright young man, he decided to have it all out at once. "I . . . I want to marry you, Julie. Have for a long time."

"Oh, yes. So have I, Cole."

"You can't marry a no-good bum."

"Can't I?" she said warmly. "Besides, you're not a bum any more."

"Well, what about your aunt?"

"I know," she said slowly and soberly. "I know, Cole."

"I'll talk to her."

"It won't do any good, Cole. We'll run away."

"No, we won't," he said flatly. *At least you won't, Julie,* he thought, *but I may have to after talking to Kit.*

He went immediately to the house and found Kit in the office. She was sitting, her feet propped on her desk, gazing moodily out the window. She swung them down quickly as he paused at the open door. She was wearing Levi's and a flannel shirt that seemed to lessen her cold, inaccessible regality. He felt more confident.

"Come in, Cole. What did you want to see me about?"

"Marrying Julie," he said, then wished he hadn't been quite so blunt.

Kit, unsurprised, regarded him bleakly. "Well, I saw it coming," she said, rather to herself. "How old are you, Cole?"

He squirmed a little. "Well . . . twenty."

"Twenty," she said dryly, "and Julie is not quite seventeen."

"Miss," he said respectfully, "this is not Boston. This is the frontier."

Kit's blue eyes went a little frosty. "And the object of that brilliant conclusion?"

"My father married when he was eighteen," Haven explained mildly, "with my mother just turned fifteen."

Kit stared at the desk top. "And what does Julie say?"

"That she'd run away with me," he said uncomfortably.

"Out of the mouths of babes," Kit responded dryly. She got up and walked around the desk to face him. "Cole," she said, more gently, "you are honest to come to me about this, even knowing, as you must, that I would refuse."

A reckless anger touched him. "Maybe Julie was right."

Kit smiled, a little sadly. "No. For if you did run away, I would spend the Maylin fortune, if I had to, hiring Pinkerton men to track you down. You wouldn't get far, Cole . . . and I am Julie's legal guardian until she is eighteen."

"So that's that," he said in a wry, tired voice.

"Not entirely. At least, I have more to say. You are penniless, while Julie, by even Eastern standards, is a rich young lady. Would you live off her?"

"I wouldn't touch a penny of it," Haven said calmly, "and I think Julie would give it up."

"No doubt," Kit said sarcastically. "Then you would go make your home as a pair of penniless nesters in a tumbledown line shack. How long do you think Julie could stand that, after the life to which she is accustomed?"

Haven was silent. It was so—he was no stranger to hardships, but Julie . . . ?

"Even assuming that what's between you is more than infatuation," Kit went on, "you can see how it is, Cole. I believe she is too young."

A wicked smile touched Haven's mouth. "How old are you, Miss Maylin?"

Kit's equanimity was shattered. She blushed and stumbled. "You . . . why, what do you mean?"

"I think you know, miss. To be plain, you may want to die an old maid, but. . . ."

Kit, very white now, interrupted quietly. "Cole, you may pack up and leave this ranch immediately, nor do I care to see you again, until . . . ," she added hesitantly, "you can show me that you can support her comfortably. However, I hardly think it is fitting Julie should marry at all till I do."

"Yeah," Haven said lugubriously as he turned to leave. "Well, no fear about her being too young then."

"Why, you . . . ," Kit began, but he was gone.

He went directly to the bunkhouse, hoping he wouldn't encounter Julie, and assembled his bedroll and saddled a bay gelding Kit had given him.

As he was lashing his bedroll to the cantle, Cass Farrell's voice said pleasantly behind him: "Where the hell you riding, son?"

"Out," Haven said briefly. "I'm through, Cass."

"Kit tell you to drag it?" Farrell inquired shrewdly. "About Julie, eh? Well, get a cinch on yourself, son. Don't go off like this. I'll talk to Kit."

There was an indulgent humor in his voice that infuriated Haven, although Farrell was only trying to help him laugh it off. He whirled about savagely. "Why in hell don't you tell Kit how you feel about her and end this foolishness?" He mimicked Kit's voice. "I hardly think it is fitting that Julie should marry till I do."

He saw the surprise and hurt move behind Cass Farrell's weathered face then, as though an old wound had been struck open. Haven felt a stab of remorse, but he didn't say anything, just stepped into the saddle and rode away from Doubletree without seeing Julie.

Tolliver was standing by the Blackjack corrals after breakfast, picking his teeth, when Cole Haven rode up. The foreman regarded him bemusedly for a moment, still picking his teeth, noting the war bag and blanket roll, then asking idly: "Kit give you the rush, kid?" There was no malice in his voice.

"That's right," Haven said disinterestedly. "Any jobs?"

Tolliver just regarded him mildly for a while, then said: "Kid, you got more gall than a twenty-mule team. You know how it stands between Doubletree and Blackjack."

"All right." Haven wasn't interested. "Any jobs?"

Anger touched Tolliver's gaze. "Yes, damn you," he said unpleasantly. "There are. Hike right up to the house. Leave the crow-bait here and I'll grain him. You'll find Peyton in his

157

study. That's the second room to the right after you go in."

Haven dismounted, handing the reins to Tolliver, said—"Thanks."—and tramped up to the house, walked in the back door, and found himself in a corridor. He knocked at the designated door.

"Come in," said a voice.

Haven walked in to face behind an oak-and-walnut desk a dark, mustached man in his thirties whose bland, well-fed face bore the sign of soft living.

"I understand you need riders."

Payton regarded him inscrutably, after a while saying: "Cole Haven, hmm?"

"So?"

"How come you left Doubletree?"

Haven told him patiently, shortly, and flatly.

Payton hunched forward across the desk. "Like to get back at Kit?" he asked confidingly.

Haven's face betrayed nothing. "Got any ideas?"

Payton's eyes coalesced oddly. "I wanted her for years. Doubletree, too. I'm going to have both. I killed old Marlin to start the ball rolling."

Haven stiffened, but said nothing.

"You can help me. You know the ranch house at Doubletree. We're going to abduct Kit and hold her until she changes her mind about me."

The man's arrogance held Haven momentarily mute. Did Payton actually think he could make Kit Maylin prefer him to dying first? When he spoke, though, he said: "What about Cass? He'll kill the man who touches Kit."

"I've got a line shack on the north boundary. Never used now since I fenced that part off. We can keep her there. Cass won't find her. And once I have her there, I can persuade her I'm the man for her."

A cold chill tremored through Haven, although the room was warm and close. He knew then that Payton had wanted Kit so long, had brooded over it so persistently, that his mind was affected on the subject. The man was probably a little crazy.

"About the job, you're hired," Payton said. "And meet me here at nine tonight. There'll be two of the other boys in on it, too . . . if you want in."

"Sure."

"Good. Thought you'd like it. And there'll be a bonus for you for your help. For now, haul your gear to the bunkhouse and go to Tolliver for orders."

"Fine," murmured Haven, "and thanks."

At nine, Haven was at the study, knocking at the oaken-paneled door. At Payton's—"Come in."—he entered, closing the door behind him. Tolliver was there, and Ollie Sears, a short, wizened 'puncher in his fifties. Both wore guns, he observed. Payton, at his desk, said: "Sit down, Cole. You're going to sketch us a plan of the house."

On a sheet of paper, Haven sketched, and Payton made plans. An hour later they rose, Payton pulling on his hat and saying: "Let's ride."

He opened a drawer and pulled out a long-barreled Remington with belt and holster that he buckled on. Haven alone was weaponless now. Payton was still cautious.

On a rise near the Doubletree outbuildings, the four paused, sitting their horses in the moonlit night. The lights were still on in the bunkhouse and ranch house.

"Get this," Payton said. "We'll go over it till you all do. Gus," this to Tolliver, "you cover between the bunkhouse and house, in case anyone gets curious. Ollie, you take the front of the house, in case anyone makes a break, but no

159

shooting till you see who it is. Cole, you come with me."

They waited on the rise, reiterating the plan, and watched the lights wink out one by one till Doubletree lay in darkness. When Payton finally, glancing at his watch, said it was midnight, they ground hitched the horses except for Payton's which they brought in nearer, within the gate that enclosed the rear patio. Then, Tolliver and Ollie having taken their stations, Haven and Payton moved onto the verandah and let themselves into the front room through the door that Haven had known would be unlocked.

From here, they moved into a corridor toward the back, but at the first door they came to, Haven hesitated.

"What's the matter?" Payton snapped. "You said Kit's room was the last door."

"Not sure now," Haven said. "Might be Julie's. Or maybe neither. One of these side rooms."

"You're a handy one," Payton said scathingly. "Get the hell outside and hold my horse ready. I'll handle this myself."

Haven deliberately left through the front door, but didn't head around back to Payton's horse. This was what he'd been waiting for—what he had stalled Payton in hopes of. Actually neither Kit nor Julie slept in any of the rooms off that corridor. Those were guest chambers. The girls' rooms were located to the very rear of the house. Let Payton search here. Haven itched for a gun. If he had had one, all of this would have ended when Payton first suggested his crazy scheme at Blackjack.

Once on the verandah, he could see Tolliver's dark, huge frame between there and the bunkhouse. Keeping silently to the shadow of the house, he circled around, back of the corrals in a wide circuit, then to the rear of the bunkhouse. He opened the back door and stepped inside, fumbling for a lamp in the darkness. He found it and struck a match. As murky illumination spread through the room, he saw Cass Farrell lying propped on one elbow in his bunk, his graying hair tousled.

"What the hell, boy?"

"Payton's after Kit. He's in the house now."

Farrell was on his feet immediately, pulling on his boots. He always slept fully dressed. With a few terse questions as he worked, he gleaned the situation, then moved over to a battered dresser in the corner, yanking a drawer open, saying: "Sent George out to Carnes Cañon to clean up some lobos. It's up to you and me."

From a drawer he pulled two heavy Colts, one in a shell belt that he buckled on; the other gun he handed to Haven. Snuffing the light then, Farrell moved silently in darkness to the front door, opening it silently, his gun ready.

Tolliver was moving forward in the moonlight toward the bunkhouse, attracted by the light. He shot now as the door opened, a bright spear of flame in the night. Farrell grunted and his leg buckled, but he was shooting even as he went down on one knee. Tolliver twisted, then his falling made a thin, gritty thud.

Haven, behind Farrell, was on his knees by the older man immediately.

"Get the hell into the house. Get him before he gets Kit," snorted Farrell.

Haven left him, running toward the house, his gun pointed before him. Before he reached the verandah, Ollie, attracted by the shots, ran around from the back and sighted him. Sensing what must have happened, Ollie shot. Haven felt the fan of the slug past his temple. He fired once, by reflex, his shot merging boomingly with Ollie's second. Ollie tripped in the act of stepping onto the verandah, pitched across it with a crash, rolled off the edge, and lay,

161

motionless, on his back.

In an instant Haven was running into the house, shouting for Julie. He found her on the floor of Kit's room, half stunned. Kit was gone. Payton had found the room. "Payton . . . he hit me . . . took her."

Hoof beats sounded a pulsing thudding from the rear. Haven charged out the back. A horse with two riders was charging for the gate. Haven shot twice. The horse stumbled, pitched with a headlong crash that splintered the flimsy fence before his down-plunging, falling weight.

"All right, Cole," Kit said wearily the next day, as she sat propped up in bed regarding Haven and Julie at her bedside. "I guess I'll have to grant your wedding after what you did. You can handle yourself like a much older man. But please, both of you, stay on here."

"Thanks, Kit," Haven said, grinning. "Hate to make you break your vow about marrying first, though."

Farrell, standing on a crutch at bedside, scraped and fidgeted."Damn it, Kit," he said suddenly. "Do you have to break it?" It was hard for him to say it. "I mean, I was never sure but what you liked Payton, but with him jailed, in prison . . . well, damn it!"

Oddly, there were tears in Kit's eyes. "You old fool," she said softly. "I was beginning to wonder if I'd have to ask you!"

Trouble from Texas

All morning Marshal McQuade had watched the Texas men riding into town, as lean, shaggy and wild-looking, after a thousand-mile trail drive, as their wiry bronchos. At this early hour things were still pretty quiet, even in the saloons where the riders had converged. Things didn't usually start to pop, even with a newly arrived trail crew in a Kansas trail town, until nightfall.

This particular crew herded for Curtis Granger, who always went out of his way to encourage his men to tear apart the railroad town of Sentinel. "My boys have to let off steam," old Granger would insist. The saloon and gambling hall owners agreed; their business rose in direct ratio to the steam-letting. But a line had to be drawn somewhere, and that was the town marshal's job.

It was John McQuade's job on this, his first year as a full marshal. He'd deputied for Gus Birnie for two years before this. Gus had been killed in a saloon fracas a month ago, and the city council had readily voted McQuade into his vacated position. Gus had been a good marshal; he'd kept the insolent trail herders in their place, confining their hell-raising within limits that satisfied the respectable elements. He'd even faced down Curtis Granger every successive year when the wealthy

Texan hit town, demanding unlimited entertainment for his boys. Gus had squelched that by putting through—and enforcing—a gun-check statute that required all visitors to turn in their side arms at the jail and not pick them up till they left town.

So far, McQuade had competently filled Gus Birnie's boots. But Granger's annual arrival was the real test, and the city fathers were watching to see how he'd handle it.

"Remember this about Granger, son," Gus had told McQuade last year, just after the old marshal had successfully bluffed the wealthy rancher for the seventh time. "If you give him a square inch, he'll take an acre."

Granger always came in himself, from his camp on the bottomlands of the river beyond Sentinel, to bully the town officer. McQuade knew he'd have to reckon with him, as Gus had for seven years.

One thing at a time, McQuade thought now, smiling at the tight anticipation the idea gave him. *Wait'll he gets here. Besides, he never gave Gus anything but lip. You can handle him.*

McQuade placed his lean shoulders against the barbershop's candy-striped pole, and continued to study the still-quiet street. A wind gust eddied miniature twisters of dust down the avenue. A kid sat on the Mercantile steps, pegging rocks at a tin can. A lone rider rode his horse down the street, past the barber shop.

McQuade's blue eyes suddenly grew alert under the shadow of his hat brim. That rider was Wirt Crandall, youngest and wildest member of Granger's crew. Last year, Crandall had entered a saloon without checking his gun and had shot up the back-bar mirrors. McQuade, then a deputy, had buffaloed him and lugged him to the jail, where he cooled his heels for five days and was fined fifty dollars for damages by Judge Rainesford.

McQuade wondered if Crandall remembered that—and had his answer when the man shot him a swift sideward glance as he passed. McQuade's muscles tightened, waiting, but Crandall rode on to the jail, where he dismounted and went in to check his gun with the jailer.

When he came out, he angled over to the Roadbrand Saloon and went in. McQuade relaxed slightly, but slanted frequent glances toward the saloon. Crandall might or might not have learned a lesson last year; he was the born-troublemaker type, and with a few drinks under his belt. . . .

McQuade forgot Crandall when Nell Breen stepped from her father's general store and leaned with folded arms against the doorway, idly casting her gaze downstreet. She saw him and waved—almost half-heartedly, McQuade couldn't help thinking. He'd courted Nell for some time; between them there was a half understanding which remained unspoken, because he hesitated to suggest marriage, knowing her strong dislike for the trail town and its rough characters in general.

She was here because she'd stuck with her father after opportunities had run out for him back East, and the West had offered fresh promise. McQuade she regarded as a quiet-spoken exception to the general run of Western men. She knew he hoped for the day of law and respectability in Sentinel. But for his way of helping to bring it about, in the violent and dangerous position of peace officer, she held strong disapproval. It stood like a wall between them.

After a moment, Nell reëntered the store. McQuade watched the saloon. A half hour wore by before Crandall came out, his face flushed with drink. He crossed the street to the jail with a weaving, unsteady step. He came out strapping on his gun belt, then started to climb into his saddle, and made it on the third try. He kicked his horse around and started down the street.

Wendell Breen, a tall, aristocratic-looking man, stepped from his store and stood for a meditative moment where his daughter had. His ascetic face lighted as he saw McQuade, standing across the way, and he left the sidewalk to cross the street to him. Then Crandall, pushing his horse at a canter, came almost abreast of Breen as the storekeeper reached the middle of the street.

He shouted: "Out of the way, grandpa, or I'll ride through you!"

Breen stopped uncertainly, his faded eyes full of confusion as he stared at the horseman bearing down on him. A gentle-natured man past middle age, he was slow of response, slow of action.

"All right, grandpa, if that's the way you want it!" Crandall said gleefully, and put his horse straight toward the old man.

McQuade had already left the walk and was running into the street. He was too late; the shoulder of Crandall's broncho nudged Breen hard enough to spin his meager frame off balance and tumble him on his back.

McQuade hauled up short. "Get down, Crandall!" he ordered.

The Texan pivoted his mount, grinning. "Just having a little fun with the ol' turnip, *mariscal*."

"You'll do to scare the women, Wirt," McQuade said contemptuously. "Get off that horse before I knock you off."

The boy's eyes, red-rimmed from days of dust and sun glare, grew impatient and short-tempered. "You and these fuddy-duddy merchants have been lording it high, wide, and handsome over us long enough. Think I'll just take care of you, *mariscal*."

He spurred his horse straight at McQuade, then pulled the animal up on a tight rein to rear high on its hind legs, towering over McQuade, iron-shod hoofs flailing inches from his head. The marshal threw himself backward to escape the hoofs, rolled over, and came to his feet. Crandall's horse came down on all fours. Now the Texan tugged at his gun, but it stuck in its stiff holster.

McQuade lunged to the stirrup, reached up to grab Crandall by the belt, and lugged him boldly out of the saddle. Crandall hit the ground on his hip and shoulder, the wind knocked out of him. With an angry yank he finally freed his gun, but McQuade kicked it out of his hand.

McQuade said to the storekeeper: "Are you all right, sir?" After receiving Breen's dazed nod, he rammed his gun into the boy's abdomen as he hauled him to his feet. "You know where the jail is."

Crandall shook his burly frame and glared at McQuade like a ringy bull. Then he swung around and started down the street. "You won't be holding me beyond tonight, *mariscal*," he bragged over his shoulder. "Not when Curt Granger hears about this. This year he's brought a crew big enough to tear your lousy town apart. And he says he hopes you'll try to stop him."

McQuade locked him up, then left the jail to go to Breen's store. Nell and her father stood in the aisle between the counters, she brushing at his dusty clothes and saying something in an angry voice, and Wendell Breen placating her.

Seeing McQuade in the doorway, Nell fell silent. He advanced into the store, pulling off his hat. It was cool in here and smelled of oiled leather. The girl turned toward McQuade, her brief emotion walled now behind an expressionless face. She was little, under middling size anyway, and wore a dark working dress that, with the way her black hair was drawn smoothly back in a bun, gave her a look of prim severity.

"For Father's sake, I should thank you," she said distantly.

McQuade looked down at his hat. "Yes, Nell," he said dryly.

"I'm sorry, John. That sounded cold. But I don't like to see you brawl."

"If you saw it, you know who started it."

"I know, but . . ."—she shook her head in a frustrated way—"I just want you out of it, John, before you have to use a *gun*."

"I can't pull out of it, Nell," he said gently, "especially not now. You know that."

"I know," she said in a brittle voice, "and I guess there's nothing more to say, is there? Not if you're determined to founder and die in a pool of your own pride."

She turned and headed for the storeroom, brushing angrily past her father. Wendell Breen heaved a deep sigh and walked over to McQuade, pulling out his pipe.

McQuade hammered a fist against the counter. "Damn it, it isn't just pride. Can't she see that? I'm no hero! It'd be a lot easier for me to give a point now and again. But doesn't she see what would happen if I did?"

"In some cases, it might be advisable," Breen said, frowningly puffing his pipe alight, "but not with Granger."

"That's what Gus used to say."

Breen tapped him on the shoulder with his pipe stem. "Remember this, boy. Nell is not unreasonable. She knows as well as any what keeping the peace must cost in sweat and blood. She hates bloodshed and violence, but she hates worse watching it run rank and wild. She's simply a woman frightened, John . . . not for herself, for you. This was her only way of showing it without declaring herself. We Breens are not the ones to wear our feelings on our sleeves. They run too personal and precious for that."

"I hope you're right," McQuade muttered.

"I damned well know I'm right," Breen said calmly. "She'll come around in her own good time."

When McQuade returned to the jail, he found Curtis Granger sitting in McQuade's swivel chair in the front office, his spurred boots propped on McQuade's desk. A pleasant-faced young man in dusty trail clothes sat on the edge of the desk. McQuade assessed this young man in a brief glance, decided that he would be more at home with the fancy mother-of-pearl stocked six-shooter he wore than with a rope in his hand, and shuttled his glance to Granger.

"You look comfortable, Curt."

Granger didn't answer immediately. He took a plug of tobacco and a knife from a coat pocket, unfolded the large blade, cut a slice from the plug, and put it in his mouth, licked the blade clean, and returned plug and knife to his pocket. He eyed the marshal mournfully, a gaunt, sour-faced, bright eyed old man in a rusty black suit.

"I heard about Gus when I hit town. It's tough, McQuade."

"On who?" McQuade asked.

"On you, sonny boy." Granger got stiffly to his feet. "You're not the man old Gus was. You're not the man I am. They don't raise 'em like old Gus and me any more. We herders want a wide-open town. Gus made us toe the line, but those days are over. Gus is dead, and there's only you, and you have no one to back you. I have." He motioned to the pleasant-faced man. "Meet Reno Dawes, McQuade."

Reno grinned, the grin quirking a puckered scar at a corner of his mouth in a way that changed his face. He looked downright wicked now. "You must be getting old," McQuade said, "when you hire gunnies to back your play."

Curtis Granger twitched a shoulder upward in a regretful shrug. "That's how the ball bounces. A man gets old, and he needs a young right arm. Reno takes my orders."

"So you'll push it to gun play."

"Why, son, it'll be any way you want to name it, any way at all. All you have to do is show sense."

"Like how?"

"You have one of my boys, Wirt Crandall, in the lock-up. Free him, for a starter. Then get that damn' fool gun-check law repealed."

McQuade looked at Reno, who was grinning and tapping the butt of his gun in a seemingly absent gesture, and he thought of Nell. She might forgive a brawl, but she would never condone gun play. Yet he couldn't afford to give an inch to Granger. McQuade tried to keep the note of desperation from his voice.

"Can't we talk this over?"

"Son, you had your warning. We've said everything. You'll be seeing us." He lounged around the desk, followed by Reno Dawes, and they left.

McQuade sank into his chair and stared at the rowel-scarred desk top without seeing it. He was sharply aroused from lethargy by the cry most dreaded in this arid country.

"Fire! Fire!"

McQuade took six swift steps to the doorway of his office. Men were pouring from saloons and business buildings and running toward Lofton's stable downstreet. He could see sooty clouds of smoke erupting from the roof. McQuade joined the bucket brigade which had formed a line from the creek to the stable and was pushing at a frenzied pace to drown the livid tongues of flame licking up the tinder-dry boards. Race Deering, the owner, with a hostler, was blindfolding the panicked horses inside and leading them out. Despite the suffocating fumes that now clogged the interior, they led all the animals to safety.

It was soon evident that the building could not be saved; flames had already consumed the roof and the loft and were spreading to the inside walls. The townsmen stopped trying to save the stable and concentrated on wetting down the adjacent buildings to prevent these from catching fire. A few storekeepers and businessmen even ascended to the roofs of their respective buildings with wet gunny sacks to smother any flying sparks that might lodge in the dry shakes.

McQuade had been one of those close to the building structure, and his face and hands were blistered by heat. As the bucket line broke up, he headed back toward his office to dress his burns. Race Deering's voice caught him up short.

"I'd like a word with you, Marshal."

Deering also owned the feed store; the destroying of his stable would not break him. But now his ruddy face was an even more fiery red than usual, from heat and anger.

"Marshal, you're supposed to be the law since Gus died. He kept those wild Texans under control. Why don't you?"

"Speak your mind plain, Mister Deering."

"All right. That Texan bunch set fire to my stable on purpose."

"That's a pretty serious charge."

"A bunch of 'em went in here a while ago to put up their horses. My hostler left the stable for a minute. When he come back, the Texas men were gone and the stable was on fire, with the flames already spreading to the loft. Only a fire started by kerosene would make the flames rush up that way."

"Are you sure? A stable filled with hay is a big tinder box."

"It was a kerosene fire! I have two lanterns hanging on hooks inside, for night work. When we were getting the horses out, I noticed that both of 'em were gone. It's pretty obvious they broke 'em on a stall partition and got the fire started in such a way it couldn't be stopped. Once it hit all that hay in the loft. . . ." Other townsmen had gathered about them to listen, and there were grim mutters and nods of agreement.

"All right, Mister Deering. I'll question the Texas men, and see if I can find any witnesses."

The liveryman snorted. "Questions! Witnesses! By Jingo, if I were you. . . ."

"You're not, though," McQuade said, his voice suddenly hard, "and no private citizens will take the law into their own hands while I'm marshal of this town."

Deering opened his mouth to say more, but something in McQuade's face and tone stopped him. McQuade was only average height, and narrowly built at that, but the circle of townsmen who'd been crowding about with the shape of menace gathering in their faces was suddenly silent. Their ranks parted swiftly as he pivoted and walked through them.

In his office, he salved and bandaged the worst of his burns. Then he went out again and spent the balance of the afternoon asking questions. Deering's hostler claimed he'd seen the three Texas men running from the stable just before he returned and discovered the fire. Even in their hurry, they'd been laughing gleefully.

The hostler went with McQuade to point out these men in a saloon, and the marshal questioned them for a half hour. All were half drunk, but even so they could not be caught off guard by his point-blank questions. They blandly said, yes, they'd left the stable after putting up their horses, but, no, they hadn't started a fire; they'd come directly to this saloon and were quite surprised to learn there'd been a fire.

McQuade left the saloon, defeated and angry. On what

charge could he have them booked—suspicion of arson, with no concrete evidence that arson had even been committed? He thought: *if I take them in on that flimsy charge, Granger's crew will tear down this town around our ears.*

He returned to his office, but paused outside with his hand on the doorknob, his eye caught by a commotion downstreet. The bulk of Granger's crew—more than a score of men— were coming up from their river camp on foot, their ranks filling the street from walk to walk, augmented constantly by other herders leaving the saloons and falling in.

There was no air of jostling camaraderie to the group. A few of these men wore fixed, nervous grins, as though they were already fearful of this thing that, once begun, could not be stopped. Granger had probably inspired them with his fierce notions—but Granger was not with them. At the front of the cavalcade walked Reno Dawes, his crooked grin flashing in his hat-shadowed face. McQuade could not see Reno's eyes from here, but he knew they were pinpointed on him.

Townsmen were gathering in small knots in the doorways and on the walks, and the sense of growing tension McQuade had marked in them before was mounting like the hum of a tautly vibrating wire. Both sides, cowboys and townsmen, had begun to work themselves into the mindless mental states of a mob, which in one moment of crazed frenzy could turn men into primal animals.

Momentarily almost caught in the spell himself, McQuade shook himself free and lashed into motion. He lunged into his office and hauled down a sawed-off Greener from the gun rack. From the cell-block drifted Crandall's harsh laugh.

"You overplayed your hand this time, *mariscal.*"

"Wirt," McQuade said coldly, "if your friends kill me, the people of this town will probably lynch *you.* Think that over."

He moved back onto the walk and took up a position by

the door, the scatter-gun under his arm and pointed at the walk. His mouth was dry, but his face showed nothing to the horde of men who began to fan out as they drew abreast of the jail, ringing him about at a three yards' radius. Reno Dawes set his hands on his lean hips and laughed silently as he surveyed the lone man on whose vest glinted a tarnished badge of office.

"Well, Marshal, do you want to give us Crandall, or do we have to take him?"

"You'll take him over my dead body."

One of the men laughed, but stopped suddenly when no one else joined him. Reno grinned, easy and friendly.

"That's just possible too, Marshal. But it doesn't make too much sense. Besides, I dislike killing a man except by myself. It doesn't seem fair, somehow, with all these other fellers behind me."

"Then tell them to clear out. You and I can settle this."

Reno Dawes smiled regretfully and shook his head. "I'd sure like that, Marshal, but I have my orders from Curt. I'm supposed to tell you to let Crandall out of the clink or we'll shoot you down, take him out anyway, and then tear the whole damn' town apart."

McQuade slowly brought the shotgun to a level, centering it on Reno's chest. "I've got two loads here," he said distinctly. "I can let both barrels off before you can bring me down. The first barrel's for you, Dawes. A sawed-off rig like this will spray to hell and gone."

There was a dangerous stir of movement among the men. Reno raised his arm unhurriedly, and the movement subsided. "That's nonsensical talk, Marshal," he said matter-of-factly. "You can't take more'n a few of us that way, and the rest'll free Crandall and carry through Mister Granger's orders. You'll die for nothing . . . and a lot of these folks will get hurt because you were stubborn."

Dead silence caught and held; the ranks of the trail herders stood, unyielding. McQuade had seen, once, what a shambles a Texas crew could make of a town. They had him over a barrel; they knew it, and he knew it. His voice, when he spoke, was thick and low.

"All right, you take him. But remember this." His eyes swept the faces that were blankly walled against a show of feeling. "I know your faces now, and I have a long memory. I'll see that you pay for this . . . every last man-jack of you."

He turned and strode into the office, pulled the key ring from the wall, unlocked Wirt Crandall's cell, and pushed him out to the walk. Then he placed his boot toe in the small of Crandall's back and pushed hard, so hard that the man lunged sprawling off the walk and plunged face first into the dust.

"He's yours," McQuade said, then lifted his voice. "Now get out, the whole damned lot of you!"

He pointed the scatter-gun at the center of the throng, and they slowly dispersed, not a man meeting his eyes. They were basically good men, most of them, ashamed now.

Wirt Crandall got to his feet, red-rimmed eyes stark with his vicious thoughts as they rested briefly on McQuade, then he spat in the dust and followed the others. Reno Dawes stared at the marshal a moment, then laughed outright, and went after Crandall, clapping him on the shoulder and drawing him toward a saloon.

McQuade let out his breath with a sigh and wiped his sweaty face with his sleeve. Remembering the guilt on the Texans' faces, he knew he had not wholly lost. But half a victory held a gray taste. He entered the office, kicked the door shut behind him, and sank into his swivel chair, leaning his elbows on the desk and his face in his hands.

The soft click of the door latch aroused him a little later, and he looked up to see Nell Breen standing in the doorway, looking small, pretty, and self-contained.

"John, may I say something?"

"It's a free country."

"I only wanted to say that I saw it, and I'm proud of you."

"Proud? I backed down."

"That's why I'm proud. You're behaving sensibly, while the rest of this town is turning into a jungle." A rush of feeling came to her face, and she bit her lip. "Oh, I guess I just want you out of this job! If we were married and I had to wait out every day wondering if they'd bring you in hurt . . . or dead . . . I think I'd go crazy. You have enough money saved to go into partnership with Dad."

He stared blankly at his desk, then looked up and saw her flush.

"I'm sorry," she said. "That was forward of me."

"No," McQuade said slowly, "just honest, Nellie. And you know how I feel about you. Only I'm wondering . . . is it a man you want, or a clothes dummy behind a counter?"

She flinched, quick pain showing in her face, then turned without a word and ran from the office. McQuade came half to his feet, then sank back into his chair. *Why did I say that?* he wondered miserably. The mounting tensions he'd encountered on every side had laid an unbearable pressure against him. Still, his words had been unfair, and he had to tell her so.

Resolutely he left the office. Pausing on the walk, he saw that Nell had almost reached her father's store, and he started after her at a half run. Then he heard the shot, Wendell Breen's angry shout, and sounds of struggle inside the store, and saw Wirt Crandall and Reno come out arm in arm, laughing.

"Father!" Nell screamed, and ran toward the store.

176

As McQuade hit the boardwalk at a full run, Reno wheeled to face him, his light quick eyes laughing. "Are you looking for someone, Marshal?"

Crandall was leaning against the building for support, laughing softly, too drunk to stand by himself. A new .45 dangled from his right hand. "Yeah, *mariscal*. You name it."

McQuade shot a sideward glance through the open doorway and saw Wendell Breen groaning on the floor, Nell on her knees beside him.

He said in a brittle voice: "What did you do in there?"

Reno said innocently: "Wirt, here, wanted to buy a new gun. He loaded it up, then figured it was only fair he get a little target practice in the bargain. So he shot at a lousy can of peaches . . . and got it dead center, too. Old man Breen let out a screech you could hear clear to Texas, and jumped the kid. So Wirt just tapped him on the head with the Forty-Five barrel. I'm telling you, it's a caution the way these old cusses buck at a little good clean fun." Reno laughed and shook his head. "Peaches in a can! What'll those Eastern folk think of next?"

"I see," McQuade said levelly. "You primed the kid with drinks, got him to tell you why he was thrown in jail, then worked on his mind till he blamed his victim for his trouble. Reno, you stink."

Reno backed away, his hands beginning to lift. He was still smiling, but his eyes glittered like agates. "Marshal, that's mighty hard talk."

The liquor he had consumed during the day had finally caught up with Crandall; glassy-eyed and aimless, he began sliding down the wall of the building and fell face down, inert and sodden across the boardwalk. *One down,* McQuade thought, and lifted his gaze to the waiting Reno.

The time of decision had come; it was unavoidable now.

Reno would not let himself or Crandall be locked up without a fight. And if McQuade let it pass, it could mean the beginning of a different Sentinel—a town where every lawless element in the territory would stake its claim. It would be living testimony to the betrayal of old Gus Birnie's work and sweat and blood, which had spared Sentinel from the bloody record of the many other wide-open cattle towns.

Reno said softly: "You're wearing a gun."

McQuade began to move forward. "I don't need a gun to handle a bully who picks on kids to hurt old men."

"You're not a kid or an old man." Reno grinned coldly. "Open the ball. I'm waiting."

"What are you speaking as now . . . a self-made killer, or one of Granger's flunkies?"

"I'm speaking just for me, Marshal. Just me, Reno Dawes."

"Good," McQuade said steadily, "because I'm going to take your gun away, Reno, beat you till you can't stand, then jail you for six months."

"And you won't pull your gun," Reno said softly, then shrugged. "Come ahead, mister. I like sure things, anyhow . . . and I always did want to notch a lawman." He dropped his hand to his gun.

McQuade began to shift his weight to start forward. He felt a tug at his holster, then saw that Nell was at his side and was covering Reno with McQuade's gun clamped in both her hands. "You dirty bully," she said, "this is all you understand!" She cocked the gun.

McQuade saw her slim fingers whiten as she brought pressure on the trigger. He knocked her arm down as the gun went off, the shot slamming with a rocketing echo into the boards of the walk. Before Reno, startled and off guard, could recover, McQuade was on him, taking two swift strides forward, then launching in a dive that drove the gunman from his feet. Reno slammed on his back, his head crashing on the boardwalk and his muscles going suddenly limp.

McQuade got slowly to his feet, letting his breath out. He stared speculatively down at the unconscious gunman, adjusted his hat with a jerk, then walked back to the white-faced girl. With a muffled moan, she buried her face in his shirt. He lifted his gun gently from her nerveless fingers and holstered it.

"Hush, now, it's done."

Curtis Granger left a saloon across the way and headed directly for them, half a dozen crew men at his heels.

"John, will Granger start anything?" Nell asked.

"I don't think so," McQuade said slowly. "But he's used to being a law unto himself. You'd better go inside, Nellie."

"No! Whatever happens, I'm with you." Courage was vibrant in her hazel eyes. "It'll be that way from now on."

He tightened an arm around her shoulders, then dropped it, and faced the rancher. Granger's weathered face was ruddy with drink, but his eyes were steady and sobered.

"I'm not backing down, you understand, McQuade," he said harshly. "But I watched it, and Reno went too far. When things get so bad young ladies take up arms. . . ." He shook his head, then said with sudden belligerence: "But, look here, McQuade, what Reno did isn't the same as my regular boys letting off a little innocent steam. When I come back next fall. . . ."

"You'll observe the usual rules," McQuade said. "You'll check your guns at the jail. There'll be no riding horses into barrooms, and no throwing bottles at windows or mirrors."

Granger broke in irritably, "I know the rules! All right, McQuade, you win. And maybe you're three quarters the man Gus was. Anyway, with a woman like yours siding you, I don't see how you can lose." He tipped his hat. "Ma'am, a Texan salutes you." He said hesitantly: "Can I have Wirt?"

"I think," McQuade said evenly, "I'll let him dry out in the clink as long as your crew's in town. You can take him back to Texas, though."

They watched Granger and his men cross the street to their horses, mount up, and volley out of town. They were returning to camp to eat, but after supper they'd be back. McQuade turned to Nell, smiling. "I have a night's work ahead. You'd better see to your dad, while I lock these men up.

"All right," Nell said. "But . . . hurry back, John."

The Reckoning

Sundog was aptly named. To say it hadn't changed in five years, Hatch thought, would be like gilding the lily. To him the town had always resembled a tired, slat-ribbed cur dozing in the sun. Clattering to life overnight as a flash-in-the-pan mining town, it had survived as a ranch supply center. But its rows of false-fronted buildings, silvered and scoured by wind and sun and weather, showed its hasty origin.

Hatch reined in his gaunted sorrel by the livery barn. He stepped stiffly out of his saddle, trying to square his bull shoulders in the ill-fitting suit coat. The suit was good black broadcloth, but sizes too small for his bulk, grayed by July dust that shifted in streamers from its creases as he tramped into the barn runway, leading the sorrel.

The place was cool and dim, smelling of musty straw and the sharp ammoniac reek of dung. An unconscious scowl knit Hatch's thick black brows as he halted in the clay-floored runway, blinking against the red ache of his eyes. This old barn hadn't changed, either, except for being more rundown than ever.

Christ. What a place for a kid to grow up.

For a moment the tingle of anticipation Hatch felt was beat down by an unaccustomed twitch of panic. What did you say to a kid after five years? Tell had been only thirteen when he'd gone away. There'd been a few letters from the boy over the first couple years. After that, nothing at all.

Jesus, five years. Time enough for a boy to shape toward manhood. To change unguessably.

"Anybody here?" His voice carried hollow between the double row of stalls; a horse whickered irritably.

Moon Forney came out of the office at the rear of the barn, an immensely fat man who swayed as he stumped down the runway. A single gallus supported his greasy leather pants over his dirty underwear. His bloodshot eyes squinted above an ambush of tangled gray whiskers. He came to a stop, his jaw dropping.

"I be damned . . . Hatch. Lucas Hatch. It really you?"

"Me all right." Hatch stuck out his hand, noting that Moon's was damp with sudden sweat as he gripped it. "Still batting the jug, eh?"

Moon gave a nervous titter. "It shows, huh?"

What the hell, thought Hatch. *He's scared.*

"Where is he, Moon?"

Moon fingered his beard, grinning vaguely. "Didn't have no idea you was getting out, Lucas. You oughta get a man word."

Hatch's hand, scarred and ham-like, shot out and seized a handful of underwear, then hauled the liveryman forward till their faces were inches apart.

"You act kind of skittery, Moon. Why is that?"

"Jeezus, Lucas! You don't need to take a-holt of a man like. . . ."

Hatch's fist twisted, forcing Moon's sagging bulk up on its toes. "Then you give a man a straight answer when he asks you. *Where's my boy, Moon?*"

"He's all right! Tell's all right . . . God's sake, Lucas, you choking me!"

Hatch slowly unclenched his hand. "It could get worse, old man. A whole sight worse. Where's Tell?"

Moon backed off a step, his wreath of chins shaking. "Now you listen, old Moon done his best, Lucas. He done his level best, you hear?"

"Moon, I ain't going to ask it again."

"He gone to work for Santee Quillan, Tell has. It wa'n't no doing of mine, Lucas."

Hatch felt a deep sinking in his belly. He didn't move, just stared at Moon, who took another step back.

"Don't be skittery," Hatch said softly. "No reason to be, less'n it's your blame."

"Lucas, I swear t' you . . . !"

"Let's step back to your office, all right?"

Moon led the way into the dirty cubbyhole. He lifted a jug from under his battered roll-top desk, yanked the cork, and took a big slug. Hatch, his stare like jagged slate, grabbed the jug away and slammed it down on the desk.

"Don't stall me, Moon. Just don't stall me."

"All right . . . all right! It happent like this. . . ."

He hadn't been able to control the boy, Moon insisted. Young Tellford had taken to hanging out with a pool-hall crowd, riding high with the young toughs on the strength of his father's reputation. About a year ago some county ranchers had started complaining of penny-ante rustling; talk was that Tell and his crowd of young hoodlums were mixed in it. Sheriff Buckhart had figured he had enough evidence to jail the lot.

But before trial, the sheriff had been shot in the back from an alley. The killer was never found. Grudge murder was the verdict of the coroner's inquest, but it was whispered that Santee Quillan was behind that killing of an honest lawman in order to cinch his growing power in the county. A gun-handy henchman of Santee's, Gauche Sevier by name, had been appointed by Santee's friend, Judge Harkness, to take over the sheriff's office. Tellford Hatch and his friends had never come to trial; Santee had put up their bail money, and then the case was quietly dropped. These days Tell was seen everywhere with Santee's hardcase bunch.

Hatch took off his hat and wiped a hand over his face, slowly rubbing his eyelids.

Lord God. Where had it all started? Ten years ago he'd been a respected rancher with a wife and a sturdy young son and a home full of love and laughter. Enough to do any man proud.

Then one stinking break after another. Tearing all of it down, tearing him down as a man. The typhoid plague and Lena's death. The drought that turned his summer graze tinder-dry. The prairie fire that wiped out his grass and buildings. The desperate trail drive to Dodge to salvage something, anything. A sudden attack of Texas fever that had left his herd strung out dead and dying along the banks of the Red River.

Back in his home country, he'd organized several equally desperate neighbors for rustling strikes against still-thriving outfits, running the stolen beeves on night drives down to the Gulf Coast and a rendezvous with crooked stock buyers. In a few years Hatch had gathered a gang of tough nuts and held them together with a hard fist and a quick gun. Lucas Hatch —gunman, rustler, gang leader. Everyone had known it; none had had the proof or the nerve to do anything about it. Hatch's headquarters had been G Town, a backwoods hellhole frequented by ne'er-do-wells and bad characters of every stripe. He'd left his growing son with Moon Forney in Sundog, paying for the boy's care.

But Hatch and his gang had gone too far when they'd

broken into a Union Pacific mail car and carried off ten thousand in government gold. Hatch had been identified by a train man. Dick Clendennon, the tough U.S. deputy marshal, had come alone to G Town and calmly walked into a dive where Hatch and his gang were drunkenly celebrating. Clendennon had hit Hatch over the head with his gun, shot one of the gang who objected, carried Hatch out, slung him over a horse, and taken him to trial and a twenty-year sentence in the penitentiary.

Hatch dropped his hand, feeling the scarred-over pain surge alive once more. *Lena, Lena!* If only she had lived. But that wasn't right, either; it was like blaming the dead. He had paved his own road; it was too late for turning back.

But there was still Tell.

Moon Forney was rummaging in his desk; he dug out a pair of tin cups and sloshed both full from the jug and handed one to Hatch. "Uh, you got a parole, huh?"

Hatch looked at the cup a moment, then swigged the raw whisky, feeling it curl like hellfire in his belly. "Yeah," he said heavily. "Lucas Hatch, the model prisoner. Feature that, Moon."

Relieved at being off the hook, Moon gave a jowl-shaking chuckle.

Hatch stared into the cup. "Santee Quillan must've taken some pepper in his craw since we rode together. He always talked a big game, but I never seen him into anything bigger'n two-bit cow-lifting."

Moon swallowed his whisky to the last drop before replying. "Yeh, yeh, he runs the county now. Got his finger in ever' damn' pie that's cut. Year after you was sent away, he busted the Alhambra Casino in a big game, bet his whole pile against the house and won that. Bought a freighting business and hired gunnies to force his rivals to sell out cheap. Now he owns all the saloons in Sundog, general store, feed company, 'most everything."

"Is that right?"

"Surest damn' thing you know." Moon lowered his voice. "Runs a local rustling combine, too. Sells stolen beef through special contacts he's got down in Williamson County. Got 'most ever' elected official hereabouts under his thumb. He ain't stopping, neither. Got him some heavy pull with a political machine up in Austin, they say. . . ."

Hatch nodded slowly.

Santee had always been slick as silk, too slick for any honest crook's taste. But his smooth ways had been helpful in disposing of the crowd's stolen beef to crooked dealers. One time when he'd tried to skip out with all the proceeds and they'd caught him, the rest had been for hanging him. But Hatch had made an object lesson of Santee instead, beating him to a pulp in front of them all.

It had seemed a good idea at the time, but Santee wasn't the kind to forget; he would hold a grudge forever, biding his time. It hadn't troubled Hatch's sleep; he'd never been all that impressed by Santee Quillan. Never turn your back on the man, that was all.

That was one more mistake you made, Hatch thought. *It could just be the biggest of them all.*

He drained his cup, hitting Moon with a slate-hard look. "You could have got word to me about Tell."

"Ha, ha, now you know I can't write none, Lucas. Anyways, locked up like you was, nothing you could do, was there?"

"Where'll he be now?"

Moon shrugged. "Kind o' early, but I'd try the Alhambra. Him and that Frenchified sheriff of Santee's are thicker'n horseflies in July. Drinkin', gamblin', wenchin' around . . . ."

Hatch didn't say any more. He walked out to the street and swung south through the midday glare toward the Alhambra's garish sign a block away. His hand curled unthinkingly along his thigh, as if to grip a gun that wasn't there. The hand began to perspire, and he wiped it dry on his coat.

Shoving through the batwing doors into a smell of sawdust and stale whisky, he swung a glance across the mahogany bar and tables. The place was deserted except for a corner table where two men were bent over cards. One threw down his hand with a curse and tilted his chair back, swinging his profile into relief.

Hatch's heart thudded to his steps, hollow on the long floor, as he crossed to the table. Neither man even glanced at him.

He cleared his throat gently.

Tell turned his head. His bored young face went slack with disbelief. He got up so quickly that his chair crashed to the floor.

"Pa . . . my God. *You?*"

Hatch had the swift, brief shock of seeing the gangling boy he remembered facing him eye-level. A second shock came with what he saw in the youth's face. They had always looked a lot alike, he and Tell, and now it was as if he faced his own mirror likeness of twenty and more years ago. But there were differences, too. Hatch had worked too hard in his youth for the kind of fast living that showed in Tell's face. *Christ. He's only eighteen.*

After a long, awkward moment he stuck out his hand, and Tell took it just as awkwardly. Another difference. His own palms wore a thick horn of callus from prison work.

"You, ah, get paroled, Pa? That it?"

Hatch nodded. He was having trouble finding words.

187

"Well, Jesus. . . ." Tell's grin streaked wide and sudden across his face. "You *look* good."

"Yeah. Outside work. We got plenty of that."

"Your pa, Tell? This so-fine-looking man is your pa?"

The other card player had a soft, lazy voice, finely accented, and his fingers, gently riffling the cards, were long and fine. He stayed lazily slack in his chair, not offering to shake hands, merely nodding with a chalky little grin as Tell jerkily performed the introductions.

Gauche Sevier. Hatch knew the name but not the man. Sevier had a full olive-tinted face, his long black hair pulled to a sleek club back of his neck. A Creole dandy from the Louisiana side of the Sabine, Hatch guessed. Sevier's gun belt was cinched low on his fawn-colored pants; a sheriff's star glinted on his brocaded vest.

"Lucas Hatch," he murmured. It was the purr of a relaxed cougar. "Your prowess of the gun was heard of to New Orleans once. It sets a man to wondering."

"Well," Hatch said, "I hope you ain't too curious."

Sevier laughed, rounding his eyes. "Ah! If one is the better, *n'est-ce pas?* But *non!* Against the father of my so, so great friend, Tell? Ah, *non.*"

"You relieve me."

Tell chuckled a little nervously. "How about a drink, Pa?"

"I want to talk to you."

"Hell, you can say it in front of Gauche."

Hatch rolled his shoulders against the tight coat, feeling the anger in him gather and focus now. *Just take it slow,* he warned himself. *Five years.*

A door opened at the rear of the long room.

"Lucas, by God!" Santee Quillan was coming forward, hand extended. "Thought I knew that voice. How you doing, boy?"

Nothing to do but set your teeth and dog it out. Somehow.

Except for the pearl-gray suit tailored to his blocky body, Santee Quillan hadn't changed. His light hair was close-cropped above an oval cherub's face. Even as a nondescript and unshaven cow thief, he'd used that bland boyish charm to pave over every bump in his crooked road. Shaved and bay-rummed, he was no different. He could afford men like Gauche Sevier to handle the bumps that wouldn't smooth, that was all.

After another pleasantry or two, Santee took a couple of cigars from a waistcoat pocket and held one out.

"No," Hatch said. "Thanks."

"Well, well." Santee clipped his cigar with a small gold cutter. "Old Lucas. I can't believe it." He was smiling the smile that never reached his eyes as he lighted the cigar. "Things have changed, you know, boy. A lot of things."

"I heard."

"Well, well. No point mincing words, then. There's a good place for you in my outfit if you want it. Where you can keep an eye on Tellford." He dropped a hand on Tell's shoulder. "Coming up quite a young man, ain't he?"

Hatch held himself in with an effort. "Like you say," he said tonelessly. "I got something to tell you, Santee. Private."

"I thought you might have. Mind stepping outside, Tell?"

Tell looked uncertain; he glanced from one to the other.

"Do it, son," Hatch said tightly.

"Well, hell, ain't I got a right . . . ?"

"You heard your daddy." Santee smiled. "Take a walk, boy."

Tell wheeled and tramped angrily out the batwing doors.

Santee flicked a fractional ash from his cigar. "Don't mind if Gauche here listens in, do you?"

"Like you said, no point mincing words, Santee. I come

189

back to Sundog for one reason. To see my boy set a straight trail. You're fouling it. So step off. Just step off it, Santee."

"Um, so Lucas Hatch seen the light and done reformed. Quite a joke, eh, Gauche?"

Sevier showed his chalky smile. "It is a great joke."

"Don't be dumb, Santee. You don't want to tangle with *state* law. He's still under age, and I'm still his father."

Santee's eyes widened mockingly. "Pardon me all to hell. Guess you didn't know the court appointed old Moon Forney Tell's legal guardian after you was sent up."

"I know it, and it don't matter. Moon'll follow my lead."

"Lucas, you just don't get it, do you? You made your last tracks five years ago. I hold the whip hand now. Moon knows it. And you know Moon."

Hatch felt a cling of sweat along his belly and back. He made his voice steady. "Santee, I know why you took Tell on. But you won't need him now."

Santee lifted his brows. "No?"

"I'm here. You can do what you want with me. You don't need to stab me through the kid. Let him go."

"Who's holding him? He likes it with me."

"You can get him off that idea."

"I swear, Lucas, you must've spent your time in prison reading bad novels. Can't think where else you'd 'a' picked up all those notions. I made you an offer. Come on. Have a drink, think it over."

Hatch shuttled a glance at Sevier who was on his feet now, standing negligently hipshot, a thumb hooked in his gun belt. Then Hatch said calmly: "All right. You're forcing my hand is all. Santee, you was in on that last hold-up. I could've turned state's evidence and knocked years off my term by turning in the lot of you."

Santee nodded unconcernedly. "You want me to thank you?"

"After my release, I told the warden to get word to the U.S. deputy marshal to come to Sundog and meet me here. He ought to be along in a day or so."

Santee's eyes narrowed. "Clendennon?"

"Clendennon was never satisfied with just nailing me. I was the only one they could identify for certain. Clendennon wanted all the men in that hold-up. He visited me in prison regularly, tried to pump me. I never broke. Be a different story when he gets here. That . . . or you shuck Tell off your payroll."

"Lucas, that's a poor bluff. You didn't know what was happening with Tell till just now. I'd swear it."

"You ever hear of a prison grapevine, Santee?"

Santee's tongue flicked over his lips; slowly he shook his head. "No, Lucas. It's a bluff. It won't wash. That time you beat me to a pulp in front of a half dozen others, no one ever done that to me. Prison put you out of my reach, but not your son. I meant to build him up to worse than the swellhead pup he is, then frame him, and throw him to the law." He laughed quietly. "No way I can hurt you like that'll hurt you. Is there, Lucas?"

A red darkness sizzled in Hatch's brain. He saw Santee's pale, smiling face. Only that. He smashed out once, solidly.

Santee back-pedaled wildly and crashed into the table, taking it over with him as he fell.

"Don't move, *m'sieu* . . . again." Sevier barely whispered the words. "It is better a man has an even break . . . eh?"

Hatch rubbed a shaking hand across his mouth. He looked at the Creole's cocked and leveled pistol and slowly, slowly, let his weight relax on his heels.

Santee got to his feet, fumbling out a silk handkerchief. He

191

dabbed at his lip. He wiped his hands, eying Hatch smilingly.

"You're a fool. How about that Sevier, eh? Ever see anyone so fast with a hogleg?"

"He dumb enough to use it?"

"Don't make that mistake. Gauche will drop you in your tracks if I say the word. Of course, Tell won't be happy about that, but. . . ." Santee let one shoulder lift and fall. "He won't be unhappy long, I guarantee it. Oh, yes, I can cover both your deaths, Lucas. Sundog's my town. I can cover any damn' thing that happens in it."

Hatch didn't reply. A sickness of defeat filled his mouth.

"About Clendennon. That *was* a bluff, eh?"

"Go to hell."

"Lucas, I can cover a deputy marshal's death, too, if I have to. You better answer up."

"All right. It was a bluff."

Santee smiled pleasantly. "I believe you. You just saved your hide, boy. Your kid's, too. Tell you what now. The stage from the north will be here at one. Its run will take you south almost to the border. From there on you can spit into Mexico. Get over the river, Lucas. Don't let me hear of you on this side of it again, all right?"

"What about Tell?"

"You can't do him no good. Won't be you he'll listen to after today. *¿Comprende?*" The smile again. "What we'll do now, we'll all amble down to Moon's and wait for that stage. They switch teams there. You'll want to say so long to Tell. But careful how you say it, Lucas. Careful."

Hatch walked out ahead of the two.

Tell was pacing slowly up and down by the livery barn as they approached it, head down, thumbs hooked in his belt. He hauled up now and dropped his hands. There was no surprise in his young face; it looked guarded and sullen.

"Your pa has got to be on his way," Santee said easily. "Too bad he can't stay a spell. Pressing business, he says, down Mexico way."

Tell didn't seem to hear him. He looked at his father. "You letting 'em hooraw you out, ain't you?"

"Like he says, that's all. You take care of yourself, boy."

"I always looked up to you." Tell's voice was soft and bitter and wondering. "Man, I always bragged you to anyone'd pay ear. Always thought if you come back, man, what a pair we'd make."

"You thought that, did you, boy?"

"Hell!" Tell half shouted it. "I know there's bad blood 'twixt you and Santee! You think I didn't hear about that? But you lost your nerve. I knew it when you walked into the Alhambra 'thout no gun on! You lost your guts, or you wouldn't 'a' come to Sundog without a gun!"

Hatch glanced at Santee drawing unconcernedly on his cigar, then at Sevier who stood idly hip-cocked, one hand resting on his hip, index finger idly tapping his gun butt. He gave Hatch the edge of a warning smile.

Even if Santee didn't hold every card, what could he say? He'd given this boy of his nothing to hold pride in but a gunman and outlaw. Now even that warped grain of respect was wiped out. It wouldn't matter what he said. The twig was bent. And Lucas Hatch—more than Santee Quillan, more than anything—had done the bending.

Santee eyed Tell, slowly nodding. "You're a bright lad, Tellford. Yes, sir. But, hell, I knew it from the first. I didn't single you out from that bunch of punks you ran with for nothing."

Tell said nothing. *Did he believe Santee?* Hatch wondered. *And what if he didn't? Would the truth matter? Tell had learned his values from a source that never drew the line. So why should*

193

Tell? Even so, Hatch thought sickly, *you can't let it go like this. There has got to be something.*

Moon Forney came from the archway of the stable, leading the teams of swing horses. He halted, seeing the four of them, and scraped a palm nervously over his whiskered jaw.

"You, uh, leaving here, Lucas? Had kind of a feeling you wouldn't be 'round long. Didn't even unrig your hoss. . . ."

"Lucas has decided to take the stage," Santee said idly. "He won't need a horse. Pay him what it's worth, Moon."

"Not much, that crowbait," mumbled Moon. "Ain't worth more'n twenty dollar."

"He'll take it. Get the money and his saddle." A wicked mockery flicked Santee's tone. "You want your saddle, don't you, Lucas? You can trade it for a barrel of sour wine down in pepper-gut country."

In a couple minutes Moon came out, lugging the saddle and dropped it to the ground. The stage, with a thunder of hoofs and rattle of harness, came rolling in from the north end of town as Moon thumbed some banknotes off a greasy wad of them and handed them to Hatch, not meeting his eyes. Hatch pocketed the bills and bent to pick up his saddle.

The stage careened to a stop in front of the archway. Santee moved over to the front boot, saying to the driver: "Any mail this trip, Bowie?"

Hatch tramped toward the rear boot, holding his saddle. He glanced through the stage window at its single passenger. Then, facing the coach broadside, he froze in his tracks, a coldness balling his guts. He saw a hawk face chiseled from brown granite, the hawk eyes fixing him like a target. For a moment he couldn't believe it. And then he didn't want to. Clendennon.

Santee was still talking to the driver, and Sevier's face was turned that way. Yet Hatch was paralyzed for the moment. Clendennon's arm thrust out the window and turned the door latch. His tall form bent almost double through the tight doorway as he began to step down.

Santee's gaze swung casually toward him. Shock blazed across Santee's face. Then his hand darted into his coat and came out with a double-barreled pocket pistol.

"Gauche . . . that's Clendennon . . . !"

Sevier's hand blurred down and up, cocking his gun as it came level.

Clendennon's hard eyes moved from Hatch to Santee. "Quillan, what the hell is this?"

"You'll never know," Santee whispered. His lips pulled back from his teeth. "You bluff better than I knew, Lucas. Now . . . there'll be an incident of sorts. The deputy marshal and a stage driver were killed in Sundog by an unknown gunman. That's all anybody will ever find out. You bluffed too damn' well, Lucas. Now you'll watch it . . . the way I said."

Tell stood white and slack-jawed as the Creole's .45 swung to cover him. Lifting Tell's gun from its holster, Sevier dropped it in his coat pocket. He twitched a faint, sorrowful shrug. "I'm sorry for this, my friend. You were a *bon camarade. . . .*"

Whirling suddenly, Hatch threw his saddle, thrusting it out with the heels of his hands and releasing his grip. The heavy rig, backed by all the force of his heavy arms and shoulders, hit Sevier in the chest and knocked the slender gunman spinning, his gun blasting off side. He fell over the coach tree and rolled between the wheeled horses.

In the same instant Hatch balled his body and lunged sideways at Santee. The pocket pistol barked almost in his face. Hatch felt a sledging impact in his arm. Then he slammed

195

full-tilt into Santee, and they went down together.

Santee landed on his back, clawing and kicking against Hatch's weight. His right arm was doubled against his chest, pinned there by Hatch's body. Then he yanked it free, clubbing his pistol blindly at Hatch's head. A savage cuff of Hatch's fist sent the weapon flying. He surged to his feet, dragging Santee with him.

A gunshot crashed behind them, but Hatch didn't turn his head. All the pent fury boiled out of him in one smashing blow. Santee's knees folded. Hatch held him erect by the fist-doubled shirtfront, pulling his other fist back for another full-arm blow.

"That's enough!"

Clendennon's voice cracked like a whip. Hatch swung a red stare at the lawman and his drawn pistol. Then he let Santee's limp body crumple to the ground.

Sevier lay face down in the dirt where he'd scrambled from beneath the team. Blood darkened the dust by his head.

"Had to shoot," Clendennon said. "He was pulling a bead on your back. You hit?"

Hatch grimaced. The numbness was going from his arm, and the pain had begun, savage and tearing. Blood dripped off the ends of his fingers. His knees felt weak. He had the deathly feel of a man reaching the end of something.

"Still no sawbones in this town, I take it," said Clendennon.

"No, sir," Moon said shakily. "I got some red-eye back in the office."

Tell was still rooted where he stood, his face white and stunned.

"You. . . ." Clendennon's voice made Tell jump as if he'd been stung. "Give your pa a hand inside."

Santee Quillan groaned. Clendennon gave Hatch a hard,

wry look, then pulled a set of handcuffs from his pocket, bent and snapped them on Santee's wrists, and hauled him to his feet.

Supported by his son, Hatch tramped down the stable runway to the office. Clendennon growled an order that held back a handful of people drawn by the ruckus, then followed with Santee in tow. Hatch settled himself on the single rickety chair in Moon's office. After he'd taken a slug of whisky, Clendennon helped him work off his coat.

"You give this garment quite a stretch," the lawman observed dryly. "That drummer's coat's just middling size."

Hatch eyed him dully. "Thought here'd be the last place the law would think I'd come. And how in hell you catch up so fast? I come straight here after busting out."

"Don't be a damned fool," Clendennon grunted. "Where else would Lucas Hatch go?"

He talked tersely as he cut away the bloody shirt from Hatch's arm with his pocketknife. He said that the warden had telegraphed his office, informing him that Hatch had escaped from a gang working outside the walls. Clendennon, judging Hatch would head nowhere but where his son was, had picked up the trail at once. His horse had gone lame on the road, the lawman said, or he'd have made better time. Clendennon had spoken with a traveling man who'd been attacked on the road by a fellow in convict's clothes, a man who'd come barreling out of the brush, leaped on the drummer's wagon, and knocked him out. When the drummer had come to, his clothes were gone and one of the horses, as well as a saddle rig from his sales stock.

"Somehow," Clendennon concluded in his dry, acid way, "I figured I was on the right track."

Moon Forney's jaw dropped. "I be dogged. They wa'n't no parole, huh? He busted out . . . ?"

"I'm wondering why," Clendennon said grimly. "He had a fine prison record. Would've got half his sentence knocked off for good behavior. He knew damn' well I'd track him into Mexico if I had to."

Hatch stirred his shoulders wearily. "Even another year in the pen was too long, way I felt. No word from my boy. Had to see him once more . . . see how he was."

Tell was leaning his back to the wall, arms folded, staring doggedly at the floor. He didn't look up. But he moved in a hurry when Clendennon, after examining the wound, snapped at him to lend a hand.

The bullet had passed clean through without touching bone, and the exit wound wasn't as bad as Hatch had feared. That lady's gun of Santee's, Clendennon observed as he cleaned and bandaged the hurt, wasn't worth shucks past a yard away.

Finished, Clendennon jerked a curt nod at Santee, sitting on the floor, cuffed hands wiping his bleeding nose with a handkerchief.

"I want to hear what happened with him. All of it."

Hatch told him, watching Tell as he talked. Before he was done, the boy was looking straight at him.

"I . . . I should have known better." Tell swallowed hard. "You was letting Santee run you out to keep us both alive. I thought . . . well, I thought you changed. . . ."

"He changed," Clendennon said in a flat, cold voice. "Cut sign of this, boy. Kind of bargain-sale guts it takes to make Santee's kind of crook ain't worth a penny on the dollar. I kept a close track on your pa in prison. It never changed him. I never seen prison make a better man of anyone. Hatch changed himself. If you don't know why he done it yet . . . well, boy, you just wasn't worth it."

Tell flushed. "Guess I see it all right."

"I reckon so will the governor. Happens to be a friend of mine." Clendennon rubbed his chin, jutting it in the way of a man who'd made up his mind. "We're that close, we don't balance out favors no more. All the same, I don't ask 'em lightly. I got to know a man. I got to know your pa pretty well, hoorawing him off and on these five years. Might've stepped for him before except he never would give me some names I wanted."

Tell's mouth opened. "You mean Pa . . . you can fetch Pa a pardon?"

"Not right off, no. Not after he busted prison. But there's his reason and some good results besides. Santee here. We been trying to get some goods on him a long time. That's enough to get things moving." Clendennon's cold glance shifted to Hatch. "He's got a lot going for him, your pa. The governor's a family man. Knows what it is to have a son to get steered the right way."

Hatch felt shaky with more than pain. He started to his feet, then winced, and sank back. "Lend me a hand, Tell. . . ."

It was good to see his son move as fast to that quiet order as he had to Clendennon's tough ones.

The Broken Spur

Rainesford left Signal's dust-rutted main street and turned right of Pogue's general store, leaving the shop-lined thoroughfare for the residential fringe of the little town. Approximately a half-block walk brought him to a brief view of whitewashed one-story frame houses, each with its distinctive touches.

Here, beneath the spreading cottonwoods lining the dirt street and flowered lawns, the cooler air was a relief after the glaring, dusty main street of late afternoon, and Rainesford pulled off his hat and fanned his head, his black hair close-ringleted with sweat damp along the temples. At a smaller house with a white picket fence he turned in, a big-shouldered, whittle-hipped man of thirty on whose gray flannel shirt glinted a dust-dulled sheriff's badge.

He stepped into the house, the door already propped open to catch any chance breeze, sailed his hat onto the leather-upholstered sofa, called—"Anyone home?"—and paused there in the doorway, his dark eyes set and somber against what must follow now.

His wife, Laura, an auburn-haired girl only a few inches shorter than he, came in from the kitchen in a frilly apron, her face flushed from the heat augmented by a hot stove, kissed him, and asked: "How was it today, breadwinner?"

"Want to know?" he asked eagerly in a voice that brought a swift, grave concern to her gray eyes.

"What is it, Lou?"

"Your Uncle Harvey. I . . . put him in jail today, Red."

Laura sank onto the sofa, her hands falling to her lap. Her eyes on him held no expression at all. "What was the charge, Lou?"

He looked carefully at the floor; his square, tough face seemed graven from mahogany. "Murder."

She repeated the word in a voice soft with terror. "Murder. He couldn't murder anyone."

"I know that," murmured Rainesford. "But Frank Sales is dead over in the hotel. With a bullet through his brain. And Harvey was found kneeling beside the body, half drunk. The desk clerk and Tracey found him."

"I don't want to hear it!" Laura said, coming to her feet, a wild timbre to her voice. She started past him toward the kitchen, then wheeled to face him. "I don't care what evidence you found. Harvey never murdered anyone!"

Rainesford pulled out his pipe, irritation cutting his voice thin. The past hour had drawn his nerves taut. "With his tonsils varnished with booze every waking minute, I grant you he wouldn't do it consciously, anyway," he said dryly.

Laura's mouth thinned, and she walked wordlessly on to the kitchen. Rainesford sifted tobacco into his pipe, tamped it down harder than necessary, and lighted it, then sank onto the sofa, hunched forward with a troubled look, his elbows on his knees. *Well, damn it, I had to tell her,* he thought. *My fault she was bound to take it that way?*

They ate supper in silence, and afterward, over coffee, he said: "Want to go down and see him?"

Without looking at him, she said: "Wait till I get my shawl."

When they stepped out, the coolness of evening was touching the air. They walked a block in silence, Rainesford pulling out his pipe in troubled introspection. Finally he said quietly: "Look at it this way, Red. It's my job. If it wasn't mine, it'd be someone else's. I'll do all I can, but first I'll do my job. That's what I'm wearing this hunk of shiny tin for."

She took his arm. "I've had time to think, Lou." She looked up at him. "It hasn't been any bed of roses for you, either."

"No," he agreed.

They turned the corner onto Main Street and came abreast of his office. He held the door open for her, and they went in. A lamp burned on the roll-top desk, and young Tracey Eagan, the deputy, sat there, playing his concertina, his boots on the desk.

"You can go and eat now, Tracey."

"Eaten," Tracey said. "Hello, Laura."

"Hello, Tracey," she said, but her anxious eyes sought the cell-block.

Rainesford pulled the big key ring from the wall, and turned to Tracey. "Listen, put your damn' feet on the floor and quit running those rowels over my desk, will you?"

Tracey grinned brashly, tilting his hat back on his corn-shock hair and not moving his feet. "Yes, boss, yes, boss." He struck up a fresh tune and sang in a soft banter, telling Susannah not to cry.

Rainesford went back to the cell-block, Laura behind him, and paused before Harvey James's cell, unlocking it and pulling it open as Harvey came to his feet, a stout, very short man with a saintly ruff of white hair encircling a shining bald dome. He was stark sober, and, because he was never accustomed to being entirely sober, his hands were shaking like a palsied man's. A single gallus supported his patched trousers over his dirty underwear.

Laura entered the cell and made him sit down. "Why did you do it?" was her first question.

"I didn't, damn it, Laura!" he said angrily. "I was in the saloon when someone gave me a note saying Frank Sales wanted to see me in his room over at the hotel."

Rainesford locked the cell door, leaned against the bars outside, smoking while he watched Harvey. The man was a weakling, he knew, a boozing lightweight—but not a murderer. Also, he thought, troubled, he was Laura's only living relative. He waited, arms folded politely, while Harvey told Laura the story he had already heard.

"Well, I went to Frank's room. He was layin' there . . . blood under his head. Then Earl Herbie, the desk clerk, was shakin' me, and Tracey, they was sniffin' my gun." His voice was trailing off pitifully.

Laura shook him. "Harvey, Harvey, who gave you the note?"

The old man buried his face in his hands. "I don't know, Laurie. I told Lou that. Why you keep heckling me? I can't remember. I was too drunk."

"But you have to!" She broke off, seeing the futility of remonstration. Then she glanced quickly at Rainesford. "Lou, he couldn't have done it if his gun wasn't fired."

Rainesford said morosely, not meeting her eyes: "It was, though, Red. One chamber had a spent slug. And when Tracey smelled his gun, he says he smelt fresh-burned powder."

Laura said desperately: "Harvey, did you hear the shot?"

"I don't remember, Laurie, I just don't. Can't you let me alone?"

She sighed. "What about the bullet, Lou?"

"We found it in the wall by the window. It was a

Forty-Five. So is Harvey's gun."

"Lou, you've got to do something!"

"I've got to do my job, Red," he said roughly.

A quick, angrily drawn breath lifted the silken basque of her dark dress. "Yes, of course . . . it would be awful if you were found lying dead in a pool of your own manly pride."

The tension in him broke on his face in a swift, pale rage. He wheeled and walked from the cell-block and out of the office, slamming the door behind him. Outside, he stood for a moment, his dead pipe clasped between his teeth. *I'll talk to Earl again,* he thought, and started through the cooling dusk toward the hotel upstreet.

One thing he hadn't mentioned to Laura was that Earl Herbie, the desk clerk, had sworn he had heard two shots, although only one had hit Sales, going through his head to embed in the wall behind him. There was only one empty chamber in Harvey's gun, yet Earl had seemed certain he had heard two shots. Sucking on his pipe, Rainesford thought, scowling: *None of it makes sense.*

The murderer was the town drunk, an ineffectual, likable old booze-head. The murdered man was a small, nattily dressed stranger who had been in town for only two days, who had stayed at the hotel, bought drinks lavishly, and asked many questions. No one knew Sales's business, although everyone knew of him, of course, in a small frontier town like Signal, and everyone speculated. Why should anyone, particularly Harvey, kill him? No one at the saloon had noticed who'd given Harvey the note from Sales.

Rainesford turned from the darkened boardwalk into the deserted hotel lobby that was empty except for Earl Herbie, who was leaning back in his chair, squinting through his glasses at an old newspaper. A lamp overhead gave meager light.

Herbie looked up as Rainesford came over to stand by the desk. The clerk was a short, balding man in his shirt sleeves. His mere face revealed nothing.

"Hello, Lou," he said, throwing the paper on the desk.

Rainesford folded his arms and leaned his elbows on the desk. "Earl, you positive you heard two shots?"

"Damn it, Lou, I'd swear to it." Earl leaned forward, frowning a little. "Harvey came about four, drunk, and asked me where Frank Sales's room was. Then he went upstairs. A few seconds later, I heard the shots. I ran over to your office and got Tracey, and we went up and found Harvey kneeling alongside of Sales."

Rainesford nodded uneasily. He had heard this story after he'd ridden in a half hour after the murder. He had been warning some squatter off Joe Kline's homestead.

"Harvey had time enough between when he left and you heard the shots to get up to Sales's room?"

Earl pursed his mouth. "He was pretty drunk. Yes, I'd say he had time." He clucked sympathetically. "Tough, him being Laura's uncle."

Rainesford thoughtfully nudged the wastebasket by the desk with his toe. "All right, Earl, I guess that's. . . ."

He was suddenly rigid all over as his gaze fixed blankly on the wastebasket, snapping into focus as it scanned the address on a half-crumpled envelope lying on top of other rubbish in the basket.

Mr. F. Sales
Signal Hotel
Signal, Arizona Terr.

In an instant, he had found the letter to Sales beneath the envelope. It was also crumpled, and he smoothed both out on the desk, and read them. The letter was in fine women's script and sent from Tucson. With care he read it through, and his dark eyes were not pleasant as he raised his gaze to regard Earl.

The clerk was sweating, trying not to look at him. His mean face gleamed ruddily, and he mopped it with his handkerchief.

Rainesford said gently, tapping the letter: "Know what's in here, Earl?"

"How would I?"

"It's to United States Marshal Frank Sales from his wife, Jane. Sales's last letter. Too bad he never got it."

Earl said automatically: "What d'you mean?"

"I mean, you've been opening Sales's letters."

"That ain't so! He flung that letter in the basket himself this afternoon after I give it to him and he read it."

Rainesford smiled slowly. "After the murder you told me Sales hadn't left his room all day." He circled the desk swiftly, caught a handful of Earl's boiled shirt front, and hauled him to his feet. "Why'd you open Sales's letter? Someone pay you?"

Earl choked a little as Rainesford twisted his shirt, but said nothing.

Rainesford said softly: "There's been a murder, Earl. I can lock you up as an accomplice, unless you talk."

"All right, Lou. Let me go. It was Chet Mallinson. He paid me to open all Sales's mail and let him read what was inside."

Mallinson, Rainesford thought disbelievingly. He let go of Earl. Mallinson was the wealthiest rancher within a hundred miles. Sales had been a United States marshal, according to this letter. It was this information Mallinson had wanted, and it must have been Mallinson who killed Sales, believing Sales was after him, then somehow threw the killing on Harvey.

"What did Mallinson want to know?"

"He didn't say. But when he read this letter, he was het up. Crumpled it up, flung it in the basket, and walked out."

"You read it, of course," Rainesford said dryly.

Earl flushed. "I couldn't make nothing of it."

"You're lying. You were damn' good and scared when Sales was murdered after Mallinson read that letter. But too scared to talk. There's a penalty for tampering with the U.S. mail, Earl. I'll see *you* later."

He turned and walked from the hotel. He stepped from the boardwalk, ducked under the rail, and angled across the street toward Gabe's saloon. Mallinson should be there; he usually made it every evening, rain or snow. Shouldering the batwings aside, he paused in the doorway, his gaze raking down the line of men at the long, crowded bar. Not seeing his man immediately, he stepped inside, and strode down to the end of the bar, identifying each man in turn through the stirring strata of tobacco smoke. Reaching the far wall, he turned and scrutinized the tables, and playing solitaire at a corner table, a whisky bottle at his elbow, was Mallinson, a great, beefy man with hard, weather-burned features, surrounded by close-cropped, snow-white hair.

Rainesford headed directly for him, and Mallinson looked up, his big hands still on the table, and Rainesford saw the guilt and fear wash thinly across his face and a quick wariness succeed this. Rainesford quickened his pace, and, knowing suddenly what had happened, Mallinson's nerve cracked, and he came to his feet, his chair crashing over in his haste, and went for the door.

Rainesford broke into a run, and they reached the batwings simultaneously. Their combined weight split the swinging doors apart with a crash, and both pitched onto the boardwalk. Rainesford reached his feet first and hauled

Mallinson up with no gentleness, an iron grip on his doubled-up shirt front.

"Speak up, Chet!" he said harshly, tightening his grasp. "Why'd you kill Sales?"

"I didn't kill Sales, damn you!"

Rainesford glared in an angry arc at the circle of gathering onlookers and addressed them: "All right, go about your business. Hurry it up."

As the crowd dispensed, muttering, Rainesford pushed Mallinson down the walk ahead of him toward his office. There, he nudged him inside. Tracey stopped playing his concertina as they entered, regarding Mallinson in surprise.

"Sit down," Rainesford said, nodding to a chair, and added to Tracey: "I thought I told you to quit marking up my desk. Now take those spurs down and damn' fast."

Some driven, harried note in his quiet voice made Tracey swing his feet off the desk, still regarding Mallinson curiously. "What'd he do, Lou?"

Rainesford sat down on the edge of the desk, swinging one leg up over the corner. "Why was Sales after you?" he asked Mallinson.

Mallinson regarded Rainesford shrewdly for a moment, and something in the sheriff's face warned him not to stall. He said heavily: "Last year I had a beef contract with the San Pimos reservation. The Indian agent there bought underweight cull scrub steers cheap from me and pocketed the difference in the allotted government funds. I was glad to get rid of the stuff." He paused and wiped the back of a hand across his ruddy, sweat-gleaming forehead. "About a month ago, I heard the Army had arrested him after some of the reservation siwashes took sick on his bad beef. I knew, if he talked, they'd be after me for violation of my contract. When Sales showed up in town and asked a lot of questions, I thought he might be a government agent, checking up preparatory to arresting me. So I bribed Earl to open his mail. I found out from the letter today he was a U.S. marshal. That's all."

"Not quite," murmured Rainesford. "You killed him and made Harvey James the goat."

"You go to hell," said Mallinson, his pale, shrewd eyes intent on Rainesford's face. "I was at Gabe's all afternoon, right there in the corner, before and after Sales was killed. You go ask Gabe."

"I will," said Rainesford. "For the time, I'll lock you up where you can't hurt anyone else."

"I didn't kill him."

"You hired someone to do it, then, which comes to the same thing. The government will be interested in your story."

He pulled his gun and motioned Mallinson toward the cell-block, putting him in the cell next to Harvey's. As he locked the door, Mallinson grasped the bars. "You can't hang me for Sales's murder, Rainesford. Ha, ha! If anyone hangs, it's Harvey."

Laura had heard everything from Harvey's cell, and she came over to the bars and gripped them. "Lou, is he right?"

He jangled the keys in his right hand. "Afraid so," he said gravely. "I'm going to take another look around Sales's room. Want to come along?"

"Yes." She patted Harvey's hand. "Don't worry, we'll find something."

Rainesford unlocked the door, let her out, and re-locked it. He left the keys with Tracey, and they walked over to the hotel. As they walked, she laced the fingers of one hand through his. "I've acted terribly."

"Agreed," he said, and that was all, and they walked on in the familiar closeness.

Rainesford went directly to the hotel desk.

"Earl, you didn't lie about hearing two shots?"

"No. It was straight, that part of it, Lou. I swear it." There was fear behind Earl's eyes, and Rainesford could believe him.

He wordlessly turned from the desk and started up the stairs, Laura at his side. Her voice was excited. "Lou, he did hear the shots!"

"That's what he says. Harvey was too drunk to remember hearing anything."

He opened the door to Sales's room and lighted the lamp. It was a small, dirty room with a dresser and bed. Sales's body had been removed to the undertaker's parlor, but recalling its position on the floor by the bed Rainesford believed that Sales had been sitting on the edge of the bed when he was shot.

He showed Laura the bullet hole in the wall by the window. "He was shot from the doorway, you see, and the bullet went on to lodge here."

Laura looked at the open window, the soiled curtains bellying inward under the night breeze. "Couldn't he have been shot from the window ledge? That would explain how the murderer got away."

He smiled tolerantly. "It doesn't explain how he got up to the window, though, Red. This is the second story. Besides, the bullet was found beside the window. If Sales was shot from the window, the murder slug would be in the opposite wall, by the desk."

"Let's look," she said, and started examining the wall by the door.

He began to laugh, then choked it off as she cried: "Look! Lou, here it is."

He dug the bullet out of the wall with his knife.

Laura's eyes shone. "This explains the second shot, Lou!"

He nodded, as he stoked up his pipe. The murderer had waited on the window ledge for Harvey to arrive, lured by a false note. When he heard Harvey's footsteps in the corridor, he shot Sales through the open window, then stepped into the room long enough to fire a second bullet into the wall by the window, so it would appear that Harvey had shot Sales from the doorway. Sales had probably been dozing on the bed, and had been rising, awakened by Harvey's footsteps in the corridor, when he was shot.

He smiled at Laura. "This clears your uncle, Red. And I still haven't got a killer, but I do have a dang' smart wife. Let's take a look around that shed."

In the lobby, he borrowed a lantern from Earl, and they went outside to search around the shed. It was a low structure of scrap slabs with tarpaper nailed over the roof. It wouldn't have been hard climbing onto it. The tarpaper was grooved where the man had slid off, and on the edge of the eaves Rainesford caught a bright twist of steel in the lantern glow. He took hold, pulled it free—a broken spur rowel that had been wedged in a split in a crack of a weather-warped roofing board, and he thought: *Caught it in here when he jumped off and broke it. Too hurried to notice.*

It was the size of a silver dollar, broken off with part of the shank. He passed it to his wife. She turned it in her hand wordlessly, then gave it back, saying wearily: "Should we advertise for the owner?"

Rainesford grinned wryly.

They returned the lantern and walked back to the office. Tracey wasn't in the office when they got back, possibly having stepped out for a drink. They went to Harvey's cell, and Laura was telling him the news and watching his face brighten when Tracey came in. Rainesford didn't have to look around to know it was Tracey.

Those damned jangling spurs! he thought, and the thought froze in his mind.

He could hear the rattle of a spur at only every other step as Tracey walked from the door to the desk. Rainesford walked from the cell over to the desk to confront Tracey who already had his feet on it and was starting to swing them down when he saw Rainesford.

"No, leave 'em there, Tracey," said Rainesford, his voice idle and pleasant.

Tracey looked surprised, but agreed.

Still pleasantly Rainesford said: "This yours?" He pulled out the broken rowel and tossed it on the desk.

Tracey picked it up. "Mine, all right. Was wondering where I lost it. Where'd you find it?"

A cold, wary excitement held Rainesford. He said softly: "Where you left it when you jumped from the ledge outside Sales's room."

For the space of four empty silent seconds, Tracey stared unmoving at Rainesford, gauging his chances, then moved, hand streaking for his holstered gun.

The shot was deafeningly contained by the small office.

Laura came running back from the cell. "Lou! Lou!"

Rainesford let out his breath. "All right, Laura. Tracey won't be using his arm for a while, though. Good thing he won't be needing it."

After the doctor had attended to Tracey's arm, Rainesford locked him up with Mallinson who admitted now that he'd hired Tracey to kill Sales. Tracey countered with an accusation of his own, and back and forth it went till it came out that Mallinson had put an expended cartridge in Harvey's gun while he was sleeping off a drunk and that Tracey had given Harvey the faked note from Sales. They were still bitterly accusing one another when Rainesford locked up the office for the night, and he and Laura and Harvey started down the street.

"That's what happens," Rainesford said gloomily, "when you hire footloose saddlebums for deputies. Tracey hasn't been with me a month."

Laura said: "I'm just glad it's over."

"Right, Laurie," said Harvey. "That cured this child. Through with booze for life."

They were opposite Gabe's now, and Harvey stepped off the walk and started across the street.

"That was a short life," observed the sheriff.

"Hell, a man's got to taper off," said Harvey James without stopping.

The Man We Called Jones

The gun? The .45 hanging over the mantel? Why, sure, look at it. Look at it, but don't handle the belt, son. It's old, over sixty years old. Leather's brittle, hasn't been worked. Like to fall apart. Why do I keep it there? I can tell you a story about it, if you want. Really a story about the man who owned it. The bravest and best man I ever knew.

It was way back, the summer of 1890. This same valley. I was seventeen the previous year. You weren't yet a twinkle in your pappy's eye, so it'll take a sight of doing for you to see it as it was then. You made your way by team, by horseback, or walked. Roads were mud, mud, mud.

The valley was all big ranches, or rather mostly one big ranch. That'd be Kurt Gavin's Anchor. Gavin came into the country early after the last tide of gold-seekers was drifting out, drove his stakes deep and far, and, being a little bigger and a little tougher than most others, he made it stick. By 1890 with the Cheyennes long pacified and the territory opened to homesteading, Gavin was the biggest man in the valley, nigh the biggest in the territory. Even his swelling herds couldn't graze the whole of the open range he laid claim to. Least, that's what the homestead farmers figured. Or sodbusters, as the cattlemen called 'em . . . the *damned*

214

sodbusters who came in with their plows and chewed up the good graze. Which is what we did in Gavin's eyes to the range he called his, because Uncle Jace and me were among the first. We'd had strong ties back in Ohio, but my ma had been dead a good many years. Typhoid pneumonia had taken Pa in 1889. Uncle Jace and Pa had been mighty close brothers. They'd run the farm together for years, and the old home held too many memories for Uncle Jace. He hadn't any family or close kin left, 'cept for me, and nothing to hold him from pulling stakes for the West, which he'd always wanted to do.

A year after Pa's death saw me and Uncle Jace running a shoe-string outfit on Gavin's east range. Gavin gave word to his riders to hooraw us off, and I tell you those high-spirited lads made our lives some miserable, what with cutting our bob-wire and riding short cuts through our fields, or riding past the house of a midnight after a drunk in town, screeching, shooting at the sky. You could call Uncle Jace a peaceable man, but he was that stubborn he wouldn't budge off what was his by law. And when Gavin's crew pulled down a whole section of fence by roping the posts and dragging it away with the ponies, Unc's temper busted. Him and me were out scouting boundary that morning when we found the fence down and some Anchor cows foraging in the young corn. They'd even left one rope on the fence to make their sign plain.

Unc was mad clean through, though not so's you could see it . . . 'less you knew Unc. Me helping, he hazed the cows out cool as you please, and we got tools and repaired the fence, Uncle Jace giving brief jerky orders in as few words as needed. Afterward, grimy and soaked with sweat, he turned to me. "Get on your horse, Howie. I'm going to see Gavin."

We cut across Anchor land on a beeline for the ranch headquarters, Uncle Jace riding ahead. He was a huge-framed man, though so leaned-down with hard work the clothes hung on him like tattered cast-offs on a scarecrow. Even so, with the big back of him erect and high in his wrath, I could almost hear his rage crackle across the space between us. Unc didn't pack a sidearm. He had his old Union issue Spencer .54 in the saddle boot under his leg, and I'd seen him drive nail heads with it, and I was some squirrelly, I tell you.

It must have been ten minutes later when we sighted the little knot of horsemen off to our left, and Unc quartered his bronc' around so we were headed for them. I caught his thought, then—that these were the jiggers who pulled the fence down and ran that Anchor beef through the break. Coming near up, we saw all five of them were mounted but now moving, and then we saw why. They were grouped under one of the big old ironwood trees you don't see any more, and there was a rope tied to a spreading bough. The end of the rope was noosed around the neck of one of them, a little fella with his hands tied at his back. They were all of them motionless, waiting on our approach.

The little one I'd never seen, but the other four all were Anchor crewmen I recognized—one of them Gavin's tough ramrod, Tod Carradine. He was a tall, pale-eyed Texan with ice in his smile, cocky, sure of himself. The others were ordinary 'punchers with the look of men ready for a dirty job they didn't relish, but held to be necessary.

"Howdy, Tod," Uncle Jace said in a voice easy-neutral without being friendly. "Hemp cravat for the man?"

"Why, yes, Devereux," said Carradine in a voice amused, also without being friendly. "You ever see this little man before?"

Unc shook his head, no, without taking his eyes off Carradine. He wasn't worried about the others.

Carradine pointed lazily at the hip of the horse the little

fella sat. It bore an Anchor brand. "We found him hypering off our range on his bronc'." Carradine smiled, altogether pleasant. "Suit you, Devereux?" he then asked in a voice suggesting he didn't give a damn how Unc was suited.

It was open and shut, far as I could see. A stranger had been caught riding off Anchor range on an Anchor horse. The answer for that was one no Westerner would argue. That's why I was surprised when Uncle Jace's glance shuttled to the little fella.

"Friend," Unc said quietly, "speak out your say. It's your right. How'd it happen?"

The little man looked up slowly. His head had been bent, and I hadn't seen his face full till now. It was shocking, pitiful, ravaged somehow in a way I couldn't explain. He gave a bare tilt of his head toward Carradine, murmured—"However he says."—and looked down again.

Carradine smiled fully at Unc. He repeated: "Suit you, Devereux?"

"Not quite." Uncle Jace frowned, looking back at the Anchor foreman.

Carradine was still smiling, but uncertainly. It had only come to him then what this was building to. He was the only Anchor man packing a gun, and I saw the instant impulse chase through his mind. Uncle Jace didn't waste time. He never wasted time, or words, either. Somehow the old Spencer cavalry carbine was ready to his hand, and he laid it light across the pommel. "Don't even think about it, Tod," Unc advised mildly. "Howie, cut the gent loose. Give him a hand down. Tod, take what's yours and keep your dogs off my fence line. Or I'll larrup you out of this valley at the end of a horsewhip."

Carradine's hands hung loosely, his eyes hot and wild-wicked. He said: "I'll mind this, Devereux!"

"Do that. I'd kind of deplore having to remind you," Unc said mildly.

We silently watched the four Anchor men out of sight. I found my voice. "Unc, we going to see Gavin?"

"We won't have to. He'll hear about this."

Uncle Jace got off his horse, only now taking a close look at the raggedy drifter, and his eyes went quick with a pitying kindness as his hand went out. "I'm Jace Devereux. My nephew, Howie. We homestead over east."

The little horse thief looked at Unc in a grave, considering way. He said in a deep bass voice, startling in such an under-size man: "My name is Jones. I'd admire to work for you. For nothin'."

Unc looked at the hand in his own, seeing it crossed with rope scars. "Well, now, as a cowman, ain't you afraid of some farm stink wearing off on you?"

"I'd admire to work for you," Jones repeated, adding: "for nothin'."

I knew a kind of warm feeling for this runty, spooky-looking gent with his sad and faded eyes looking up from the shadow of his Stetson at Unc's great height. And glancing at Uncle Jace, I saw he felt the same.

Unc said in his rich, big voice: "Come along, and hang up your hat, Jones."

That was the way of it, and Jones settled into the workaday routine of the farm, as natural a part of it as the buildings themselves, already dry and gray and weather-beaten. Jones was all of those, too. He was that colorless he might have been anywhere from thirty-five to fifty-five. He fitted to the new work like an old hand, so quiet you'd hardly know he was there but for the new-improving ways the farm began to shape up.

He stayed, and we called him Jones, just Jones. He never

gave another name, and we never asked. I reckoned Unc had been shamed into hiring him. Shamed by the little fella's offering his services for nothing, though the main reason he'd saved Jones was to retaliate on Anchor and show what he thought of all its power. Jones must have known that. How could life kick a man into such a corner he could be so beggar-grateful? It was as though no one'd done him even a half-hearted kindness till now.

I saw him right off as a man a boy could tie to. He worked alongside Uncle Jace who was twice his size and three times his power, and he let Unc set the pace. He'd be so tired he could barely stand, and never a whisper. Watching him hump alongside Uncle Jace in the fields, he cut a comical, earnest figure that made you want to laugh and cry all at once. It might be that I'd laugh, and sometimes, if you laughed too hard, he had a way of looking at you that made you feel you'd need a ladder to reach a snake's belly. But there was another special way he could look, a way that made you feel two feet taller, like the wry grin of him when I'd lick him in our nightly games in the kitchen. He was mighty proud of his checker game, was Jones. It was the one little vanity he had, yet he was the best loser ever I saw.

We got close, the two of us. Mind, I was just seventeen, a hard time of growing up. You get that age, you'll know what I mean. A lot of things are confusing to a fellow. In the one month he was with us, it was Jones helped me see my way to the end of more than one bad time. He had a way of looking at things, of talking them out so they'd seem a lot clearer. Fact, he was as much pa as I ever knew after my own pa died. He sort of took up that empty place in one boy's life that Uncle Jace, for all he was as big a man inside him as outside, couldn't quite fill.

Jones would go into the settlement of Oglala now and then

to get supplies, and Gavin's riders hoorawed him every time and sent him packing out of town. Never hazed him if Unc or I was along, so I never seen it. Heard plenty, though. Neighbors saw to that. Folks would snicker behind their hands, watching Jace Devereux's new man go out of his way to walk around trouble. Never carried a gun, either. Not even a rifle on his saddle.

Never spoke of his past, did Jones. But he had one behind the face he showed the world. Remember, he'd come to us a reprieved horse thief. And strange how Uncle Jace in taking him on hadn't thought, being a middling cautious man, that he might be getting a pig in a poke. But seemed like it hadn't even occurred to Unc.

Uncle Jace was right that Gavin had heard his warning to leave us be. His riders hauled off their war of nerves, at least on Unc and me and our fences and crops, and rode herd on the other homesteaders—and, of course, Jones. Gavin had soft-pedaled on us, but we only wondered what he had up his sleeve. We found out about a month after Jones came to the farm. Gavin himself, sided by Tod Carradine, came riding into the yard one night after supper, as Uncle Jace and Jones and me was sitting on the front steps, breaking in some new cob pipes.

Gavin's hardness was a legend in the territory, and it was easy to see that age hadn't softened him. He was a blocky, well-fed man in the slightly dust-soiled dignity of a black suit, and his habit of authority sat him like a heavy fist. There was even a touch of arrogance to the way he bent the hand holding his cigar.

Uncle Jace got off the step, knocking out his pipe. "Light down a spell, Gavin. You, too, Tod."

"I'll speak my piece from here," Gavin said. "Your tracks are big, Devereux. Big enough so I respect 'em." He paused, and Unc didn't speak, wondering, like me, where this was leading to.

Gavin said it then: "I need men like you, Devereux. Sign on with me for double wages. The boy, too."

Unc said—"No."—instantly, as I knew he would. We Devereux aren't that way where we work for other people. And even if Unc was, it wouldn't be he'd work for the likes of Gavin.

The rancher didn't look mad, not even greatly concerned. He'd had his own way for too many years. There was only a faint irritation in his voice. "You go, Devereux. You go this week . . . or next week you'll crawl out of this valley on your belly."

He turned his horse in a violent way and rode out of the yard.

Carradine's soft drawling chuckle slid into the quiet like a gliding rattler. "I always suspicioned you was a Sunday man, Devereux. Now we'll see."

"A Sunday man?"

"A man who's a man one day . . . when he talks big. I don't think you'll back up what you said when you saved that horse-stealer." Carradine smiled with full insolence. "I don't think you can."

"You tell me that with Anchor behind you," Uncle Jace said, the snap of an icicle in his voice, "which by my lights makes you a yellow dog, Tod."

Carradine smiled, ever so gentle. "I'll be in town tomorrow afternoon . . . in front of Red Mike's. You be there, and we'll see if you're man enough to call me that again. Or send your big bad hired man. . . ."

So the issue was in the open now.

When the sound of Carradine's riding off had died on the still, evening air, I turned to Unc. "He's a mean one, Uncle

Jace. With a gun. There's stories followed him from Texas."

"And I offer there's something to 'em," Jones said softly, his voice startling us. He could kind of fade back so you forgot he was there. "It's why he needled you. I reckon you'd better not take him up, Jace."

"And I reckon I had," Unc said grimly.

Jones only nodded. "I figured so," he said, and walked around back.

I wanted to say more to Uncle Jace, but a look in his face warned me, and in a minute I followed Jones around back where he was working with the axe on some stove wood. He had his shirt off against the heat, and the scrawny, knobby upper body of him gleaming with sweat made him look like a plucked chicken.

Jones paused, leaned on the axe, and mopped his face with his shirt. "Why has Gavin got his sights primed for your Unc, Howie? There's other farmers squattin' on his land, and more comin'."

Squatting was the word a cattleman would use for a legal government homestead. It was Jones saying it, though, so I let it ride. You didn't get mad at Jones.

"The others got no heart to 'em," I said with contempt. "Unc's got more gall than a government mule, and the homesteaders know it as well as Gavin. If he can stampede Unc, the others'll follow suit."

"Hum," said Jones, and went back to his work. I got the other axe and helped. But a couple times I caught him leaning on his axe and looking off toward the hills with that air like a considerable thought was riling him.

I didn't sleep much that night, thinking about the next day, with Carradine's waiting in front of Red Mike's bar and Unc dead set on meeting him. Uncle Jace was no gunman. He knew it. I knew it. Even Jones knew it.

So I was near relieved when about noon of the next day Jones came into the kitchen where I was fixing some grub and quietly told me that Uncle Jace's leg had got broken. They'd been heisting the massive ridgepole timber of the barn Unc had finally got to building, raising it into place, and it fell.

Between the two of us, we splinted up Unc's leg and got him into bed. His face was white and drawn, and his eyes near starting from his head with the pain.

Jones said in his gentle voice: "I reckon this is in the way of a lifesaver for you, Jace."

"But won't they say Unc ran away from it?" I asked.

"They'll say more," Uncle Jace said bitterly between set teeth. "They'll say I got stove up a-purpose to get out of meeting Tod. And it'll be a spell before I can call any of 'em a liar and back it. By that time the farmers will be out, and Gavin'll swallow up their homesteads."

Jones and I looked at each other. Unc was right. He was the backbone of the homesteaders. With him broken, they'd cut and run.

"That leg'll need a sawbones," Jones said, unruffled. "I'm going into town, and I'll send one."

There was a note in Jones's voice that left me curious, and after a while, when Uncle Jace was resting more easy, I followed Jones out to the harness shed where he'd rigged his bunk. I came to a stand in the doorway as I saw him, and I almost fell over.

Jones didn't see me. He was facing a shard of mirror he had nailed on the wall over an old packing crate that held his possibles—and there was a gun in his hand. For thirty seconds I stood and watched as he drew and fixed a mock bead on his own reflection, the hammer falling on an empty chamber each time. I tell you, he made that fine-balanced gun do tricks.

The truth all rushed down on me at once. I'd had it figured how Jones's hell-born past was that of any rabbity little gent who couldn't hold up his head in a world of big men. But the man who could make a cutter do his will like this one—why, he was head and shoulders above the biggest man. It was the gun—that was the hell in Jones's life. That's why he'd never packed it, why he walked soft and gave Gavin's loud-mouths a wide berth. It wasn't them he was afraid of, it was himself. His own skill, his deadly skill. That was the real truth and tragedy of his back trail.

While the rest of us, rancher and homesteader, talked war and prized ourselves for it, Jones was already fighting his own private battle, a harder one than any of us would ever know. Now he'd lost his war. Lost it in the way a real man would— by facing out the enemy of the only one who ever befriended him.

He'd loaded the gun while my thoughts raced. Like magic, that gun was again in the fine-tooled holster, and then he swung toward the door and saw me.

For a full five seconds he didn't speak. "I'm going to see Carradine, Howie. You won't try to stop me." There was the thinnest under-core of steel to his voice, and I wouldn't have tried, even if I'd been of a mind to. But I was going with him, and I said so. He didn't comment, and it was that way the whole ride. Neither of us spoke a word till we'd nearly reached Oglala.

"Jones," I said.

He grunted.

"Jones, I wouldn't be surprised you let that beam slip on purpose to keep Uncle Jace from going out."

"You talk too much," he said mildly, and that was all. I didn't care. I was that sure he'd saved Unc's life.

Oglala was drowsing in the westering sun. One horse

stood hipshot at the tie rail in front of Red Mike's. Carradine's blaze-face sorrel.

Jones hauled up across the street, stepping down and throwing his reins. His gaze was fixed at Red Mike's as he said to me: "You get in this store and stay there."

I didn't, but I got back on the walk and out of the way, and he didn't even look at me.

"Carradine!" That was Jones's silence-shattering voice. A big voice for a little man. Maybe as big as the real Jones.

After a little, the batwing doors parted and Tod Carradine stood tall in the shadow of the weather-beaten false front. Stepping off the walk, bareheaded, the sun caught on his face, showing it red with heat and whisky. He'd been drinking, but he wasn't drunk.

When he saw who it was hailed him, he looked ready to laugh. Almost. He peered sharp at Jones, and something seemed to shut it off in his throat before it started.

"Carradine," Jones said. "Carradine, you brag something fierce. Back it."

Carradine began to smile, understanding, his teeth showing very white. He cut a mighty handsome figure in the sun. "All right, bravo," he said. "All right, bravo."

But I watched Jones. And I watched it happen.

Carradine was fast. Mighty fast. But Jones was the man. The last of a dying breed. Not one of your patent-leather movie cowboys with their gun-fanning foolery and their two fast-blazing six-guns. The man Jones knew you couldn't hit a barn fanning. He got his gun out right fast, but then took his time as you had to when it was a heavy single-action Colt you were handling. Carradine got two fast shots off before Jones's one bullet buckled him in the middle and smashed him into the walk on his back.

Carradine didn't touch Jones; the other fellow did. The

one in the alley between the store and the feed barn, at our back. Stationed there in case this happened. I heard this dirty son's gun from the alley, and I saw Jones's scrawny body flung forward off balance.

Before the shot sound died, I saw Jones haul around, his gun blasting, and this bushwhacker, hard hit, flung out away from the alley with his gun going off in the hot blue face of the sky. He went down and moved no more.

Jones was sinking to his knees, the light going from his eyes and a funny little smile on his face. It was the first, the last time, I saw him smile with all a smile should mean.

When I reached him and caught him as he slipped down, he looked up, recognizing me, and said: "Tell your unc . . . you tell him to keep that peg dusted, Howie. My hat won't be on it. . . ." The smile was gone as he lifted his head to stare at me with a fierce intensity. "Howie, mind what I say. If you forget everything else about me, never forget what I learned . . . the hard way. You can't run from what you made of yourself. You can't run that far. . . ."

The voice trailed, and the eyes looked on, not at me—at anything.

I eased down the meager body of the man we called Jones, and wanted to cover his face from the prying, question-rattling crowd. I remember I had to do that, and there was only my ragged pocket bandanna. When I'd finished and looked up, there was someone standing over me I didn't at first recognize for the wet blurring in my eyes. But then I blinked and saw it was Gavin.

He was holding his cigar in his arrogant way, frowning around at his two dead hirelings and at Jones, and not believing it. I went up and after him with my fists doubled. Then a big man with a close-clipped Vandyke threw a beefy arm across my chest.

"Hold it, son. I have a word for Mister Gavin."

Gavin fixed his cold stare on the newcomer. "Who the hell are you?"

"Baines, special agent for the U.S. Land Office. Washington has been getting notices about your terrorizing government homesteaders. And I've seen enough to validate it. You and I'll discuss that shortly." The big man turned back to me and nodded down at Jones. "He a friend of yours, son?"

I managed to find words. "Jones was the best."

"Jones?" Baines eyed me closely. "I reckon you don't know him very well. Suggest you write to the sheriff at Cheyenne. He'll give you particulars. So can a lot of others."

That's about all. Within weeks, a new flood of homesteaders filled the valley. I saw Gavin a few times after, a broken old man. I don't know what Baines told him, but the hand of the government can be right heavy.

About Jones? Yes, I could've written to Cheyenne and found out. But I didn't. I never wanted to find out. All I can tell you is what he was to me—friend of the Devereux, the bravest and best man I ever knew. The man we called Jones.

About the Author

T. V. Olsen was born in Rhinelander, Wisconsin, where he continued to live all his life. "My childhood was unremarkable except for an inordinate preoccupation with Zane Grey and Edgar Rice Burroughs." Having read such accomplished Western authors as Les Savage, Jr., Luke Short, and Elmore Leonard, he began writing Western fiction and went on to become one of the most widely respected and widely read authors of Western fiction in the second half of the 20th Century. Even early works such as HIGH LAWLESS (1960) and GUNSWIFT (1960) are brilliantly plotted with involving characters and situations and a simple, powerfully evocative style. Olsen went on to write such important Western novels as THE STALKING MOON (1965) and ARROW IN THE SUN (1969) which were made into classic Western films as well, the former starring Gregory Peck and the latter under the title SOLDIER BLUE (Avco-Embassy, 1970), starring Candice Bergen. His novels have been translated into numerous European languages, including French, Spanish, Italian, Swedish, Serbo-Croatian, and Czech. His novel, THE GOLDEN CHANCE (1992), won the Spur Award from the Western Writers of America in 1993, and several of the characters in this story return in DEADLY PURSUIT (Five Star

Westerns, 1995). His work will surely abide. Any Olsen story is guaranteed to combine drama and memorable characters with an authentic background of historical fact and an accurate portrayal of the terrain.

Acknowledgments

"Man Without a Past" first appeared under the title "The Man Without a Past" in *Ranch Romances* (2nd May Number: 5/17/57). Copyright © 1957 by Literary Enterprises, Inc. Copyright © renewed 1985 by T.V. Olsen. Copyright © 2001 by Beverly Butler Olsen for restored material.

"A Time to Fight" first appeared in *Ranch Romances* (1st August Number: 7/27/56). Copyright © 1956 by Literary Enterprises, Inc. Copyright © renewed 1984 by T.V. Olsen. Copyright © 2001 by Beverly Butler Olsen for restored material.

"The Ambush" appears here for the first time. Copyright © 2001 by Beverly Butler Olsen.

"Tenderfoot" appears here for the first time. Copyright © 2001 by Beverly Butler Olsen.

"End of the Trail" first appeared in *Ranch Romances* (1st August Number: 7/26/57). Copyright © 1957 by Literary Enterprises, Inc. Copyright © renewed 1985 by T.V. Olsen. Copyright © 2001 by Beverly Butler Olsen for restored material.

"Deadline Day" appears here for the first time. Copyright © 2001 by Beverly Butler Olsen.

"Killer's Law" first appeared in *Ranch Romances* (1st